They turned up a dirt road. On either side of them there was a stone wall made of big, round rocks that looked like it was going to topple over.

They rolled down a long driveway and pulled up in front of a small house. Zinnie opened her window all the way. The air smelled sweet and sunny and green. She saw a face in the window, and then the door flung open.

THE SILVER SISTERS STORIES
by Leila Howland
*The Forget-Me-Not Summer*
*The Brightest Stars of Summer*

# the Forget-Me-Not Summer

## LEILA HOWLAND

Illustrations by Ji-Hyuk Kim

**HARPER**

*An Imprint of HarperCollinsPublishers*

When cooking, it is important to keep safety in mind.
Children should always ask permission from an adult before
cooking and should be supervised by an adult in the kitchen
at all times. The publisher and author disclaim any liability
from any injury that might result from the use, proper
or improper, of the recipe contained in this book.

The Forget-Me-Not Summer
Text copyright © 2015 by Leila Howland
Illustrations copyright © 2015 by Ji-Hyuk Kim

Library of Congress Cataloging-in-Publication Data
Howland, Leila.
  The forget-me-not summer / Leila Howland. — First edition.
    pages  cm
  Summary: When their parents, a screenwriter and a film editor, go
off on summer projects, Marigold, twelve, Zinnia, eleven, and Lily, five,
must visit their Great Aunt Sunny in Cape Cod, where they learn much
about themselves and each other and grow closer than ever.
  ISBN 978-0-06-231870-1
  [1. Sisters—Fiction. 2. Interpersonal relations—Fiction. 3. Great aunts—
Fiction. 4. Actors and actresses—Fiction. 5. Cape Cod (Mass.)—Fiction.]
I. Title. II. Kim, Ji-Hyuk, ill.
PZ7.H8465For 2015                                          2014027413
[Fic]—dc23                                                          CIP
                                                                    AC

Typography by Kate J. Engbring
16  17  18  19  20    OPM    10  9  8  7  6  5  4  3  2  1
❖
First paperback edition, 2016

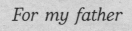

*For my father*

# 1 · Zinnie

It was the third Saturday in June, school had been out for a whole week, and Zinnia Silver, who was usually up to the gills in homework and after-school activities, had a lot of extra time on her hands. So this morning she had given herself a mission. She was going to straighten her crazy, unruly hair. She stood in front of her bathroom mirror determined to tame her mane. She was eleven years old and tired of being the funny-looking sister.

To Zinnia, or Zinnie for short, there was no one on the planet more beautiful than her older sister, Marigold. Marigold was a just a touch tall for her age, which was twelve, with a smile so bright and winning that during her brief stint with braces, she had somehow managed to make them seem like the ultimate accessory. And like their mom, Marigold had honey-blond hair that was heavy, shiny, and straight. When it was down, it moved like silk, in one smooth piece (so easy to toss, so ready for a moment's flip), and when it was up in a ponytail, it swung from high on her head, almost like it was keeping the beat to a pop song. Zinnie had plenty of time to study the back of Marigold's head, for though she was only a year younger and just one grade behind her at Miss Hadley's School for Girls, she was always a few steps behind.

Lily, the youngest sister, who was five years old and alarmingly cute, also had their mom's hair. It was so blond it was nearly white and had a bit of curl so that when the sun hit it just right, her face was framed by soft loops of light. Her cheeks were round and rosy and delightfully chubby, inviting kisses and gentle pinches and coos. Berta, Lily's nanny, had warned the older Silver sisters never to take their eyes off Lily in public.

"¡Ah dios mio!" Berta exclaimed once as she made fajitas. "Someone will think she's an angel and kidnap her!"

Marigold gasped, and Zinnie threw a brave hand over her heart and swore on her life that under no circumstances would Lily ever be left unattended. Zinnie knew this duty would fall to her. Lily must be protected from kidnappers, and Marigold must be free to pursue her greatness. A middle sister's job was not an easy one.

While Zinnie knew her almost-black hair would never look right blond, she felt sure that if it were straight like Marigold's, she would be a little closer to being as pretty as her sisters. She uncapped the straightening foam that she had saved up for, squeezed a puff of it into her palm, and applied it to the top of her wet head. "Style as usual," the directions read. So she brushed the goop through, making sure no strand was left untouched, and blow-dried.

The result was not good. The top of her head looked greasy, and the bottom half of her hair seemed to have taken on an extra two inches of fuzz. She felt like Sampson, the poodle down the street, whose over-the-top haircut was a family joke. "Fine! Just . . . just frizz away," she said into the mirror. She let the can of straightening goop crash into the sink. "I surrender."

She'd thought this was a private drama, but she'd left the bathroom door open and her dad had witnessed this moment. He leaned in the doorframe.

"It looks like you got my hair. Sorry, Zinnie," he said.

"But Daddy," Zinnie said, "you're bald." And they both burst into laughter, even though Zinnie felt like crying.

"Good news is the hair comes with a sense of humor," he said as he swept her into a big coffee-smelling hug.

"Do you still have writer's block?" Zinnie asked.

Her dad was a screenwriter. His office was in the little guesthouse in the backyard, a place the girls had to be invited into to enter. It was his private thinking space. Every morning he hid away in there to write, emerging only for coffee refills, sandwiches, chips, and, if he was really on a roll, Chinese food delivery. The girls were not even supposed to knock on the door between the hours of eight a.m. and two p.m., Monday through Friday. Except, of course, if there was a emergency, and that did not include arguments over TV time, fights over what was fair, anything to do with clothing, or second opinions on permission to do something to which their mother or Berta had already said no.

If Dad wasn't in the office in the morning on a weekday, it meant he had writer's block. When that happened, which seemed to be more often these days, he wandered around the house looking tired and nervous. Now that Zinnie thought about it, he had seemed extra worried lately. He hadn't taken her to the movie theater for classics on Tuesdays like he usually did, even during the school year (because *good* movies are an education, he always said), nor had they gone to the Santa Monica Pier, which he'd promised they would as soon as school got out.

"'Cause you look like you have writer's block," Zinnie said, studying the dark circles under his eyes.

"Well, I've had a tough decision to make," he said, and sighed. "But I think I've finally made it." For a second Zinnie thought he looked like he was the one who wanted to cry, but before she could ask him any more questions, he smiled, piled her hair on her head, turned so that they both faced the mirror, and said, "What about this for a new look?"

The way he held up her hair smack on top of her head did look silly, but it also gave Zinnie an idea. "I could do my hair like Alisha!" she said. Alisha was the name of the warrior princess character in the last movie her dad had written, *American Robot 3: Robots' Revenge*. It was Zinnie's favorite of the three robot movies Dad had written because the hero, Alisha, was a girl. Alisha had serious martial arts skills. The actress who had played her had worn her hair in a high bun held together with chopsticks. Zinnie struck a kung fu pose in the mirror.

"And you know who has a whole drawer full of chopsticks?" Dad asked.

"You," Zinnie said.

"Come on, let's go to my office."

Zinnie followed her dad through the backyard to his office, which, as usual, was almost as messy as her room. There were stacks of scripts on the floor, movie posters on the walls, and piles of DVDs on the shelves. His silver laptop sat on his desk along with a half dozen notebooks, piles of paper, a mug of change (mostly pennies), and two used coffee cups with the spoons still in them. Still, even with the clutter,

Zinnie's eyes were drawn to the bright-green Post-it attached to his computer screen. "Call Marty at 10."

"Who's Marty?" Zinnie asked.

"My lawyer."

"Why do you have to call a lawyer?" Zinnie asked as Dad handed her a set of chopsticks. She couldn't help thinking of the billboard that their car pool passed every day on the way to school. It had a guy with wavy hair and a toothy smile on it. He was leaning out of a red sports car. Below his picture were the words DALLAS PERRY, THE LAWYER WHO PUTS YOUR DIVORCE IN THE FAST LANE! A kernel of worry popped into Zinnie's head. Three of her classmates' parents had divorced this year.

"Grown-up stuff. Nothing for you to worry about." He glanced at his watch. "Oh, it's almost time for my call. Let me know how the new hairdo turns out, okay?"

"No one calls it a hairdo, Dad. It's a hair*style*."

"Well, excuse me," he said with a smile, tousled her hair, and shut the door behind her.

Zinnie sharpened the chopsticks against each other on her way back into the house and upstairs, wondering if she should consult Marigold about this lawyer thing, when she remembered that Marigold had an important meeting today. She knew that Marigold was upstairs in her room. But her door had been shut all morning, which meant that she did not want to be interrupted. As if Zinnie didn't have enough reasons to worship her sister, Marigold was also an actress. She had already been on TV, and today she had her first interview with an agent. Marigold had explained that she needed to prepare for this very important meeting and made Zinnie promise to leave her alone. She had even commanded her to swear with her right hand on the newest *Night Sprites* book, the one that they had waited in line almost two hours for at the bookstore.

*I will keep my promise to Marigold,* Zinnie thought. After all, she had sworn on her favorite book. She rewashed her hair in the sink to scrub out the goop. She towel dried her hair, watched a YouTube video on buns, and set about creating the perfectly messy but neat pile of hair on her head. As she was placing the second chopstick in at just the right angle, she reassured herself that there was no reason to think her parents were getting a divorce. She hadn't heard them fighting or anything, not the way Marigold's friend Pilar had said her parents had before her dad moved to Albuquerque.

*Besides, Dad told me it was nothing to worry about,* Zinnie reasoned as she made her way to his office to show off her new look. She passed Lily's room, where her sister was singing to herself. Then she went down the stairs, which she took two at a time; skipped across the black-and-white-tiled kitchen floor, touching only the black squares; and sashayed through the backyard with its lemon, orange, and avocado trees.

But when she arrived at Dad's office, the door was shut. This meant he was still on the phone with the lawyer. She had already pivoted back toward the house when she decided there was no harm in making sure this was really "nothing to worry about," as her dad put it. She pressed her ear against the door and listened.

"Look, Marty," she heard Dad say, "I'm as sad about this separation as anyone. We had some good times, some good years, but frankly, I'm stuck. If I'm going to continue to grow, I need a change. It's time to split. If feelings get hurt, so be it."

A separation? A change? Time to split? That sounded like something to worry about! A hundred kernels of worry popped at once, filling Zinnie's head and spilling down into her belly. Was that what his big decision had been about? Would he move to Albuquerque? What about Saturday cartoon marathons and watching concert rehearsals at the Hollywood Bowl on summer afternoons? And what about the father-daughter dance at school? Did her mother even know that he was planning on leaving?

She needed to talk to Marigold immediately. Marigold always knew what to do. They had to come up with a plan, and fast. Zinnie needed to speak with her before she left the house, no matter how mad Marigold was going to be.

Zinnie darted back through the yard and across the

kitchen, not caring about what happened to her carefully constructed bun or what color tiles she stepped on. She flew up the stairs and down the hall, slipping a little on the smooth wooden floors as she passed Lily's open door.

"You have sticks on your head!" Lily called after her.

"Yup," Zinnie said over her shoulder. *Lily will not find out,* Zinnie swore to herself. *Marigold and I will fix this.* She was out of breath as she arrived in front of Marigold's closed door. She raised her hand to knock and paused. Not only did Marigold have the DO NOT DISTURB sign on her door, she'd added the word "important" in bubble letters and outlined it in pink highlighter. Marigold was going to be as mad as the troll in the first *Night Sprites* book when the fairies awakened him from his one-thousand-year slumber. But what was Zinnie supposed to do? *Not* tell her older sister that their parents were getting a divorce? Unthinkable. Zinnie took a deep breath. Then she knocked.

"Marigold," she said, "I need to talk to you!"

"You're going to get in biiiiig trouble," Lily said, appearing next to her in a purple tutu and red rain boots, her bunny in her outstretched arms. "Here. Take Benny for protection."

## 2 · Marigold

Marigold had begged her whole family to please, *pretty please with sugar on top*, not bother her on the most important morning of her entire life. She was going to audition for Jill Dreyfus, the best acting agent for kids in all of Hollywood, in less than a half hour. She needed to focus. Mom had put the interview on the family calendar in blue ink, and Marigold had rewritten it in red ink, indicating it was an event of the highest priority. Marigold had added "Marigold's private time" in the hours leading up to it, also in red ink, and then, just as an insurance policy, put the DO NOT DISTURB sign on the door. And *still* Zinnie was knocking! She took a deep, calming breath and tried to ignore her younger sister.

She had been looking forward to today for two whole weeks, practicing her monologue and vocal exercises every morning. She had made collages of outfits to wear for the audition from pictures in magazines. She'd shown her mom the collage and even included a list of stores where they could buy the outfits, but her mother had said the clothes were too grown-up. Marigold had then gone through her closet three times until she settled on a blue-and-green tie-dyed dress and gold wedges. She was putting the final touches on her hair (one barrette, left side, a few dangling wisps) when Zinnie knocked again.

"Zinnie wants to talk to you," Lily said through the door, and added some tiny but firm knocks of her own.

Marigold stifled a scream. Why did no one in her family seem to understand what a big deal today was? Zinnie and Lily were bugging her, and her parents were not even going to allow her to wear makeup. Sometimes it seemed as if no one cared that this was her dream. Her parents had been the ones to take her to the premieres of the *American Robot* movies. That's where Marigold had first seen the actresses in their glamorous dresses, smiling at the flashing cameras. But it wasn't the fancy clothes and red carpets that made Marigold love acting (though she had to admit it didn't hurt).

For Marigold, acting was about the way she felt when she pretended to be someone else: bright, awake, calm on the inside no matter if she was crying or laughing on the outside. Marigold wasn't like Zinnie, who could make everyone laugh with a single word or facial expression. Grown-ups always said what a pretty girl Marigold was, but then they'd turn to Zinnie and laugh with sparkling eyes. Marigold had once overheard their grandmother describe Zinnie as captivating. Marigold had never heard the word "captivating" before, but somehow she knew just what it meant, and it was better than "pretty."

It had been such a sweet surprise when, right after winter vacation, Marigold had tagged along with a classmate to an acting class at the Ronald P. Harp Acting Studio. She found that when she was reading a script, she knew what to do. She could slip in and out of other people's words as easily as sliding in and out of a costume. It was like there was a little bit of gold inside her that was hers and hers alone. She was captivating.

Later that evening Marigold asked her parents if she could join the class. She was surprised when they said they had to think about it. They always wanted the girls to try out new activities. In sixth grade alone, Marigold had taken Bollywood dancing, yoga, Spanish, and cake decorating. But those classes were all at the after-school program at Miss Hadley's. The Ronald P. Harp Studio was a twenty-minute drive away. She'd had to ask a few times before they said yes. Once they saw how much Marigold was enjoying the class, however, they seemed happy to take her every week. So she thought her pleading was behind her when, two months later, she asked if she could sign up for a special one-day auditioning-for-television workshop, taught by an actual, real-life casting director.

"The casting lady is really looking for kids to put on that new show *Seasons*. You know the one with the big billboard on Melrose? This is basically like a real TV audition," Marigold said, practically bursting out of her skin, she was so thrilled by the possibility. But instead of sharing in her excitement, Dad sighed and put his head in his hands, and her mother said no without even taking a breath.

"But why not?" Marigold asked. She didn't understand. Acting was her favorite thing in the world. Her parents always talked about how it was important to try lots of activities so that she could find out what she liked. Now she'd found something that made her as happy as a big slice of birthday cake with a whole frosting flower on top, and they were saying no?

"I'm sorry, honey," Mom said. "Acting for fun is great. But acting for money, that's different. The entertainment industry is no place for kids."

"I'm not even sure it's a place for adults," Dad added. "Don't you want to be on the swim team again this year?" Marigold shook her head, mystified by this resistance. She was always coming in second or third to last at the swim meets. Even though the coach said that winning didn't matter, it sure felt like it did when the ribbons were passed out and Marigold never got one. Besides, the chlorine made her skin itch.

"It's my dream to be an actress," Marigold said. "Just like Dad's dream is being a writer. And Mom's dream is to be a mom."

"A mom *and* a film editor," Mom corrected her. She frowned and fiddled with her wedding ring. "Which I was, you know, before you were born."

"Oh, yeah. Sorry." Marigold could forget how sensitive Mom was when it came to her old job. "So, um, can I just do this class? Please? It's just one afternoon. You wouldn't let anything stop you from following your dream, would you?"

"No," Dad said, running a hand over his head. "I wouldn't."

"Then why would you stop me from following mine?" Marigold asked.

Her parents exchanged a look and asked her to leave for a moment so they could speak in private. Marigold stood in the pantry, staring at the boxes of pasta, cans of tomato sauce, and jars of artichoke hearts, as her parents whispered in the kitchen.

"Here's the deal, sweetie," Dad said when they called her back in. "Show business is really tough. The chances that you're going to get to be on a TV show are small. And I'm not saying this because I don't believe in you. Trust me, this has nothing to do with talent. It's just the business, and we don't want you to be disappointed."

"I won't be," Marigold said. "I promise. No matter what happens. I won't be disappointed."

"You can't promise that," Mom said, tucking Marigold's hair behind her ear.

"But I can promise that if it stops being fun, I'll quit," Marigold said.

"Okay," Dad said, lifting his hands in surrender. "You can take the class."

Marigold smiled and hugged them. She knew someplace quiet and shimmering inside her that she would not be disappointed. She knew that this was just the beginning.

And she was right. After Marigold's turn in front of the camera, the casting director clapped and cheered. She called the Silvers' house that very night and offered Marigold the role of Jenny, the new neighbor girl, on *Seasons*. The casting director told Marigold that she would have two whole lines and get to eat an ice cream sundae on camera. Her parents let her take the job under three conditions: Acting could never get in the way of her schoolwork, they had the right to pull her out of it at any time if they felt she was growing up too fast, and all her earnings would go into a college fund. Marigold agreed to their conditions. She would have agreed to anything, even sniffing the cafeteria garbage every day, if that was what it would take to get her parents to let her accept the part.

That had been a few months ago. Since then she'd

been in three episodes of *Seasons*. And now, in just twenty-five minutes, she would meet with a very important acting agent. She had begun to recite her monologue to her mirror one final time when Zinnie burst into her room with a pair of chopsticks in her hair.

"I know I shouldn't interrupt, but it's an emergency!" Zinnie said.

The expression on Zinnie's face was the same as when she'd accidentally set off the emergency exit alarm at the Gap. Lily jumped in behind her, looking back and forth at her sisters with great anticipation. Before Marigold could say a word to either of them, Mom stepped into the room with her pocketbook over her shoulder, keys in her hand, and sunglasses on her head.

"What's an emergency, Zinnie?" Mom asked.

"Yeah, what's the emergency?" Lily asked.

"Nothing," Zinnie said, paling a little as she stared at Mom. "Nothing at all. Are you okay, Mom?"

"Um, I'm fine," Mom said.

"Are you sure?" Zinnie asked.

"Of course. Are *you* okay?" Mom asked.

Zinnie nodded, looking at the floor.

"Then why would you burst into my room like that?" Marigold asked, ready to put an end to the shenanigans. "When the sign is up and everything?"

"It was a . . . hair emergency," Zinnie said, touching the chopsticks.

"I'll say," Marigold said. Zinnie's face flushed with hurt. Sometimes things just flew out of Marigold's mouth before she could stop them. *I need to be nicer to Zinnie*, she thought.

"I think you look cute, Zin," Mom said, putting an arm around her. "Will you show me how you did it later?"

"Anything for you, Mom," Zinnie said, and hugged her. "Anything in the world."

*Ugh, never mind,* Marigold thought. *Zinnie is such a kiss-up!*

"Marigold, are you ready?" Mom asked.

"I think so," Marigold said.

"Can I come?" Zinnie asked. "Please? I need to talk to Marigold."

"Whatever you need to say, you can say in front of me," Mom said.

"Never mind," Zinnie said.

Marigold raised an eyebrow. What was Zinnie trying to tell her?

"Then I guess you're going to have to wait," Mom said, "because you have acting class, remember?"

"What about me?" Lily asked. "Do I have anything important to do today?"

"Berta will be here any minute to take you to the zoo," Mom said, patting Lily on the head. "Get your shoes on, Zinnie. Samantha's mom is picking you up in five minutes."

# 3 · Acting for Beginners

"Oh, Zinnia," Ronald P. Harp said, his voice breathy with lament as he sat in his director's chair and shook his head.

Zinnie had just finished performing a scene from *Alice in Wonderland,* in which she'd finally been allowed to play Alice rather than a boy's part. (Girls outnumbered boys by two to one in the class, and Zinnie often had to play the boy. Or the mom. Or an animal.) She knew she'd been distracted. How could she not be after she'd listened in on her dad's phone conversation about a separation? Her family was on the verge of falling apart, but unless she'd wanted to make a big scene in front of her mother, who might not have even known about her dad's talk with the lawyer, she'd had no choice but to go to acting class as if everything were normal. As difficult as it was,

Zinnie was determined not to panic until she was able to discuss the whole situation with Marigold.

"Oh, Zinnia," Ronald repeated, removing his glasses and massaging his temples. While it was true that she'd messed up some of her lines in the scene, Zinnie didn't think she'd been *that* bad. Ronald was squinting like she'd given him a headache, and it wasn't the first time he'd made this face.

The weird thing was this wasn't one of the classes that her parents made her take, like piano or chorus. She'd really wanted to take this class, figuring that if Marigold loved acting so much, so would she. Her parents agreed to let her sign up as long as she also gave piano lessons another shot. Marigold was annoyed that they'd let Zinnie enroll without much of a fuss when she'd had to beg and plead. "You have no idea how easy you have it!" Marigold had said. "Older sisters have to do all the hard work around here!"

Zinnie hoped the two of them could be acting sisters. She wanted them to go to parties together and be interviewed as a duo. If Zinnie had her way, the *Seasons* people would even write a part for her. She would play Marigold's character's forgotten sister. She would have escaped from an orphanage, traveled cross-country by train, and arrived on the doorstep of the *Seasons* house in tattered clothes with patches on them.

This class was the key to that dream, but it was turning out to be harder than she'd imagined. Zinnie had always thought that if she tried her hardest at something, eventually she'd get good at it. That was what teachers always said. But it was becoming more obvious with every class that acting didn't work like that. In fact, trying harder only seemed to make it worse. Still, she wasn't ready to give up. She took a deep breath and listened as Ronald spoke.

"You're thinking from up here," Ronald said, gesturing to his forehead. Then he clutched his chest. "Instead of from here."

"Huh?" Zinnie asked. Her brain was in her head, so of course that was where she was thinking from! As usual, Zinnie didn't get it.

"I don't really understand what you mean," Zinnie said.

"What do I mean? What do I mean?" Ronald ran a long-fingered hand over his goatee. He looked tired. Tired of Zinnie. This was her second time taking Acting for Beginners, and she hadn't made any progress. "Can anyone in here explain what I mean?"

"She has no emotional connection," Samantha Wise said. Samantha had been in a commercial last year, and everyone knew she was up for a part in a TV show as a beautiful deaf girl. "But it's not just her words," Samantha continued, pulling her long, spiderlike legs into her chest and resting her chin on her kneecaps. "Her facial expressions are so huge that they're . . .

like a clown's." Her butt-length hair draped around her shoulders like a curtain.

*Get a haircut*, Zinnie thought meanly. She made a mental note to ask her mom to figure out a new carpool situation as soon as possible.

"What do we call that, class?" Ronald asked.

"Pulling faces," they answered. Zinnie wanted to melt into the sofa, just become part of the fabric, and wear away with time. Pulling faces was a mortal sin at the Ronald P. Harp Acting Studio.

"You must find your way into the character. First, I think you must find your way into Zinnia Silver. Who is the real Zinnia? Where is she?"

Zinnie had no idea how to answer these questions, and yet Ronald was looking at her like she should. She'd bet he never asked Marigold these questions. She was probably just perfect from the beginning. It didn't seem fair. Zinnie felt like crying, but she didn't. She swallowed hard.

"Don't bury your feelings, Zinnia," Ronald said. "Let them live. Let them breathe! Wake up and bloom, Zinnia! Bloom!"

At the end of the class Ronald pulled her aside and told her she would not be allowed to continue at his acting studio. He was nicer to her in that moment than he had ever been, which was confusing. "Acting isn't for you, Zinnia," he said. Zinnie nodded and smiled and held her breath. He put a hand on her shoulder and added, "But that doesn't mean you don't belong in the theater. Just think of all the jobs that need to get done backstage. Why, you could even be a stage manager one day!"

# 4 · A Star on the Balcony

The lobby at the Jill Dreyfus Agency for Young Performers was large and sunny, with big windows and a balcony that had a view of the Hollywood sign. A girl was talking on a cell phone out there. She was in a blue sundress, and as a breeze blew, her long dark hair fanned out against the green-brown hills in the distance. As Mom talked to the receptionist, Marigold scanned the framed movie posters on the walls. They featured Jill Dreyfus's most famous clients. There was Max Jordan riding a bicycle into the wind in *Race to the Top*. There was Tamika Garcia driving a school bus in *Field Trip Fiasco*. And there was Amanda Mills making a face at herself in the mirror in *Double Trouble*.

*Maybe one day I'll be on this wall*, Marigold thought, and the idea sent a shiver from her head to her toes, which were already tingling with anticipation. Actually, her feet were sweating so much she was slipping a little in her wedges. All the relaxation exercises from this morning had worn off.

Marigold was imagining what her movie poster would look like when the girl on the balcony turned around. Marigold gasped and grabbed Mom's hand when she saw that it was the real Amanda Mills. Marigold looked from the poster back to Amanda just to be sure. It was the same girl!

Amanda Mills wasn't just any actress. She was also a pop star who had been discovered on *America Sings* when she was only ten and now, at thirteen, had a hit album and her own TV show and was rumored to have landed the lead in the movie version of *Night Sprites.*

"OMG, Mom, that's Amanda Mills!" Marigold said as they took a seat on a big white sofa. "I wish I could talk to her."

"Go and say hi," Mom said.

"But I don't know her," Marigold said.

"Well, introduce yourself," Mom said. "She's not talking to anyone." It was true. Amanda had hung up the phone and was just standing there, leaning against the railing, as the traffic whizzed by on Sunset Boulevard. "We have a few minutes. The receptionist said Jill is running late. I'll be right back. I'm going to find the ladies' room. It must be down that hall."

Before she could think too much about it, Marigold took a deep breath, smoothed out her dress, and walked up to Amanda, who was now staring at her cell phone as if willing it to ring.

"Hi," Marigold said. In addition to her feet, her palms were sweating now, too. "You're Amanda, right?"

"Yup," Amanda said. "That's me." Marigold couldn't believe it. She sounded exactly like she did on TV!

"Nice to meet you. My name is Marigold Silver."

"Cool name," Amanda said. She placed a hand on her forehead to shield her eyes from the sun, looked right at Marigold, and smiled. Marigold beamed back. Without all her makeup on, Amanda looked like a regular girl instead of an international megastar.

"So I just have to ask, is it true that you're going to be playing Seraphina in the *Night Sprites* movie?" Marigold asked.

"Yeah," Amanda said. "I just signed the contract."

"I love those books! I've read them all like five times. Which one is your favorite?" Marigold asked, still amazed that this conversation was actually happening. "Let me guess! *Whispers of Winter*? Or no, wait, *Dares of Dawn*?"

"Oh, I haven't read them," Amanda said.

"Really?" Marigold had to summon up all her acting skills in order to hide her shock. She didn't know of a single person her age who hadn't read the books. Even her dad had read the first one. "They're awesome."

Amanda nodded and then checked her cell phone again.

"Waiting for a call?" Marigold asked, rocking on her heels in hopes that some air might sneak into her wedges and cool off the bottoms of her perspiring feet.

"My mom was supposed to pick me up, and she's late," Amanda said.

"I'm sure she'll be here soon," Marigold said.

"Yeah, right," Amanda said, her face full of shadows. "She always does this."

"Well, I think it's epic that you're going to be Seraphina," Marigold said, switching the subject to something positive. "I would do anything to be in that movie."

"I think they're doing more casting in July," Amanda said, "but they're probably just looking for stars, you know?"

"Oh," Marigold said, feeling a little sizzle of pain like a prick of hot oil from Berta's griddle. She wasn't a star.

"I mean, unless you wanted to be an extra," Amanda said. "But who would want that? I always feel bad for them. The other day one of them was following me everywhere. It was so weird."

"I'd never want to be an extra," Marigold said, even though she knew that just seconds ago she would've jumped at the chance, especially for the *Night Sprites* movie.

"Um, I think I'd better go inside," Amanda said. "I'm getting a sunburn."

"Me, too," Marigold said. She trailed Amanda back into the lobby, wondering if she should ask Jill Dreyfus about auditioning for *Night Sprites* before or after she performed her monologue. Marigold was now more determined than ever to try out even if she wasn't a star—yet. As Amanda approached the receptionist's desk, Marigold took a seat on the big white sofa. She didn't want to be following Amanda around like that extra.

"Did you get ahold of my mom?" Amanda asked the receptionist.

"We can't reach her," the receptionist said, "but I'm going to keep trying."

"She was supposed to be here an hour ago," Amanda said.

"I know, hon. I ordered you some sushi. It's in the kitchen, okay?"

"Fine," Amanda said. "Whatever."

"See you later," Marigold said as Amanda walked away.

"Yeah, see ya," Amanda said.

Speaking of moms, Marigold was wondering where hers was. She wasn't in the lobby, and she wasn't on the balcony. She headed toward the hallway to see if she was still in the bathroom. Marigold was starting to think that maybe not being able to locate her mother would give her something else to talk to Amanda about when she spotted her, standing in an empty conference room, speaking into her cell phone.

"To tell you the truth," Marigold overheard Mom say, "I think a change from L.A. will be refreshing. I don't care if it's the middle of nowhere Canada. The apartment sounds great. I'm sure we'll settle right in and make a home of it."

They were leaving L.A.? For *Canada*? Now? Right when all her dreams were about to come true? Marigold felt her very center erode, as if her home, this edge of the world called California, had suddenly broken off and slipped into the sea.

"Marigold," the receptionist said. "There you are. Jill will see you now. Are you ready?"

# 5 · Family Meeting

When Samantha's mother dropped Zinnie off at home that afternoon, Zinnie finally released the tears she'd been holding back the whole car ride. She dried her eyes with the sleeve of her T-shirt (a Marigold hand-me-down, which as usual didn't look nearly as good on her as it had on her sister). Then she made herself a cup of hot cocoa and put a slice of Berta's chocolate chip banana bread in the microwave. Now that she had been kicked out of acting class, her dream of being a movie star with Marigold was crushed.

As she watched the microwave rotate the banana bread, she thought about the fact that she was never going to play the long-lost orphan sister on *Seasons*. There would be no important meetings that she and Marigold would go to in coordinated outfits, nor would there be magazine articles about the amazing Silver sisters, starring in their very own movies. Was she always going to be on the outside of Marigold's fabulous life, just looking in? She plucked a napkin from a stack and wiped her eyes.

And yet Zinnie was also relieved. Nothing that Ronald had ever said made any sense to her. Acting class wasn't fun, and now she wouldn't have to go back. As she added a few extra minimarshmallows to her mug, she realized that she felt lighter. A weight had been lifted, even if it had left a dusting of disappointment.

The microwave beeped. Zinnie removed the banana bread and carried her snack toward the sunporch, which she thought was the nicest room in the Silvers' house. She liked the cozy chair with its sun-bleached cushion and a matching ottoman that Mom had picked up at a flea market. It was the only place Zinnie could find true peace. Lily burst into her room a minimum of three times a day, wanting to watch cartoons or raid Zinnie's art supplies, and Marigold barged in whenever she needed Zinnie's pencil sharpener or a hair band.

Usually, no one ever thought to look for her on the sunporch, but today, when she crossed the sunny threshold with her cocoa and banana bread in hand, she nearly tripped in the doorway. Her whole family was sitting there, looking as if they'd been waiting for her. Had Ronald P. Harp called ahead to tell them all the news of her failure?

"I didn't see it coming," Zinnie said. "I'm sorry if I've disappointed you!"

"What are you talking about?" Dad asked.

"Ronald P. Harp didn't call to tell you I'd been kicked out of the class," Zinnie asked, "because I'm not good enough to be in it?"

"No, Zin," Mom said, wincing as if she were also feeling the sharp pain of being rejected. "Are you okay, honey?"

Zinnie felt tears gathering behind her eyes again.

"That man is a fool," Dad said.

"He is not," Marigold said, crossing her arms. She was sitting on the sofa. Lily was next to her, patting a small coffee stain with her hand.

"Sorry, Marigold," Dad said. "I shouldn't have said that. And Zinnie, no, he didn't call and tell us."

"So, are we all here to celebrate because Marigold has an agent now?" Zinnie asked, hoping to change the subject.

"We don't know yet," Mom said. "We should hear very soon."

"But the audition went well. Jill Dreyfus said she had a great feeling about me," Marigold said. She seemed oddly sullen about the good news.

"You were fantastic," Mom said. "And of course she had a great feeling about you. You're a great kid."

"What's the point now, though? I don't know if it matters anymore," Marigold said, shaking her head in defeat. "I don't know if anything matters."

"Okay, what's going on?" Zinnie asked.

"We're having a family meeting," Mom said with a smile, as though this were something the Silver family did.

"We're moving!" Marigold said. "To Canada!"

"Canada?" Zinnie asked, totally confused.

"Marigold, I already told you that wasn't true," Mom said.

"Then why are we having a family meeting?" Marigold asked.

Zinnie gasped, realizing this was the dreaded divorce talk. She had been momentarily distracted by her acting class, but it was all coming together now. "Don't you see? They're getting a divorce!"

"Zinnia Jane Silver!" Mom said, sitting upright. "That is absolutely not true."

"Are you bored with us?" Zinnie asked Dad. "Are you stuck? Do you need to move on?"

"No," Dad said. "I could never be bored with you, sweetheart."

"What's a divorce?" Lily asked.

"It's when people aren't married anymore because"—Zinnie glared at Dad—"they need a change or"—a new and terrible thought occurred to her—"they're in love with someone else."

"You're not in love with Daddy?" Lily asked Mom.

"No, sweet pea," Mom said.

"You aren't?" Marigold said.

"That's not what I said," Mom said.

"So you're leaving him?" Zinnie asked.

"Girls," Dad said, "no one is leaving anyone."

"Then what is going on?" Marigold asked. "Because if it weren't a big deal, you wouldn't have to have us seated all together like this on the freaking sunporch."

"If you can listen for a minute, we'll explain," Mom said, and took a deep breath. "We certainly aren't getting a divorce."

"But we're in a bit of a second-act slump," Dad said.

"Oh, Joe, don't say that. You'll confuse them," Mom said.

"Just spit it out!" Marigold said.

"I've had writer's block for a year," Dad said, standing up. "And it's been killing me."

"Is that all this is about?" Zinnie said. "You've had writer's block before. You always get over it."

"Not like this," Dad said. "I don't know who I am when I'm not writing."

"You're Daddy," Lily said.

"Yes, I am," Dad said, and gave Lily's knee a reassuring pat. "So here's the deal. I was thinking how I needed to get out of this crazy town, where you're over the hill at thirty. I was thinking we all should get out of this place."

"See! We *are* moving," Marigold said, slamming her fists into the sofa.

"Then the most amazing thing happened." Dad continued, giving Marigold a "calm down" gesture. "About a week ago I got a phone call from my old college roommate, Bobby. He's a redwood expert now. He's just discovered a patch of old-growth trees on private land, one of which he thinks is the tallest tree in the world. It could be four hundred feet tall. He's going to measure it with his team, and I'm going to film it as a documentary. If we can raise enough money, we can buy the land and save not just the tallest tree but the whole forest. Otherwise, the landowners might sell it to a lumber company. But Bobby and his team are amazing and this is a great story and it's just the kind of project I've been looking for. Nothing to do with robots."

"So why did you tell the lawyer that you needed a change?" Zinnie asked.

"That was business. That was about my agent, who doesn't want me to take this project. After ten years we're going to part ways. Wait, were you listening to my phone call?" Dad asked. Zinnie avoided his gaze. "We'll talk about that later, Zinnia."

"Where is this tree?" Lily asked.

"It's in a secret location," Dad said.

"But we don't keep secrets in this family," Lily said, repeating what her parents had said so many times before.

"I don't even know exactly where it is. The only thing I can tell you is that it's near Big Sur," Dad said. "And that I'll be gone for most of July."

"But that's not all," Mom added. "I'm going to Canada."

"Why?" Marigold asked. "Are we going, too?"

"We're getting to that," Dad said.

"It's just me going, Marigold. If you'll give me a chance, I'll explain. You know how I've been wanting to go back to work," Mom said. "The same day your dad got his phone call, I was offered an editing job for a big director."

"Who?" Marigold asked.

"Katherine Jackson," Mom said.

"The Oscar nominee," Dad added. Marigold nodded with approval.

"But I have to be on set in the middle of Canada, working pretty much around the clock for three weeks in July," Mom said. "I've been agonizing over whether or not to take the job for days, but finally I realized that I need to take it. This is my chance. If I do a good job with this, I'll have my pick of jobs in L.A. next year."

"So Dad's going to Big Sur and you're going to Canada." Zinnie was interested in the practical facts. It was not easy to live with so many people and their dreams. There was a lot to keep track of. "Where does that leave us kids?"

"Who's going to stay with us?" Marigold asked.

"Berta?" Zinnie asked.

"Berta!" Lily clapped.

"Berta's going back to Oaxaca for the summer," Dad said. "Unfortunately, her mother isn't well."

"We'll go with her to Mexico," Lily said.

"I can't leave the country! Not when my career is just getting started," Marigold said.

"Actually," Mom said, "we're sending you back east for three weeks in July, to Pruet, Massachusetts. To stay with my aunt Sunny."

"Massachusetts?" Marigold practically spit the state's name.

"You're going to love Cape Cod," Dad said.

"Who's Aunt Sunny?" Lily asked.

"An old lady we barely know!" Marigold said.

"My favorite aunt," Mom said. "Marigold and Zinnie met her when they were very young."

"When are we leaving?" Zinnie asked.

"Next week," Dad said.

"I'm going to miss auditions," Marigold said. "How can you do this to me?"

"There's more to life than auditions," Dad said.

"Like what?" Marigold asked.

"Like smelling the salt air and building sand castles with your sisters," Mom said. "Living an actual life. It's not even for a month."

"There's a really cool estuary in Pruet," Dad said.

"You think I care about estuaries? How do you expect me to get a job if I can't audition?"

"Here's the thing, Marigold. I don't expect you to get a job," Dad said.

Marigold let this sink in, and Zinnie watched her try to formulate a response. When none came, Marigold stood up and stormed out of the room.

The rest of the family sat in silence until Lily announced, "I don't even know what an estuary is!"

# 6 · Back East

The girls had been to the East Coast only twice in their lives. When Marigold was six and Zinnie was five, they visited Boston, where their mom had gone to college. They rode on the T, which is what people call the subway in Boston, saw statues of important men in old-fashioned clothes, and watched fireworks on the Charles River on the Fourth of July. It was on this trip that they visited Pruet, though only for an afternoon. Lily wasn't born yet.

On their second trip east, they visited New York, where Dad had gone to college, at Christmastime. They stayed in a fancy hotel with a doorman, ice-skated at Rockefeller Center, went window-shopping, and saw a Broadway show. Zinnie had loved it there. She loved the cold on her cheeks and the smell of roasting peanuts. They went for a horse-and-carriage ride, and it snowed. Her mother bought Marigold and her matching red coats with fake fur collars.

This was when Marigold was nine and Zinnie was eight, back when Marigold would hold her hand and make up songs with her. ("We're two girls who walk when the walk sign says walk, so let's walk-a-walk-a-walk-a right now!") When she brought up the New York trip to Marigold, Marigold acted like she didn't remember. "It was so cold," she'd say. Or "It smelled like pee everywhere," Or "Those ice skates hurt my ankles." This reaction confused Zinnie, because she remembered magical shop windows and Christmas ballerinas and steaming, salty hot dogs in the park.

Lily stayed home with Berta because she was so little. Zinnie remembered liking that trip so much in part because she got to be the youngest again. Lily had been getting all the attention back home. But on that vacation, Zinnie was the one who swung between her parents' hands and always somehow seemed to get her way. It felt like the way it used to be, back when there were only two Silver sisters, when Marigold wasn't into acting yet, and it felt like they were both stars.

# 7 · The Plan

"I have an agent!" Marigold said when she burst into Zinnie's room the next night in her perfectly-too-big sweatshirt, a huge grin on her face. This was a major mood swing from yesterday and this morning, when Marigold had been slamming doors, pouting, and even threatening to go on a hunger strike if their parents didn't change their minds about Massachusetts. Her attitude had not gone over well. Mom and Dad said they wouldn't respond to such behavior, and if Marigold wanted to talk about it, she would have to do so in a calm, responsible manner. Now Marigold danced across Zinnie's carpet and squealed. "Jill Dreyfus just called, and she wants to represent me. Can you believe it?"

"That's awesome!" Zinnie said, afraid to remind her that this wonderful news didn't change the other news about their going away for three weeks in July, but she didn't want to ruin the moment. Zinnie loved it when Marigold was this happy. Instead of being like a puzzle Zinnie had to figure out, she was like a piñata raining candy.

"I'm so psyched!" Marigold said, jumping up and down. "This is the best news of my life."

"You're going to be famous!" Zinnie said, jumping with her sister. They hopped onto Zinnie's bed and jumped until they both collapsed, breathless and giggling. "You're going to be in movies!"

"I hope so!" Marigold said. She rolled onto her stomach and drummed the mattress with her fingers, suddenly serious. "The one I really want to be in more than anything is *Night Sprites*, and Jill said there's only one more day of casting for some of the secondary roles, and it's on July seventh. Mr. Rathbone travels all the time, and that's the only day he'll be here in Los Angeles. Jill thinks she can get me an appointment. So there's no way in the world that I'm going to Massachusetts now. You and I need to come up with a plan." She sat up. "We need to change their minds, we need to do it fast, and we need to do it in a calm and responsible way."

Zinnie sprang to her feet, swept up in this call to action. "I know. We could run away. Like vagabonds. Maybe we could sneak into the *Seasons* house and sleep in the bedrooms and then leave in the morning before anyone discovers us!"

"People live there," Marigold said. "They only use the outside of the house for filming; the rest is done on the studio lot. Besides, that's not calm and responsible."

"Oh, right," Zinnie said. She sat in her desk chair. "Just kidding."

"There are other options. There have to be. Let's make a list."

"Okay," Zinnie said. She sat there awkwardly for a minute before she realized that Marigold was waiting for her to write stuff down. "Oh," she said, tapping her laptop awake. Last year in school she had learned how to use a slide show presentation program, and she'd gotten pretty good at it. Mr. Herrera, her fifth-grade teacher, told her he thought she had a real talent for presentations. She opened a new project and wrote on the first slide: "July Options for Silver Sisters."

"We could get Grammy to stay with us," Marigold said. "It would be easy and convenient."

"Easy and convenient," Zinnie repeated as she typed, then added the sparkle dust effect, so that the words would appear as if sprinkled there by a very accurate fairy. "Also, we would be spending quality time with Grammy, which is good because she's so old."

"Yeah, that's good," Marigold said. "Write that. Now for option two." Marigold began as Zinnie dutifully opened a fresh slide, her fingers poised above the keyboard in anticipation of Marigold's next idea.

"Um, let's see here, we could stay with friends. Right? I mean, why not?"

"Got it," Zinnie said, switching fonts to "jaunty Milan," her favorite. "Because . . . ," Zinnie prompted, anxious to add bullet points that could speed in like rockets.

"Because it would be fun for us and . . . it would save them the cost of the plane tickets! Yeah, write that. Save money."

"Okay," Zinnie said after she'd typed "save money" and added rockets with flaming tails. "We need another. Mr. Herrera says three is the magic number."

"Hmm," Marigold said, taking a seat on Zinnie's bed.

Lily wandered in, carrying Benny, whose nose had all but disappeared. She believed rubbing his nose brought good luck, though no one was sure how she'd decided this. "What are you doing?" she asked.

"Well," Marigold said, and lifted Lily onto her lap, "we're thinking of ways we can stay here for the three weeks Mom and Dad will be gone, instead of going to Pruet."

"Maybe Berta's mommy can come stay with us," Lily said. "And Berta will be in charge of all of us."

"Hey," Zinnie said as she searched images on her computer to find a good backdrop for the final slide, "that's actually a great idea."

"It is?" Lily asked, smiling.

"Yes, it is," Marigold said, and kissed her head, taking a good long whiff of her golden, fruity-scented curls while she was at it. "Because it's realistic."

Zinnie typed it in, then consulted her sisters on the final image. "What do you guys think? Chairs on a beach or a tropical waterfall?"

"Can I make something on the computer now?" Lily asked.

"This is my computer," Zinnie said, deciding on the waterfall and clicking it into place. "You can use Mom's."

"But Mom's computer doesn't have this game," Lily said. She reached over and touched the keyboard, accidentally erasing the last slide.

"Lily, stop," Zinnie said. She sighed and clicked Undo until the waterfall reappeared.

"Not fair." Lily pouted. "I want a turn."

"Don't yell at her, Zinnie," Marigold said, and scooped Lily up.

"You would kill me if I touched your computer, Marigold," Zinnie said. "But if Lily does something annoying, you don't care. No one ever gets mad at Lily."

"Because Lily's so cute and little," Marigold said.

"I'm not little," Lily said. "I'm big."

"Hurry up, Zinnie," Marigold said. "I want to get Mom while she's in the bathtub."

"Good point," Zinnie said, saving her work and

unplugging her laptop. The best time to ask Mom for something was at the end of the day when she was in her nightly bath. She was so relaxed that she was much more likely to say yes. Marigold led the charge as the three sisters made their way down the hallway into their parents' room and knocked on the bathroom door.

# 8 · The Presentation

"It's us," Marigold said.

"All of you?" Mom asked from inside.

"Yes," Lily answered.

"Well, come on in," Mom said. "I guess it's a party."

"We have something to show you," Marigold said.

Zinnie followed her into the bathroom with the computer under her arm.

"I had ideas too," Lily added, taking a seat on the bath mat.

"I can't wait to see it," Mom said. She was covered up to her neck in a fluffy blanket of bubbles.

"We came up with this presentation to show you in a *calm and responsible* way that we have realistic options for staying in L.A."

Zinnie placed the computer on the sink and pulled up the title slide. In a last-minute decision, she cued up the classical music that Mr. Herrera played during independent study time. The first dramatic notes always made Zinnie feel serious and important. She turned up the volume, pressed Play, and a resounding *duh duh duh duh* filled the room. Mom sat up a little in surprise. Marigold jumped. Lily covered her ears. It was louder than Zinnie had intended, not having taken into account the small space and the tile floor. She lowered the volume as the music continued into a gentler-but-no-less-important-sounding melody.

"You definitely have my attention now," Mom said with a smile.

"Here are three good options for July that allow us to stay in L.A.," Marigold said. Zinnie opened the next slide. "First, Grammy can come stay with us. It will be easy and convenient. We hardly ever see Grammy, and it's important to spend time with her now that she's so old."

Zinnie watched the corners of Mom's mouth turn up, and she was pretty sure that was because of the sparkle effect. She opened the next slide.

"A second idea is that we could stay with friends," Marigold said. "You always say how valuable true friendship is. This time will give us a chance to really get to know our friends in a way that we can't just by going to school with them."

Mom pressed her lips together and nodded. Zinnie wondered if she was trying not to laugh.

"Also"—Marigold continued—"this will save you money on plane tickets. As the old saying goes, a penny saved is a penny earned. And finally"—Zinnie opened the slide for option three—"Berta and her mother could both stay here. We all love Berta, and she loves us, and we can all take turns taking care of her sick mother. The end!" Marigold took a bow.

Zinnie ended the slide show with the picture of the waterfall and raised the volume for a moment to finish with a bang.

"Brava, girls," Mom said. She clapped, and bubbles slid down her wrists. "The opening was my favorite part. No—maybe the rockets. Actually, I like the waterfall."

"See," Marigold said, "we don't have to go. We have three good options."

"Well, Grammy is too old to be looking after three girls by herself. So that's out. And I'm not having you stay with friends for three weeks. It's too much to ask."

"Why?" Marigold said.

"Who would you stay with?" Mom asked.

"Pilar. Anyone. I bet I could stay with Clint." Clint Lee was the very handsome star of *Seasons*. He always said hi to Marigold on set and sometimes even joked around with her.

"Clint Lee? Oh, no," Mom said.

"Not to be his girlfriend or anything," Marigold said, feeling her cheeks color.

"Oh, well, that's good," Mom said, and laughed.

"What about the third option then?" Marigold said, quickly changing the subject. "With Berta."

"My idea," Lily said.

"It makes sense, Mom," Zinnie added.

"Her mother isn't able to leave Mexico. She's very sick," Mom said. "Besides, you guys are going to love Aunt Sunny. She taught science to kids for twenty years. She knows everything about everything."

"How old is she?" Zinnie asked.

"What color is her hair?" Lily wanted to know.

"Does she know I'm allergic to strawberries?" Zinnie asked.

But Marigold raised a hand to silence them. "Mom, I need to talk to you alone."

# 9 · The Great Opportunity

**M**om left a trail of damp footprints on the carpet as she headed toward her closet and changed into her pajamas.

"Mom, how could you do this to me? Do you even know what a big deal getting an agent is? Do you care?" Marigold asked, following her.

"She'll still be your agent in August. You'll only be gone for three weeks," Mom said, smoothing some lotion on her face. "And of course I care. I care about *you*."

"But they're auditioning for *Night Sprites* on July seventh. Remember? It's just one day, and Jill told me she might be able to get me an audition."

"Those books are not exactly literature," Mom said, taking a seat on her bed.

"They're literature to me," Marigold said, and sat next to her mother. "Mom, have you ever wanted something so badly that it was all you could think about?"

"Yes," she said. "When I was your age, I wanted a perm."

"Really?" Marigold asked. Mom's straight, shiny blond hair was her crowning glory. People sometimes stopped her on the street to tell her what beautiful hair she had. Marigold couldn't imagine her wanting to change it in any way.

"Oh, yes, all the girls in my class were getting them, but Grammy said no way. She said the other girls looked like they'd stuck their finger in a socket, and why would I do that to myself?" Marigold laughed. Mom continued. "I begged, I pleaded, I cried, but Grammy wouldn't budge until finally I threatened to let Joanie MacDonald, my best friend's older sister, give me one herself. She was in beauty school and needed someone to experiment on."

"Did Grammy finally let you do it?" Marigold leaned in a little closer. This was getting good.

"Nope. Instead, she took me to her hairdresser, who set my hair in rollers and made me sit under one of those big dryers to show me what I would look like if I went through with it."

"How did it look?" Marigold asked.

"It was awful," Mom said, laughing as she remembered. "I washed it out as soon as I got home, and I was so glad my mother had saved me from months of terrible, embarrassing hair."

"I guess that this audition is like my perm," Marigold said, trying to refocus the conversation. "Only imagine if that perm was the best thing that ever happened to you."

"Look," Mom said, "the truth is, your dad and I don't want you to get too swept up in this whole acting thing. We know how excited you are that you have an agent, and we want to support your dreams, but we have a job as your parents to do what we think is best for you. We think it's more important that you have this experience with your great-aunt and your sisters. You only get to be a kid once."

"But I want to be like Amanda Mills."

"No, you don't," Mom said. "Do you have any idea how messed up her life is? Poor girl didn't even know her mom until she was nine years old, And remember how late her mom was picking her up from Jill's office? I think Amanda is probably very troubled."

Dad wandered into the room, carrying a scribbled-on script. "I can practically feel the drama from downstairs," he said, kicking off his shoes and sitting on the sofa opposite the bed. He dropped the script on the floor and folded his hands behind his head. "So is this a tragedy or a comedy?"

Mom tilted her head, considering. "I think a dramedy," she said.

"What?" Marigold said, hunching over and pressing her fists to her tired eyes. "It's not funny. It's not funny at all. Daddy," she pleaded, "please don't make me go away. Please let me stay. I have an agent and a chance to audition for my dream movie. This is the opportunity of a lifetime. "

"You have a lot of lifetime ahead of you, kiddo," Dad said.

"The answer is no, Marigold," Mom added. "Let it go."

## 10 · Zinnie in Midair

"Do you think we'll see a whale from up here?" Zinnie asked when their gondola reached the top of the Ferris wheel at the Santa Monica Pier. The gondola was a circle-shaped bench with a high back and little swinging door for people to get on and off the ride. Zinnie, Dad, Marigold, and Mom were seated inside.

"Not without binoculars," Mom said. "Shoot! We should have brought them."

Zinnie made a visor with her hands and scanned the horizon, hoping that with just her naked eyes she'd still be able to see a whale or a pod of dolphins. She'd even settle for one dolphin. She just wanted something to remember California by. They were leaving for the East Coast in two days for three whole weeks, and her parents had agreed to take them to the pier as long as they were packed for Pruet. Zinnie and Lily, with Berta's help, both had their suitcases ready to go in about a half hour. Marigold, on the other hand, had spent the entire morning packing, and they hadn't been able to leave the house until after lunch.

After some pretty bad traffic and an emergency frozen yogurt stop, they were finally here, though not all of them were on the Ferris wheel. Lily and Berta were at the carousel, which was back by the bridge, much closer to the road. Lily was terrified of the ocean and refused to walk out beyond the old-fashioned ice cream parlor.

Zinnie, however, thought all the fun started once she walked past the carousel and ice cream parlor, went beyond the fruit carts and the tourist shops and the arcade, and arrived at the amusement park. Even if they weren't as scary or as fast as the ones at Universal Studios or as elaborate as those at Disneyland, she loved the rides that swept and looped and suspended her above the Pacific Ocean. She wasn't about to take off for three whole weeks without reminding Dad that he had promised they would come here once school was out.

The Ferris wheel paused at the tippy top of its cycle, and Zinnie held her breath as she looked down at the crowds on the pier and beach below. People were eating hot dogs, tacos, ice cream, and funnel cake. They were playing tag and splashing barefoot in the surf. Boyfriends and girlfriends were holding hands and hugging. One family was even swimming, even though it was chilly enough for Zinnie to wear a light jacket. Mom wouldn't let them go in the water here because she said it was polluted, but the blue-green waves looked clean and inviting from where Zinnie sat. Behind her was the city of Santa Monica with its office buildings and shopping malls. To the left were the fancy hotels where Marigold said some girls in her class were going to have their bat mitzvahs next year. And to the right was Malibu with its mansions and rugged pink cliffs.

Above it all, swinging over the sea, with a chilly salt breeze blowing on her face, Zinnie felt peaceful. She wondered if the beach was what she would miss most about California. Mom said there was a beach in Pruet, but she'd also mentioned that it didn't have an amusement park attached to it, or a mall down the street, or the best taco truck in the whole wide world parked on the street nearby.

"Do they have any taco trucks at all in Pruet?" Zinnie asked, wondering if she could actually survive without good taquitos, burritos, or churros for three whole weeks.

"I don't think so, Zin," Dad said, putting an arm around her. She leaned against his shoulder.

Now that Zinnie thought of it, she was going to miss a lot of things about California. Her mom kept saying that three weeks wasn't that long, but it felt that way when it meant that she wasn't going to be able to go to the summer program at Miss Hadley's with her best friends, Milly and McKenzie, who were probably at this very moment deciding what classes to sign up for. And Miss Hadley's summer program was totally different from school. It had classes like fashion design and ice cream making and field trips to Dodgers games and a real animation studio. As hard as Zinnie was trying to have a good attitude, Pruet sounded boring in comparison with all that she would miss.

The Ferris wheel started again. This was Zinnie's favorite part, when the gondola began its descent, because there was always a moment when it felt like she was flying. They tipped forward, and her stomach fluttered with suspense. Zinnie held tight to Dad's hand and, looking at the ocean through cracks of the swinging door, delighting in the tingling thrill that there was nothing but air between her and the watery depths below.

Marigold had always loved this Ferris wheel too, but her eyes were totally glued to her cell phone. How could she be texting right now?

"Can you put that phone away?" Mom asked Marigold. "The point of today is to spend time together."

"It's Pilar," Marigold said. "I need to see my best friend before I leave. Can I hang out with her tomorrow night?"

"Only if you put that away," Mom said.

"Just let me finish this one thing . . . ," Marigold said, not even looking up.

"But you're missing the best part," Zinnie said, reaching to cover the screen of Marigold's cell phone. Zinnie was too forceful, and Marigold's phone slipped from her hands and fell to the metal floor. Zinnie's stomach clenched as the phone slid toward the opening.

"Zinnie!" Marigold shrieked just as her dad's foot stopped the phone from falling through the crack.

"I didn't mean it!" Zinnie said.

"What were you thinking?" Marigold asked, her cheeks pink with anger.

"Relax," Dad said, bending to pick up the phone and handing it to Marigold.

"If you had lost my phone, I would have—" Marigold began to say. Their mom didn't let her finish.

"But she didn't," Mom said. "The phone is safe. So it's all good."

But it didn't feel all good. Marigold was scowling even though her phone was safely back in her hands, and Zinnie couldn't help wondering what Marigold would have said to her if their dad hadn't caught the phone with his foot. And the Ferris wheel was already at the boring bottom, and the attendant was standing ready to open the door for them to get out.

"But I missed the right-over-the-ocean part," Zinnie said.

"Then it's lucky we still have time for one more go-round, isn't it?" Dad said, wrapping his arm around her.

# 11 · Fake Kiss

The day before Marigold's dreaded departure to Pruet, Massachusetts, she and Pilar had plans to go to the Farmers Market, a historic marketplace with about a hundred restaurant stalls and farm stands. It was one of Marigold's favorite places to go in L.A. She loved all the different kinds of food there, especially the kimchi at the Korean stall, the pancakes at the 1950s diner, and the pupusas at the Salvadoran stand. And it was dessert heaven! There was ice cream, French crepes, and, Marigold's personal favorite, the Periwinkle Pie Shop, the oldest pie shop in Los Angeles.

She also loved the knickknack stores because she could always find at least one thing that she could afford with her allowance, like a package of stickers to seal the notes she passed in class or a piece of English toffee. And of course she loved the fancy outdoor mall behind the Farmers Market. It had all the coolest clothing stores. Even if she couldn't buy anything, it was still fun to try stuff on.

The girls were going to the Farmers Market to get something delicious and discuss their summer plans. At least that was the story. What they were really doing, Pilar said, was meeting up with Alex Key, the cutest seventh-grade boy at Epiphany, the boys' school down the street from Miss Hadley's. Alex Key had dark-blond hair and eyes the color of green Jolly Ranchers, and he smelled ever so faintly of Right Guard "fresh scent" deodorant (Pilar and her sharp nose had memorized the scent when they all were dancing to a fast song at the Winter Snowball, reported back, and initiated a research investigation at Rite Aid). He could snowboard, skateboard, breakdance, and beatbox. Now that he'd gotten his braces off and had a cool surfer haircut, Pilar had nicknamed him California Dreamin', after the Mamas and Papas song that played on her grandma's favorite radio station once an hour.

Pilar had heard through the Miss Hadley's grapevine that Alex Key thought Marigold was cute. Despite her own crush on him, Pilar was determined that someone should go out with Alex Key, even if she wasn't the one. She also knew that Marigold, who was prone to shyness around the opposite sex, had never held hands with a boy. Pilar wanted her friends to be in the loop and on the cutting edge. Pilar wanted Marigold to get kissed.

So did Marigold.

In fact, when she hadn't been thinking about landing a part in *Night Sprites*, she had been thinking about kissing.

Marigold's secret was that she had been kissed a month ago on *Seasons*. Thankfully, the scene had been cut, so no one knew about it. When she'd read the kissing moment in the script, she put a hand over her mouth and yelped. Her belly clenched. It wasn't fair. She didn't want to kiss anyone. Especially not Martin Goldblatt, the young actor who played the boy. He was only eleven! And he chewed with his mouth open! But she was too shy to voice her concern. Ronald P. Harp had taught her to always be professional. So when the director called action, Marigold ignored her churning stomach, puckered up, and touched her tremulous lips with Martin Goldblatt's. Even though their mouths were closed, she could smell the nachos he had eaten at the craft services table. His hand was on her knee, and it was so light that it tickled her.

"Did you fart?" he asked afterward. She stared at him unable to speak. Had she? She wasn't sure. It was true that something didn't smell right. But before she could deny it or defend herself, he was back at the craft services table, eating more nachos. She speed walked toward her dressing room and nearly knocked over Clint Lee on the way.

"Hey, you okay?" Clint asked.

"Yeah," she said, and bit her lip.

"You sure?" Clint asked. Marigold nodded. Clint put a reassuring hand on her shoulder. "Just remember, that was your character's first kiss"—he looked her in the eye and gave her shoulder a light squeeze—"not yours." She nearly burst into tears of pure relief.

"So it's like it never happened?" she asked.

"That's right." He smiled his magical smile, the very one that earned him millions, and she felt her cheeks burn. Suddenly she wanted him to kiss her.

## 12 · Real Kiss

In fact, kissing had been on Marigold's mind ever since her run-in with Clint. She'd even practiced on her pillow once or twice. Or okay, maybe ten times. But Clint Lee was way too old for her. He was twenty-one. When Marigold was eighteen, he'd be twenty-seven, and they could get married and have babies named Topaz, Opal, and Aquamarine. But that was a long way away. And she was going to have to get some kissing practice in before then, and not just on her pillow. Why not with Alex Key? He was really cute. Also, she wanted to extinguish the kiss of Martin Goldblatt as soon as possible. The longer his kiss remained her only one, the more reality it seemed to accumulate.

Marigold stood in the kitchen, staring out the window, waiting for Pilar's French au pair, Sylvie, to pick her up and take them all to the Farmers Market. Mom was on the computer, making arrangements for her trip to Canada. Berta was humming softly as she chopped fresh fruit. Zinnie and Lily were gobbling down their favorite Berta dish, chicken flautas. Finally a car horn beeped.

"Oh, that's Sylvie," Marigold said. "Gotta go."

"Wait a sec," Mom said. "Who's Sylvie?"

"She's Pilar's new au pair," Marigold said, taking a quick look at herself in her camera phone. "Remember? She's the one who'll be watching us at the Farmers Market."

"Can I come?" Zinnie asked.

"No," Marigold said, and headed toward the door.

"Why not?" Mom asked.

"I'd like to spend my last hours in civilization with my best friend," Marigold said. "Besides, Zinnie is eating dinner. And all we're doing is going out to dinner. So I don't see why she'd even want to come."

Mom tilted her head and raised her eyebrows as if to say, "Give me a break."

Zinnie pushed her plate with the remaining bites of flautas on it away from her, which showed her commitment to joining Marigold on her outing, because she really loved those flautas. "Please can I come?" Zinnie asked. "I won't even speak. I won't talk at all." She ran a pretend zipper across her lips.

"I said no," Marigold said.

"She just wants to be with you, Marigold," Mom said.

"And I just want to do my own thing. Why is that a crime? I should be allowed to go on my own, right, Berta?"

"I'm staying out of this one," Berta said.

"Can I go?" Lily asked.

"You're staying home with me," Berta said. "We're going to make pan dulce for tomorrow morning."

"And watch a DVD?" Lily asked.

"I said no more DVDs today," Mom said. Lily looked like she was about to cry, and Mom quickly added, "Okay, one more, but that's it."

It was impossible to say no to Lily.

The car horn beeped again.

"Please." Zinnie begged. "I want to be in civilization, too!"

"Lose the attitude, Marigold," Mom said, folding her arms across her chest. "I'm not sure you should go if you can't include your sister."

"No!" Zinnie said. "Don't keep Marigold home because of me, Mom."

Guilt pressed on Marigold like a Lily-sized foot. "Fine," Marigold said. "Come on. Just don't embarrass me."

"Keep your cell phones on!" Mom called as Zinnie sprang from the table and followed Marigold down the hallway and out the front door.

"Hi, Marigold," Pilar said from the front seat as

Marigold and Zinnie climbed into the backseat. "Zinnie, you're coming, too?" Zinnie nodded, and Pilar gave her a high five.

"But I'm not allowed to talk." Zinnie buckled her seat belt. "I'm just along for the ride."

"Zat's horrible!" Sylvie said from the front. Marigold shrank in her seat. This had been the story of her life. Babysitters always liked Zinnie better. Ever since she was a baby, Zinnie had a way of drawing people toward her. Marigold knew that she wasn't doing it on purpose, but it didn't mean that it was any less painful when just as Marigold was about to make a new friend or start a game on the playground, Zinnie would magically appear, beaming like a patch of sunshine on a cloudy day. Sometimes Marigold just wanted to do things in her own way, in her own time, without having to worry that she'd be left in the shadows.

Sylvie stopped at the red light at Beverly and La Brea. "In zis car, anyone may say what zay sink. It eez ze French way."

"*Vive la France!*" Zinnie said, and Sylvie exploded with laughter.

"You can talk, okay?" Marigold snapped.

"What's your problem?" Pilar asked.

"Nothing," Marigold said, and gazed out the window, regretting that she had allowed Zinnie to come. Pilar was an only child, so she didn't understand just how annoying a little sister could be.

"So Zinnie, do you want my advice for middle school?" Pilar asked.

"Uh . . ." Zinnie looked to Marigold for approval. Marigold nodded. "Sure."

"Don't put a penny in your penny loafers," Pilar said. "That's not cool. And request Mr. Bonito for your adviser. Oh, and don't join too many clubs; just pick one or two. Yearbook and Irish dancing are good."

"Irish dancing sounds fun," Zinnie said.

Marigold rolled down the window as far as it would go. They drove past the gates of a major TV network where people were lined up around the block with sleeping bags and folding chairs, hoping to be first in line the next day to maybe audition for a game show or be in the audience for the finale of *America Sings*. As they turned left onto Fairfax Avenue, Marigold's eyes were drawn to a giant billboard advertising the latest *Night Sprite*s book. She could only hope that kissing would distract her from the dream she wouldn't have the chance to fight for.

# 13 · Unkissed

"Okay, act casual, but the eagle has landed," Pilar said, and dabbed her mouth with a napkin. The girls were finishing their cheeseburgers. They were seated at a prime table at the Farmers Market, right near the French crepe place, which was where Alex Key was going to meet them. Sylvie had agreed to keep her distance as long as the girls stayed within her line of sight. She was drinking a milk shake at the 1950s diner counter, acting like she didn't know them, just like she'd promised.

"An American bald eagle!" Zinnie said, looking alarmed. "Where?" She was about to stand up when Marigold pulled her back into her seat. "What?" Zinnie asked. "They're very rare, especially in the Farmers Mar . . ." Zinnie trailed off when she saw the other girls laughing. "What?"

"'The eagle has landed' is a code phrase. It means a cute boy just showed up," Pilar said. "Alex Key. Marigold's future boyfriend."

"Ooooh," Zinnie said, "Alex Key."

"Hey, ladies," Alex said in his surfer drawl when he spotted them and approached the table.

"Heeeyyy," they all answered at once.

"What's up?" he asked.

Pilar waited for Marigold to reply, but after a few awkward seconds passed, Pilar piped up. "Not much. Um, you know Marigold. This is her little sister, Zinnie."

"Hi," Zinnie said. "I've heard a lot about you."

"A lot, huh?" Alex asked.

"A ton," Zinnie answered.

Marigold and Pilar turned pink. "Well, we've just finished our dinner," Pilar said, rising to the occasion. "Why don't Marigold and Alex get Presto Gelato, and Zinnie and I will get some pie?"

"Sounds good," Alex said.

"But I want to get Presto—" Zinnie started to say.

Pilar pulled her away. "Nope, we're getting pie," Pilar said.

"Oooh, right!" Zinnie said. "I just lo-o-o-ove pie!" Pilar giggled and looped her arms through Zinnie's.

"So," Alex said to Marigold as they made their way toward Presto Gelato, "how's that TV show going? Are you, like, filming and stuff?"

"Not now," Marigold said. "We're on hiatus." Alex gave her a funny look. "A break."

"Oh," Alex said as they pushed through a crowd by a popular Mexican place. "That's cool."

"I've tried all of the flavors except lavender honey," Marigold said proudly.

"Why?" Alex asked.

"I just wanted to, I guess," Marigold said.

"Girls are weird," Alex said.

Marigold wasn't sure how to respond. She was proud of having tried almost every flavor and thought it was pretty interesting. They stood in the long line at Presto in complete silence for several minutes. Then, out of nowhere, Alex put an arm around her shoulder. What was she supposed to do? Put a hand on his back? Her limbs suddenly felt awkward and extra long, and she seemed unable to move them.

"What flavor do you think you're going to get?" she asked him, grateful that her mouth still worked, at least. She would need that later for kissing.

"S'mores," he said.

"I love that kind," she said.

"Course you do. It's awesome." Alex smiled. "What are you going to get?"

"Lavender honey, of course," she said.

"That sounds like soap," Alex said. Marigold laughed. This was getting easier. He dropped his arm as they moved up in line, and while Marigold was relieved to not have the heavy limb draped over her shoulder, she also kind of missed its being there.

They ordered their gelati and found seats at a table that was sort of off by itself. The conversation started to flow. It turned out that they both liked sushi, dogs that didn't lick too much, and Zuma Beach in Malibu. And lavender honey wasn't that bad. Under the table, one of Alex's knees touched hers. Then he closed his eyes and leaned toward her. Martin Goldblatt's kiss was on the verge of being completely erased from her life, replaced by a real first kiss with Alex Key, when Pilar rushed over, flustered and stressed.

"Oh, my God, there you are," she said. "You've got to come quick. Zinnie is all puffy and itchy. Sylvie wants to take her to the hospital!"

"Did she eat a strawberry?" Marigold asked.

"Yes! Oh, God, oh, God! Yes!" Pilar said. "There are strawberries in the rhubarb pie!"

"She knows she shouldn't eat strawberries," Marigold said.

"Is she going to die?" Pilar asked. "Because if I even breathe nut dust, I'm a goner."

"No," Marigold said, crumpling her napkin. "She's just going to look weird and get some hives."

"Sylvie wants us to go," Pilar said. Marigold didn't want to go. She wanted to stay. "Don't just sit there, Marigold. Hurry up."

"Okay," Marigold said. "Fine."

"I'll see you around," Alex said.

"Yeah," Marigold said, stood up, and gathered her purse. "Sure."

Except she wouldn't. Because she was going to Massachusetts the next day. She was going to remain unkissed for the whole summer, and it was all Zinnie's fault. Luckily, she had a five-hour plane ride to think of how to get back at her.

# 14 · Good-bye, Home

"Hey, Zin. It's time to wake up. We're leaving for the airport in twenty minutes," Dad said, gently shaking her shoulder. Zinnie opened her eyes, which were still a little swollen from her reaction to the strawberries, and saw that the sky outside her window was purple dark. "I know it's early," he said, "but we have to get a move on."

Dad looked different this early in the morning, Zinnie thought. He seemed softer around the edges. Or maybe it was the medicine. She'd taken her allergy pills last night, and they always made her a little fuzzy the next morning. "Mom, Lily, and Marigold are downstairs eating breakfast. We thought we'd let you sleep in a little, but it's time to roll." Dad put his coffee on the table and offered her his hands, but instead of leaping out of bed, Zinnie threw her arms around him.

"I'll miss you," she said.

"I'll be thinking of you every day," Dad said, and hugged her back.

"While you're up in the trees?"

"And camping under the stars. I'll look up and know that no matter how far away you are, we'll be looking up at the same moon." Zinnie smiled at the idea. "Now, how about you wash your face and brush your teeth while I put your suitcases in the car. Okay?"

"Okay," she said, and kicked off the covers.

"Is that all you have?" he asked, pointing to her roller bag and backpack. She'd packed shorts, jeans, undies, socks, T-shirts, her two favorite bathing suits, a couple of sweatshirts, sneakers, flip-flops, three *Night Sprite* books, a notebook and pen, and her hair goop, in case she had the courage to try it again.

"Should I have packed more?" she asked. "Mom said just the basics."

"No," Dad said. "It's just that Marigold is bringing three times this much."

"Yeah, well," Zinnie said, thinking about how Marigold hadn't said one word to her in the car ride home from the Farmers Market, "Marigold has issues."

"We can talk about it downstairs," Dad said, picking up her suitcase.

"I just need to pack up my laptop and charge my phone," Zinnie said, plugging her phone into the charger. "I forgot to do it last night."

"You won't need your computer, honey," Dad said. "Why don't you leave it here? Go wash your face and come grab some breakfast when you're done. Berta came to say good-bye. She made pan dulce and your favorite, champurrado."

"Mmm," Zinnie said. Champurrado was a treat, and usually a wintertime one. Zinnie guessed that Lily had made a special request, and she was so glad. The idea of the warm, spicy cinnamon-and-chocolate drink made her momentarily forget about Marigold and her dirty looks.

But she couldn't forget for long. As soon as Zinnie entered the kitchen and took her usual seat at the table, Marigold stood up, brought her plate to the sink, and declared that she would be waiting in the car.

"By yourself?" Lily asked.

"We're leaving in five minutes," Dad said. "Can you wait five minutes so that we can finish breakfast as a family?"

"No," Marigold said, giving Berta a hug and kiss good-bye before she charged out the door.

Zinnie stood up to follow her, but Berta said, "Let her cool off, *mija*. She's almost a teenager, and teenagers need their space." She ladled champurrado into Zinnie's favorite mug, the one with the Hollywood sign on it, and handed it to Zinnie. "Have some besos," Berta said, nodding toward the basket of sugar-dusted pastries with raspberry jam filling.

"Thanks, Berta," Zinnie said, already feeling a little better. Besos were Zinnie's favorite type of pan dulce.

"What happened between you two?" Mom asked, combing Zinnie's hair with her fingers and pulling it into a ponytail.

"She's mad that I ate a strawberry," Zinnie said.

"Are you sure it's not something else?" Dad asked. Like a detective in one of the old movies they watched during Classics on Tuesdays, he could always sense missing information. "It takes two to tango, you know."

"Or rumba!" Berta said, shaking her shoulders, and Lily laughed.

"You're going to have to try to get along for Aunt Sunny," Mom said.

"I always try to get along," Zinnie said. "She's the one who hates me!"

"She doesn't hate you, honey," Mom said. "She loves you."

"And she admires you," Berta said from across the table as she sipped her champurrado. "She just doesn't know it yet."

"Yeah, right!" Zinnie said. "Berta, that's crazy. She thinks I'm a dork."

"Berta's not crazy!" Lily said. "She knows everything. She put the string back in my sweatshirt hood this morning using magic."

"My angel!" Berta said, turning her attention to

Lily. "I'm going to need at least five more hugs before you go."

"Five more, and then it's time to go," Dad said as Lily and Berta began counting hugs aloud.

"One . . . two . . . ," they counted together as they hugged.

"Come on, Zin. You can finish your breakfast in the car," Mom said.

"Three . . . four . . . four and a half . . . four and three-quarters." Berta and Lily continued as Zinnie wrapped her pan dulce in a napkin.

"How are we going to even know who Aunt Sunny is?" Zinnie asked, taking extra besos for the road. "What if we get in the car with the wrong lady?"

"Fiiiiive!" Berta and Lily said, elongating their final embrace.

"Sunny's not picking you up," Mom said, grabbing her keys off the counter. "We didn't want her to have to drive to and from Boston in rush hour, so a driver is going to meet you at the airport in Boston to take you to Pruet. She'll be waiting for you with a big sign that has your names on it."

"How long is the ride from the airport?" Zinnie asked, following Mom out the door as a million other questions rushed into her brain, like: What did Aunt Sunny usually make for breakfast? Could she make champurrado? Had Mom told her that they were allowed to watch TV after dinner and on weekends?

Did Aunt Sunny have lots of rules? Would they have to clean their rooms every day? Would she allow Zinnie to stay up late reading if she couldn't fall asleep? How many days exactly were they going to be apart from California and their parents and Berta and their bedrooms and all their stuff? How many hours, how many minutes would they be thousands of miles away from home?

# 15 · A Different Ocean

When they stepped off the plane and made their way to baggage claim, Zinnie spotted a round, smiley lady holding a sign that said SILVER SISTERS. At first she thought she was Aunt Sunny, but then Marigold reminded them that she was the driver and Pruet was an hour and a half away.

Once in the car, after they'd collected their luggage, Zinnie looked out the window and contemplated her situation. Lily was asleep in the middle, and Marigold was seated as far from Zinnie as possible, her face turned toward the opposite window.

The plane ride had been turbulent for Zinnie, and not just because they'd hit weather over the Rocky Mountains. And not just because her seat back wasn't reclining or because she'd finished rereading the one *Night Sprites* book in her carry-on somewhere over the

Mississippi River, forcing her to play tic-tac-toe with herself and make origami out of the pages of the in-flight magazines.

It had been a rough ride because Marigold was furious with Zinnie for getting in the way of her kiss, even though it had been a complete mistake on Zinnie's part. Marigold was refusing to even acknowledge her except for the one time she called her number two. Zinnie knew darn well that number two wasn't only her birth order. The punishment did not fit the crime, Zinnie thought, because there hadn't even been a crime. There'd only been a mistake.

Zinnie had tried to explain to Marigold at least five times that she hadn't realized that rhubarb pie had strawberries in it. She'd never had rhubarb. She didn't know what it was. Pilar had been raving about it to the point that Zinnie was going to feel like a jerk if she didn't get it. Zinnie knew she was supposed to ask if things contained strawberries, but a pie usually said exactly what it had in it. Peach pie had peaches. Apple pie had apples. Blueberry pie had blueberries. None of those pies had secret strawberries in them, so why should rhubarb? Did Marigold think that she liked breaking out in hives? That she enjoyed being itchy and swollen?

Or maybe it was about more than the kiss. After Marigold had walked off toward the gelato shop with Alex, Pilar and Zinnie had gone into a store and Zinnie had held up an enormous bra and said in her best grown-up voice, "This will be perfect for my big bazoombas! Does it come with matching underpants?" Pilar had laughed so hard Zinnie thought she was going to wet her pants. It inspired Zinnie to keep going. She grabbed a pair of leopard-print underwear and said to no one in particular, "Which way to the zoo? I'm an animal!" This had sent Pilar to the floor in convulsions. Zinnie wished Ronald P. Harp had been there so he could see that in real life people liked it when she pulled faces.

She also wished Marigold had been there. She wished Marigold had been the one laughing.

Zinnie had always had a feeling that Pilar liked her a lot. Even though Zinnie was still in the lower school, which made her totally uncool to middle schoolers, Pilar talked to her every day, in the library or on the playground or in the locker room. It was almost like Zinnie and Pilar had their own friendship. After last night, when Pilar had laughed so hard that she cried, Zinnie was starting to wonder if Pilar liked her more than her own sister did. After the way Marigold ignored her or merely tolerated her, it had felt good to be appreciated.

As the driver turned off the freeway onto a smaller road, Zinnie had to admit that it had also felt good to get so much attention from Pilar, to take something away from Marigold.

"Almost there," the driver said. They drove over a small bridge, down a long, leafy street, through a little town with an ice cream place, a café, a general store, some small shops, Ed's Fish 'n' Tackle, and a tiny post office. A little farther up the road was something called a boatyard. A yard for boats? As they rounded the corner, a harbor came into full view. This place was so different from Los Angeles, where the roads were big, even, and smooth; and the freeways, alive with speeding cars, crossed over and under one another like snakes; and tall palm trees guarded the sidewalks. As they bumped down the road, Zinnie felt as if they were in the pages of a book about summertime. The houses along the little road, which were covered in gray shingles and had bright white or red or green shutters and flowers in the window boxes, were like cottages. The water was dark blue, calm and sparkling. Sailboats crossed in the distance. The trees with their green canopies seemed just the type to be occupied by talking animals.

"I thought we were going far away from California," Lily said.

"We are," Zinnie said. "We're just about as far away as you can get and still be in America."

"Then why is the ocean right there?" Lily asked.

"It's a different ocean," Zinnie said.

"A different ocean?" Lily asked. Her face tightened

with fear as she held Benny close. They turned up a dirt road. On either side of them there was a stone wall made of big, round rocks that looked like it was going to topple over.

They rolled down a long driveway and pulled up in front of a small house. Zinnie opened her window all the way. The air smelled sweet and sunny and green. She saw a face in the window, and then the door flung open.

# 16 · Aunt Sunny

Aunt Sunny bounded out of the little house. She had short gray hair, small glasses, and a big smile. She greeted them all, getting a good long look at each of them and shaking their hands. Zinnie liked the way Aunt Sunny looked her in the eye, the way her favorite teachers did. "Oh, I can't stand it," Aunt Sunny said. "I've got to give you all a hug." She wrapped her arms around all three of them and squeezed. She smelled a little bit like pumpkin pie. As soon as she let them go, Lily stood shyly behind Zinnie. Marigold took a step backward and checked her cell phone's reception.

"Um, I don't have a signal, and we need to call Mom and Dad to let them know we arrived safely," Marigold said.

Zinnie felt in her pockets for her phone. Maybe hers would get a signal. "Oh, no," she said, rechecking the pockets of her jeans and her sweatshirt. "I left mine in L.A."

"Are you sure?" Marigold asked.

Zinnie nodded. She could picture her phone still plugged into the wall. She had left in such a rush this morning.

"You won't need it. We don't get really get any cell reception out here anyway," Aunt Sunny said. Zinnie watched the color drain from Marigold's face. "But don't worry. You can call from the house. Okay." Aunt Sunny clapped her hands three times. "Time for the grand tour."

They followed her inside, dragging their luggage behind them.

The house was the strangest Zinnie had ever seen. It was like something out of a fairy tale. The front door was inside a stone archway and had a little latch that opened it instead of a doorknob. And everything was made of wood: wooden floors, wooden walls, wooden ceilings. In the kitchen, the countertops were made of wood. So was the table. So were the two long benches on either side of the table. And it was like a maze. It was full of tiny rooms, one leading into another, with either a step up or a step down between them. How was Zinnie going to find the kitchen at night if she needed a glass of water? She would have to make a map.

And there were pictures of boats everywhere: photographs of boats, paintings of boats, and drawings of boats. There were tiny, intricate boat models. The other decorations were also ocean or boat related. There were paintings of waves, postcards of beaches, collections of shells in the windowsills, and a whale's tail carved out of wood on a side table.

Zinnie paused in front of one of the photographs in the study. It was black and white. There was a couple sitting inside a little sailboat, waving at whoever had taken the picture.

"Great picture, isn't it?" Sunny asked.

"Who are they?" Zinnie asked.

"Why, that's me," Aunt Sunny said, pointing to the young lady with the long braid. Zinnie recognized Aunt Sunny's eyes. "I was with Ham in *Tippy*, our little catboat. She was a beauty, *Tippy* was."

"I don't see any ham," Lily said.

Zinnie nudged Lily and whispered, "I think Ham is a person."

"Oh, was he ever!" Sunny said, her face opening into a smile that sent wrinkles in six directions. "Hamish Holt. He was a handsome devil, wasn't he? He was my husband."

"Where is he?" Zinnie asked.

"I lost him to cancer many years ago," Sunny said.

"I'm so sorry," Marigold said. Despite their arguing, Zinnie felt proud of Marigold in that moment. It was the right thing to say.

"I think Berta's mother has cancer," Lily said.

"Some people who have cancer get better," Aunt Sunny said. "But not Ham. Now I visit him at the Pisquatuit Head Cemetery."

"Where's the rest of him?"

"What do you mean?" Aunt Sunny said, leaning against the big wooden desk.

"Well, if that's where his head is buried, where's the rest of him?" Lily asked.

Zinnie bit her lip. This was the strangest conversation! Marigold covered her mouth with her hands. Aunt Sunny put her hand on Lily's shoulder and laughed and laughed.

"Oh, dear me," Aunt Sunny said, and took her hand off Lily's shoulder to remove her glasses and wipe her eyes. "They buried him in one piece. Pisquatuit Head is the name of the land where the cemetery is. Come on now, shall we complete the tour?"

Sunny led them down another low-ceiling hallway and over a step and through a little archway to a room with a fireplace and sofa and some big comfy chairs. "And here's the living room," she said, "which gets the most heavenly afternoon sunshine and is the best place to read a good book." There was a large window that looked out onto a garden and, beyond that, the ocean. There was also a rug with a mermaid on it.

"Excuse me, but where's your TV?" Zinnie asked.

"I don't have one," Aunt Sunny said, and gestured to the picture window. "I find nature puts on a fine show.

From here you can actually watch a summer storm move across the sky. And there's a family of foxes that lives just east of that tree."

Lily was busy looking for the family of foxes while Zinnie and Marigold exchanged the first sisterly look since before the strawberry incident. No TV? Dad had written for TV, and Marigold was on TV. All three Silver sisters had TV shows they watched regularly. It was one of the few things that they could do together without fighting.

"Um, do you have internet?" Marigold asked.

"Of course! I don't live in the Dark Ages. Come along now," Aunt Sunny said. "I'll show you where you'll be sleeping."

## 17 · The Barracks

*U*p the narrow staircase they went: Aunt Sunny, then Marigold, then Zinnie, and finally Lily. From her position two steps below Aunt Sunny on the staircase, Marigold couldn't help looking at the back of her aunt's legs, which were tan and strong for an old lady.

At the top was a bedroom with a ceiling that slanted on both sides and a window that looked out over the backyard. The whole room was painted white: the ceiling, the floor, the walls, and even the old radiator. There were four doors no taller than Lily that fastened with wooden latches.

"Are these secret passageways?" Zinnie asked, referring to the little doors.

"They're closets," Aunt Sunny said, opening one to demonstrate.

Marigold turned her attention to the two narrow little beds parallel to one another, each with a pale-blue blanket, the sheet folded over in a band of white, and a single pillow at the top. These beds were pretty much the exact opposite of the pink, duvet-covered fluffiness the girls enjoyed at home, where no Silver bed suffered from any fewer than four color-coordinated pillows at a time, be they square, rectangle, or tubular.

If it hadn't been for the colorful hooked rugs on the floor, which sort of matched and sort of didn't, the two painted white dressers, and the dollhouse that seemed straight out of *Little House on the Prairie* times, Marigold thought, it would look as if the girls had joined the army. Clint Lee had been in a movie about the army, and the beds the soldiers slept in were almost exactly like these, only with green blankets instead of blue.

"They may not look like much, but these beds are quite comfortable. Ham built them himself. They're just like the berths he built in his boats. Just a piece of canvas stretched across a wooden frame. They suit a body nicely." Lily and Zinnie each sat on a bed. Zinnie was smiling, her eyes lit up. Marigold guessed that she was pretending she was a stowaway.

The big relief was that there were only two beds in here, which meant that Marigold would be sleeping somewhere else. Marigold needed her privacy. She needed to be able to shut the door and block out her sisters. She needed her own space: her own closet, her own window, her own four walls. Marigold was very particular about the way things needed to be set up. Zinnie was so messy, it gave Marigold anxiety to think of her room back home, with the clothes on the floor and the homework all over her desk. Marigold had lowered her expectations and didn't think she'd be lucky enough to have her own bathroom, but she took comfort from the thought that there had to be another room, another space, for her. No one would expect her to sleep on the floor, and these beds were way too small for sharing.

"I hope you girls will be happy here," Aunt Sunny said. Marigold noticed Aunt Sunny's accent then. "Here" sounded like *hee-ah*. "I know it's simple"—Aunt Sunny continued—"but simple things are often the best."

"Don't worry," Marigold said. "I'll help them get settled just as soon as I put my things in the room where I'll be staying."

Aunt Sunny smiled, walked across the floor, and unfastened a latch on the wall, and presto—another boat bed.

"A secret bed!" Lily clapped. Zinnie smiled. Marigold swallowed.

"Isn't that neat?" Aunt Sunny asked. "You'll all be here together. Three beds for three sisters. Now raise your hands, who wants a hamburger for dinner?"

While Aunt Sunny made hamburgers on the grill, the girls called home. The phone was in the middle of Aunt Sunny's living room, and the talking-into part was attached to the dialing part with an old-fashioned curly cord, the kind that was in the classrooms at school. Marigold didn't even know it existed in people's homes. With no cell phone reception and only one phone in the whole house, Marigold felt all hope of the privacy she treasured evaporate. Since she was the eldest, it was understood that she would be the one to make the call. She picked up the phone and dialed.

"Hello?" Mom said.

"Hi, Mom," Marigold said, and out of absolutely nowhere a big lump formed in her throat. This was the first time Marigold was going to be away from her parents for more than a weekend. She had expected to miss Pilar and her bedroom and all her things, and she was prepared to take care of Zinnie and Lily if they missed their parents. She and Mom had talked about that. But she hadn't expected to be the one to be sad. Maybe it was because she was the oldest, and everyone depended on her to be strong. Or maybe it was because she'd been so mad about missing the audition for *Night Sprites* that she hadn't processed that they were going to be all the way across the country without their parents for three whole weeks. Or maybe she was just tired from a long, bumpy plane ride and fighting with Zinnie. But whatever the reason, Marigold hadn't anticipated that the sound of Mom's voice, so warm and familiar, would make her feel like crying.

"How are you, honey?" Mom asked. "How was the flight?"

"Okay," Marigold said. Zinnie and Lily were sitting on the couch, staring up at her with their big brown eyes. Marigold couldn't let them know that she was on the verge of tears. As angry as she was at Zinnie for ruining her first kiss, she knew that if Zinnie saw her cry, she would cry, too, and then so would Lily. Marigold took a deep breath and said, "We just wanted to let you know we're safe."

"Oh, good. I love you so much," Mom said.

"Me too," Marigold answered. "Here's Zinnie." She passed the phone off and turned away as fast as she could so that no one would see the two tiny tears that had escaped despite her best efforts to hold them back.

# 18 · Pancakes and Dreams

The next morning Zinnie woke up to the smell of pancakes. Lily wasn't there, though her small body had left an imprint on the sheet and the blue blanket was all bunched up at the bottom of the bed. Marigold was asleep, one arm flung dramatically over her head, the other resting on her heart. Zinnie walked downstairs in her pajamas and saw Lily standing on a chair over the stove, pouring pancake batter out of a ladle onto a black griddle that was frothy and hissing with butter. Aunt Sunny, already dressed, stood beside her. She was guiding Lily's hand as she poured three small circles of batter. Zinnie's mouth watered in response to the delicious smell of almost-burning butter.

"Good morning, Zinnia," Aunt Sunny said. "There's juice on the table, and the tap is perfectly fine for water. Blueberry pancakes will be up shortly. Your young sister is doing a fabulous job here with the last few. How'd you sleep?"

"Fine," Zinnie said, and poured herself some juice. "Do you know how to make champurrado?"

"Shampoo what now?" Aunt Sunny asked.

"Not shampoo!" Lily said, laughing. "Champurrado."

"It's a Mexican drink. Kind of like hot chocolate?" Zinnie said.

"I'm afraid not, but maybe you can teach me," Aunt Sunny said.

"Only Berta knows how to make it," Lily said sadly.

"We might be able to find a recipe online," Zinnie said. She paused for a moment, her mind half remembering something odd, something she couldn't quite grasp. "Oh, I had a weird dream."

"Tell us," Aunt Sunny said as she put a plate of blueberry pancakes in the center of the table. "People have claimed to have had wonderfully vivid dreams in those beds."

Zinnie sipped some orange juice and tried to remember. "There was a fairy there, flying in the darkness."

"Poetic," Aunt Sunny said, "perhaps spiritual." She used her hands to distribute the pancakes among four plates. "Was this fairy friendly or threatening?"

Zinnie put her orange juice on the table. "Wait, there were two fairies. One good and one evil."

"Ah, two sides of life, the light and the dark," Aunt Sunny said.

Zinnie was thinking about this, about how she sometimes felt she was probably the nicest person in the world, like when she'd helped Lily into her Pull-Ups last night and assured her that sometimes even big girls needed a little extra protection, but also how just twenty-four hours earlier she'd enjoyed stealing Marigold's friend. Light and dark. It was a lot to think about over blueberry pancakes. Just then Marigold traipsed down the stairs in her T-shirt and leggings.

"Good morning," Aunt Sunny said. "Come join our feast. Then I thought we could go to the beach for a swim."

"Not Lily," Zinnie said. "She's afraid of the water."

"Is that so?" Aunt Sunny said. "Why?"

"When I was little, a big wave knocked me over and I went tumbling and rolling and I couldn't breathe . . . and I almost died," Lily told her, saying the last bit in a whisper. "My daddy saved me."

"Terrifying," Aunt Sunny said. "That California surf can be a beast."

"She was caught in the undertow," Marigold said. "And she hasn't been in the water since."

"Oh, no," Aunt Sunny said, "How frightening."

"But that's okay," Lily said. "Because my nanny, Berta, doesn't swim either."

"Well, then, Lily can build a sand castle. Or she could stay here with me and work in my garden, and you girls can walk into town and see what's what,"

Aunt Sunny said. "I'll draw you a map."

"We can go by ourselves?" Zinnie asked.

"Sure," Aunt Sunny said.

"It's just that back in L.A. only I'm allowed to walk to the neighborhood stores without an adult. Zinnie needs a grown-up," Marigold said. Zinnie shot her a dirty look.

"Well, Pruet is a lot safer than Los Angeles, so I think it'll be just fine," Aunt Sunny said. "As long as you sisters stick together."

Zinnie grinned and sopped as much maple syrup as possible onto her last bite of pancake.

# 19 · Making Contact

Marigold carried her clothes to the little bathroom in the attic and put on her white sundress and the gold wedges that gave her an extra two inches of height. This might be some dinky little town, but it didn't mean that she had to dress like a loser. The only mirror in the bathroom was about as big as a math book and kind of blurry. It was pretty much only good for brushing teeth and making sure your hair wasn't standing up. Still, she applied a little lip gloss and, because her mother wasn't here, some mascara. She brushed her hair and put her cell phone in her purse.

Finding a cell phone signal was the mission of the day. She didn't care how far she had to walk to find it. She would walk out into the ocean if she had to. After her moment of homesickness last night, Marigold decided that she couldn't sit around for three weeks being sad. She needed to take action. The plan was to get in touch with her brand-new agent. She was determined to go to the audition for *Night Sprites*, no matter what her parents said. Marigold had an emergency credit card, and she would use it to get herself back to Los Angeles if she had to. They would understand when she was a movie star. She would even treat them all to a family vacation in Hawaii, she'd decided.

"Ready?" Zinnie asked as she bounded into the bathroom. "Wow, you look like a teenager, but one who hasn't . . . developed yet."

"Ha-ha," Marigold said, observing Zinnie in her shorts and T-shirt with her hair pulled back and an old sweatshirt tied around her waist. "Well, you look like my little brother. And why are you wearing that thing around your waist?"

"Aunt Sunny said the weather here is very unpredictable, so it's always good to have layers. Now come on, let's go."

Marigold and Zinnie followed Aunt Sunny's map and set off down Anchor Lane. The street was shady, with rambling stone walls on either side.

"Look!" Zinnie said, stopping to look at two horses in a field, their heads bent and their tails swishing. Marigold paused, but only to check her phone. Still no signal.

"Let's keep going," Marigold said.

At the end of the field they turned onto Harbor Road, which led right into the little village. After only a few minutes one of the bars on Marigold's cell phone flickered. Marigold looked up to see that they were standing in front of a big driveway and a sign that said PRUET YACHT CLUB. She took a few steps past the sign into a parking lot, and the signal strengthened for a second.

"Follow me," Marigold said.

"Okay," Zinnie said. "Except, um, are we allowed?"

Marigold had to admit this did not seem like a place where everyone could just wander in. There was a guy with a clipboard sitting at a table checking cars as they drove in. She was going to use a strategy she'd learned in acting class: the "magic if." She could almost hear Ronald P. Harp's voice in her head as she asked herself how she would act *if* she did know the clipboard guy and *if* she did come here all the time and *if* she knew exactly where she was headed.

"Just be casual," Marigold said to Zinnie through one of her winning smiles. The clipboard guy squinted as he watched them pass.

"Hi!" Marigold called. She waved to him as *if* she'd known him her whole life. He smiled, waved, and turned back to his clipboard. Success!

The girls walked down the long pebbled driveway, past a gray shingled building roughly the size of the Silvers' house and a bright-green lawn with a flagpole, to find four docks stretching out into a small harbor. Boats were tied up along all sides, and others floated farther out. It felt oddly familiar, even though Marigold had never been here before. The closest thing to this she'd seen had been a marina near L.A.

The Silvers had gone out for a special Mother's Day brunch in Marina del Rey a few years ago, and the view from the restaurant had been of a harbor full of boats. But it had been different from this. There had been ten times as many boats, and they all had seemed gigantic. The Silvers had walked along the docks that afternoon, and Marigold had run ahead. For a moment she got lost. She couldn't see her family. The docks felt like a maze, and the boats were so big with their huge motors and high, wide sides. Loud music was blaring from one of the yachts. It smelled strongly of gasoline. Marigold panicked for several seconds until her family came back into view.

It would be impossible to get lost here, Marigold thought as she took in the peaceful harbor with some big boats, but plenty of small ones, too. A family of ducks swam under one of the docks. The flag's rope clanked pleasantly against the pole. A gentle breeze tousled her hair. Marigold paused for a moment, thinking how everything here—the ocean, the buildings, the world—seemed smaller than in California. Even the seagulls. But then she moved on. She had a phone call to make before she and Zinnie were discovered as trespassers. She headed down one of the docks, Zinnie trailing behind.

"That one boy is looking at you," Zinnie said. Marigold turned to see a group of kids who looked about their age. They were all wearing the same blue T-shirts that said PRUET SAILING TEAM. There were about eight of them, mostly boys, and they were standing on the dock, listening to a coach demonstrate something from inside a sailboat. Sure enough, a boy was looking at her. His hair was red and cut very short, unlike the boys' in California, who liked their hair long so they could shake it out of their eyes as they did their skateboard tricks.

"Hot tamale," Zinnie said, and wiggled her eyebrows. "With salsa caliente on the side."

"Don't be weird," Marigold said, and glanced back at her cell phone. "Oh, my God, I have a whole bar. I'm going to call Jill!" Marigold dialed Jill's number as she walked, but the call wouldn't go through. Marigold paced the end of the dock. "It's better over here," she said, standing as far to the left as possible. There was a small sailboat tied up right there. Marigold hopped aboard the boat and caught her balance as she landed.

"Uh, Marigold," Zinnie said, "I don't know if we're allowed there."

"I've got two bars out here," Marigold said, stepping farther out in the boat. "Two bars!"

"Mar-i-gold," Zinnie whispered, gesturing for her to come back.

"Oh, it's ringing!" Marigold jumped, and the boat rocked. She bent her knees to catch her balance.

"Hello? Yes, this is Marigold Silver! For Jill!" Marigold shouted. Zinnie was gesturing for her to be quiet when the phone went silent.

"Shoot!" Marigold exclaimed. "I lost it!" She stomped her foot. "I dropped the call!"

"I really think we should go," Zinnie said.

"Will you chill?" Marigold said.

"People are looking at us," Zinnie said.

Marigold noticed that the whole sailing team was staring at them. She flipped her hair and tucked her phone into her purse. "Fine. We'll walk down to the ice cream store. Maybe there's reception there." Marigold's phone buzzed. "Oh, I bet that's her," Marigold said, but as she turned to reach for her phone, her wedge caught on a rope and she lost her balance. *Splash!* She plunged into the murky chin-deep water.

# 20 · Sink or Swim, Marigold

"Marigold!" Zinnie called. Marigold bobbed to the surface, gasping, her hair slicked back against her head. Zinnie clutched the end of the dock. "There's a ladder over here!" Even if she'd never been the best on the team, Marigold was a pretty good swimmer, so it was no surprise that she made her way quickly to the dock or that she had managed to hold on to her purse, which she tossed up to Zinnie as soon as she reached the ladder. Zinnie caught the purse. It was soaked. She peered down to see Marigold reaching to collect her floating shoes and toss them onto the dock. Then she climbed the ladder and hauled herself up, shivering and dripping, her eyes squeezed tight against the salt water.

Marigold's filmy white sundress, which just an hour ago had looked so fancy and grown-up, was now soaked through to her skin and completely see-through. Zinnie could see her white underpants with blue stars on them. Marigold crossed her arms protectively over her chest as she coughed and spit out salt water. Zinnie felt short of breath. She would much rather Marigold act imperious and haughty than look like a half-drowned kitten. If she could've traded places with her, she would've in a second.

"Are you girls okay?" a voice called. Zinnie turned around and saw the sailing coach running toward them, followed by the entire sailing class.

"We're fine," Zinnie called, hoping against hope that the coach and those kids would turn around and go back to their business.

"Oh, no," Marigold said under her breath, teeth chattering. "This sucks."

"Quick," Zinnie said. She untied her sweatshirt from around her waist and threw it over Marigold's head. Marigold pulled it on, stretching it down to her thighs, just as the team surrounded them.

"Are you sure you're okay?" the coach asked.

"I'm fine," Marigold said, and stood up tall to prove it.

"You girls should not be here unsupervised," the coach said. "Where are your parents?"

"They're not here today," Marigold said. "My sister and I were just going out for a sail."

"I've never seen you before. Do you even belong to this yacht club?" the boy with the very short hair asked.

"Why would we even be here if we didn't belong?" Marigold asked as she squeezed out her ponytail and water splattered on the dock. Zinnie felt the panic in her chest loosen its grip as she basked in the glow of her sister's confidence. Somehow, Marigold was going to make this all okay.

"I've definitely seen you before," the coach said to Marigold. Zinnie bit her smile. He didn't know that he'd seen her on TV! "But unless you girls really know what you're doing, you really shouldn't be taking out a boat."

"Okay," Marigold said.

"Let's get back to practice, kids," he said to his team. "And you girls, I don't want to see you out here alone again. You're either registered for sailing school or with an adult."

"Got it," Marigold said.

Zinnie and Marigold started down the dock. Even though Marigold's feet squished in her gold wedges and the purse flung over her shoulder was dripping wet, she walked with her head held high and her shoulders pulled back like she was president of the place.

## 21 · Peter Pasque

They had almost reached the end of the dock when Marigold felt a tap on her shoulder. She turned around to see the boy with the short red hair.

"I don't believe you," he said.

"Believe what?" Marigold asked, narrowing her eyes.

"I don't believe you're here to go sailing," he said. "First of all, I've never seen you before. And I know everyone at the PYC because my dad's the manager."

"Maybe you just never noticed us," Marigold said, her ears adjusting to his accent. When he said "before," it sounded like *befo-ah,* and "manager" sounded like *managah.*

"I would have noticed you," he said, blushing, then quickly added, "And second of all, your shoes. No one goes sailing in high heels."

"These aren't high heels; they're wedges," Marigold said.

"Whatever they are, they're not meant for sailing."

"These are very sturdy. And you just haven't met us before because we happen to be new in town," Marigold said, smiling. "Okay?"

"What's your name?" he asked.

"Seraphina," Marigold said. "And this is my sister . . ."

"Xiomara," Zinnie said, naming another Night Spite.

"I mean, what's your last name?" he asked Zinnie. Marigold flinched. The Night Sprites didn't have last names.

"Snoopy," Zinnie said.

It was so ridiculous Marigold almost laughed. And she knew why Zinnie had thought of it. Right in front of them was a white motorboat with the name Snoopy painted in gold on the back. She bit her cheeks. She had to keep it together. The boy raised a disbelieving eyebrow, but she was not about to let him outwit her. In acting, it was important to commit to the imaginary circumstances.

"You heard her," Marigold said. "We're the Snoopys. What's your name?"

"Peter," he said. *Peet-ah.* "Peter Pasque." It was like they were having some kind of staring contest. His eyes were certainly blue. Almost as blue as Clint Lee's.

"Well, we gotta go, Peter," Zinnie said, and tugged

at Marigold's arm. "Come on, Seraphina."

"Wait a second," Peter said. "If you're a sailor, then you know how to tie a bowline." He smiled and held out a rope that was coiled on the dock. "Here, use this line."

"Tie a what?" Marigold asked, gathering that a rope was called a line on a sailboat.

"A bowline. It's a knot," he said.

"I know that. It's just . . . I'm really not in the mood," Marigold said.

"That's what I figured," Peter said, and spit off to the side.

*"Ew!"* Marigold eyed him with disgust. "Anyway, I just got this manicure." She wiggled her fingers daintily. The dark-purple color on her nails was called No You Didn't.

"Tell you what: if you can tie a bowline, then I'll pay for your new mani—whatever it is," Peter said.

Marigold put her hand on her hip. He just wasn't going to give up, was he? "Well, in that case," Marigold said. Then, with her hair still dripping wet, her white ruffled sundress sticking to her legs, and her toes sliding to the front of her sopping-wet sandals, she extended her hand. Peter gave her the rope. Her fingers started to fly. Zinnie's jaw dropped.

"Bowline," Marigold said, and handed the knot to him.

Peter examined it and then looked back up to

Marigold in disbelief. "Not bad, Miss Snoopy."

"Someone owes me a manicure," Marigold said. "Now excuse me, but Xiomara and I have horses to see and ice cream to eat. See ya around."

"Yeah," Zinnie said. "See ya around!"

As Marigold sauntered away, she was so glad Zinnie's sweatshirt was covering her butt. She had to admit that sometimes little sisters came in very handy.

So did Girl Scouts.

## 22 · The Angel Takes a Bath

That night, after dinner, Marigold attempted to log on to her email account through Aunt Sunny's computer. She had just about recovered from her unexpected dip into Pruet Harbor and was dying to tell Pilar all about the crazy incident with Peter, the redheaded boy. But Aunt Sunny's computer had to be plugged into the phone in order to connect to the internet. As she was waiting for the home page to load, Aunt Sunny asked Marigold if she would mind helping with Lily's bath.

"I promised to do some paperwork for the Piping Plover Society," Aunt Sunny said. "Zinnia is doing the dishes, and it would be a great help if you could give Lily her bath."

"Um, sure," Marigold said. At least it sounded better than doing dishes.

"And I think she'll be more comfortable if her sister

helps her with this," Aunt Sunny said.

"Oh, no. Marigold can't give me a bath either," Lily said. "Only Berta knows how I like my baths."

"Berta's not here, my dear," Aunt Sunny said.

"I can wait until I get back to California," Lily said.

"You would be so dirty, you might start sprouting turnips!" Aunt Sunny said.

"Turnips?" Lily asked.

"Come on," Marigold said, and dragged her upstairs to their little attic bathroom. It was true that she'd never given Lily, or any little kid, a bath before. Even though she was the oldest sister, she hadn't done much babysitting. She had been too close in age to Zinnie to babysit her, and as soon as Lily was born, there was Berta, who took care of Lily most of the time. But how hard could it be to give her sister a bath?

She filled the tub and told Lily to get in.

"Not without bubbles," Lily said.

"Lily, come on, we don't have bubbles here," Marigold said. "Just get in."

"You could make some bubbles with the soap. That's what Berta does," Lily said.

"Fine," Marigold said, and rolled up the sleeves of her sweatshirt. She took the bar of soap from the dish and rubbed it under the running water until there were at least a few bubbles. "Okay?"

Lily nodded and then dipped a pointed toe in. "Too hot!"

"It is not too hot," Marigold said, testing the water again.

"If the water's too hot, it dries out my skin, and I get itchy," Lily said.

Marigold rolled her eyes and added some cold. "Try it now."

Lily tested it again with her finger. She was about to climb in when she stopped and said, "Where are the bath toys? I need at least three."

"Lily," Marigold said, "just get in the tub."

"I can't have a bath without any toys," Lily said. "It'll be boring."

"No wonder Berta looks so tired at the end of the day!" Marigold said. "I'll be right back." She ran downstairs to the kitchen, where Zinnie was finishing with the dishes. "I'm giving Lily a bath," Marigold announced, "and she's being a brat. She won't get in without toys."

"I told you!" Zinnie said as she dried a plate. "Lily gets away with everything! Here, give her these." She handed her some plastic measuring cups she'd just washed.

"Good enough," Marigold said, and ran back upstairs.

"Measuring cups?" Lily asked when Marigold returned.

"Or hats," Marigold said, putting one on her head. "Or boats," she added, floating another in the tub. "Now get in."

"Okay, okay," Lily said, and sat in the tub.

"Get your hair wet," Marigold said.

"Don't rush me!" Lily said.

"Dunk!" Marigold said.

"Berta uses the hand-held shower," Lily said.

"Berta spoils you," Marigold said.

"I'm her angel!" Lily said.

"You need to learn how to do things yourself, Lily," Marigold said.

"Fine," Lily said. She held her nose and lay back, dunking herself.

Aunt Sunny appeared in the doorway just as Lily resurfaced. "Just thought I'd check in on you. How's it going?"

"Okay," Marigold said.

"Why, you're not afraid of the water," Aunt Sunny said to Lily.

"Of course not," Lily said. "I'm afraid of the ocean."

"This whole time I thought you were terrified of going underwater," Aunt Sunny said.

"Not in a bathtub," Marigold said as she lathered up Lily's hair with shampoo.

"I know what you need," Aunt Sunny said as Marigold used a measuring cup to rinse Lily's hair. "Swimming lessons. In a pool. We'll head over to the YMCA tomorrow!"

"I'm ready to get out now," Lily said. "You can go warm up my towels in the dryer, Marigold."

"Oh, my," Aunt Sunny said.

"Just kidding?" Lily said.

"Yes," Marigold said, snapping open a room-temperature towel. "Definitely just kidding."

# 23 · The Town Beach

For the next several days Marigold and Zinnie didn't venture back to the Pruet Yacht Club. Marigold's phone had been completely ruined by her unexpected dip in the harbor, so the temptation of cell phone reception was gone. And Zinnie didn't want to risk running into the sailing coach again. He had been firm in his warning that the girls couldn't be there unsupervised, and Zinnie didn't know what kind of trouble they would get into if he saw them again. But the biggest reason not to go back to the PYC, Marigold had whispered in the dark one night in the barracks, was Peter Pasque.

Marigold had confessed that although she had been the first in her Girl Scout troop to earn her knot-tying badge, it had been a few years ago, and she didn't think she remembered any of the other knots. She said that she would die of embarrassment if Peter asked her to try something more advanced before she had a chance to practice.

"And," Zinnie whispered, "what if he asked his father, the *managah,* about the Snoopy family? He'd know we were lying, and we'd have to admit that he had been right all along!"

"OMG, we can never see him again!" Marigold said.

"Yeah, no way!" Zinnie said, putting the sheet up to her chin and smiling into the darkness.

So Zinnie thought it was a little odd that while they hadn't been back to the PYC, they hadn't exactly avoided walking past it. For the past three days, while Lily accompanied Aunt Sunny on errands or helped in the garden, Marigold and Zinnie had been going to the town beach. There was an alternate way to get there that, although it included a shortcut through someone's yard, would have allowed them to avoid passing the entrance to the yacht club. But they just took their usual route back and forth to town. This meant they had passed the yacht club a total of six times. Zinnie suspected that although Marigold *claimed* she didn't want to see Peter again, she secretly did. But when she confronted Marigold about this as they walked past the yacht club for the fourth day in a row, Marigold flipped her hair and said, "There are more bugs that way!"

The town beach was tiny compared with the

beaches in California. If they weren't going to Santa Monica, with its amusement park, arcade, volleyball nets, and wide concrete pathway with people whooshing by on bicycles and in-line skates, the Silver family went to Malibu for a beach day. There the ocean roared. Often the waves were big enough for tough-looking grown-ups in wet suits to go surfing, and the undertows were so dangerous and powerful that sometimes even their parents wouldn't go in past their ankles. And although it was almost always sunny in Southern California, the water was often too cold for swimming, at least for the sisters. Of course there were plenty of days in the summer when the water was calm and warm enough for a swim, but the Silver family caught only a few of those days a year. The beaches were at least an hour's drive from the Silvers' home, depending on the traffic.

But Zinnie and Marigold could walk to the Pruet Town Beach in ten minutes or less. Instead of taking a freeway to get there, they simply walked down Aunt Sunny's long driveway, along the shady road lined with mossy stone walls, and down the grassy path between the fishing store and the sandwich shop. Dotted with colored umbrellas, beach chairs, and towels, the town beach wasn't even as big as the parking lot at the Santa Monica Pier. And because it was nestled in the harbor, there were hardly any waves at all. The only creatures surfing here were the small brown crabs Zinnie and Marigold had spotted scuttling along the shore. But the sand was soft, and the water was always warm enough for swimming, even on a cloudy day. There was a little snack bar that sold soda, ice pops, hot dogs, french fries, candy bars, and little containers of ice cream that came with small, flat wooden spoons attached to their lids. Aunt Sunny said that as long as Marigold and Zinnie stuck together and didn't swim past the floating dock, they could go by themselves as often as they liked.

Walking to the town beach without an adult was a whole new level of freedom for Zinnie. Without the constant gaze of a parent, babysitter, or teacher, Zinnie felt both more grown-up and a little wilder. Her first thought was that she wouldn't have to be *appropriate* all the time. "Appropriate" was a favorite word of teachers and parents. It was used so often that it had become impossible to put her finger on exactly what it meant. Yet she was disappointed to find the only thing she could think of to do that was *inappropriate* was make fart noises, and Marigold didn't find them very funny.

Even though this was only their fourth visit to this beach, when they arrived that morning, Zinnie was starting to feel like it belonged to her and Marigold. They had a favorite spot off to the left, near the lifeguard's chair, close to the water. They had even started to get to know the teenagers who worked at the snack bar. The girl with the bangs had an accent like Peter Pasque's, only stronger. By their second visit to the town beach, Zinnie knew that her name was Ashley, she was fourteen, this was her first summer job, and she wanted to find a boyfriend. Today Ashley saw Zinnie approaching the snack bar and produced a red ice pop before she even asked for it.

"Can I also get a water?" Zinnie asked.

"Why don't you just get a drink at the bubblah?" Ashley asked.

"Bubblah?" Zinnie repeated, confused.

"Yeah, y'know, the bubblah," Ashley said, pointing at the water fountain attached to the snack bar.

"Oh, okay," Zinnie said. As she turned the handle of the water fountain and a burst of water gushed up her nose, she thought that "bubblah" was a much better name than "water fountain." Ashley started to sing along with the radio. "You have a really pretty voice," Zinnie said, wiping her mouth. "You should go on *America Sings*."

"You think so?" Ashley asked as she restocked the candy bars.

"I'd vote for you," Zinnie said. "Like ten times, and that's the maximum they allow from the same number."

"Thanks," Ashley said. "Maybe I'll try out someday."

As Zinnie walked back to Marigold, she couldn't

wait to tell her about this new word. *Bubblah,* Zinnie said to herself, and giggled.

Marigold was stretched out on a towel in her favorite bathing suit. It had a single delicate strap that wrapped around her neck, navy stripes, and the words *"Excusez-moi, s'il vous plaît"* written in glittery silver sequins across it. Zinnie's plain blue suit was less stylish. Technically, it wasn't even called a bathing suit. It was a rash guard, which was what surfers wore. The top was like a T-shirt and the bottom like shorts. She liked that there was no way it would slip off when she jumped off the floating dock, as she'd done at least five times a day since they'd arrived. Also, she never had to worry about her shoulders or back getting sunburned, and because it was a two-piece, trips to the bathroom were a breeze. Though Zinnie did have to admit that Marigold looked like a movie star in training in her fancy one-piece and matching heart-shaped sunglasses as she listlessly flipped through the latest *Young & Lovely* magazine.

Zinnie knew that the loss of Marigold's cell phone had been devastating to her. Without it, Marigold couldn't communicate with her new agent. She couldn't use the house phone to call and beg for a way to audition because Aunt Sunny had explained that her phone plan allowed only a certain number of long-distance minutes a month. It was even going to be hard for them to talk to their parents.

Aunt Sunny told them that Mom, Dad, and the girls were in three different time zones. Not only that, but Dad was going to be in the forest without reception, and Mom would be in another country, making calls to her very expensive, and they had totally different work schedules. So Mom, Dad, and Aunt Sunny had decided they would limit phone time to a couple of family conference calls while the girls were in Massachusetts. If there was an emergency, the girls could use Aunt Sunny's landline to leave a voice mail on Mom's cell phone or to call a special number to reach the cabin that was home base for Dad's documentary team. Dad probably wouldn't be there because he'd be up in the trees, but someone would be able to get the message to him.

But it wasn't just the lack of communication with her agent and family that upset Marigold. Without her phone, she couldn't text with Pilar, play around with her fashion apps, or surf the web. Aunt Sunny's internet was pretty much useless. Marigold had confessed to Zinnie during a late-night chat in the barracks that she felt as though she'd been stranded on a desert island.

"Isn't 'bubblah' a funny word?" Zinnie asked, plopping down in the sand next to her sister.

"I guess," Marigold said, not even looking up.

"I'll race you to floating dock?" Zinnie asked.

"Maybe in a little bit," Marigold said.

Zinnie sighed and decided to go for a walk. She was going to see if she could find more of those thin pearly shells that she was planning on turning into a necklace. As she stood up, she noticed that Marigold was looking out at the harbor, where a fleet of small sailboats was racing.

"I bet Peter's on one of those boats," Zinnie said.

"Who?" Marigold asked.

"You know who," Zinnie said, and dusted sand from her backside. "Peter Pasque."

"You forgot your change," said a voice behind them. Zinnie turned around to see Ashley, who was holding a quarter in her outstretched palm.

"Oh, thanks," Zinnie said, taking the quarter.

"You know Peter Pasque?" Ashley asked.

"Yeah," Zinnie said. "We met him the other day, but we told him our names were Seraphina and Xiomara. You know, like the Night Sprites? I said our last name was Snoopy. And Marigold told him we had a boat and that we could sail!" Zinnie said, laughing. Marigold lifted her sunglasses and glared at Zinnie. Zinnie covered her mouth even though it was too late.

"You two are a couple of kooks," Ashley said, shaking her head. "And you'll get to see Peter tomorrow. He'll be here at the beach for my brother's birthday party."

"Really?" Zinnie asked. She was dying to know

what Marigold thought they should do, but her sister had lowered her sunglasses back over her eyes and was reading *Young & Lovely* as if it contained the answers to the world's most burning questions.

# 24 · Aunt Sunny's Famous Surprise Brownies

"The clambake starts at noon, and we've got several batches of my famous surprise brownies to make, so we'd better get crackin'," Aunt Sunny said the next morning after Zinnie and Lily had finished their pancakes and Marigold, who had read in *Young & Lovely* that sugar was bad for the complexion, had polished off her bowl of plain yogurt.

"Actually, I think we're going to the beach," Marigold said. Ever since Ashley had told them that the sailing team was going to be at the beach today, Marigold had been thinking about how fun it had been to tie that knot in front of Peter. She was wondering what else she could beat him at. She was pretty sure that he would at least provide some new entertainment.

She and Zinnie had done the same thing for the past

four days. They walked to the beach in morning, ⸤s⸥ping at the general store for a magazine or for postcards to send to Pilar, Berta, Mom, or Dad. They sat in their usual spot, and Zinnie read her book while Marigold read her magazine. Then they'd switch. They bought ice pops from the snack stand. They swam to the floating dock and practiced cannonballs and jackknives. They searched for shells (Zinnie was making some kind of weird necklace). They played tic-tac-toe in the sand. Then they walked back to Aunt Sunny's for lunch, passing by the post office to mail their postcards. After lunch they went back to the beach and did the whole thing all over again, only in the afternoon they visited Edith's Ice Cream Shop instead of the general store.

Marigold was ready to break up the routine. She was ready for a challenge. She was ready to see Peter Pasque. And because the last time she'd seen him she'd looked like such a mess, she'd spent a lot of time that morning getting ready. She'd blow-dried her hair and was wearing her cherry-red tankini with the ruffle on the bottom.

"Zinnie and I were going to make sand angels today, right, Zinnie?" Marigold said.

"Um, we were?" Zinnie asked.

Marigold pinched Zinnie's thigh under the table.

"Ouch," Zinnie said, and rubbed her leg.

"Or maybe I could just go to the beach *alone*?" Marigold offered.

we're going to the clambake," Aunt Sunny
...ed two mixing bowls from a cabinet.

...ul of disappointment heaped on Marigold's
...was starting to get the feeling that she was
never going to get to do her own thing here in Pruet.
Aunt Sunny didn't seem to understand that the sisters
didn't always have to do things together. Even though
her mom liked it when Marigold included Zinnie and
could sometimes be strict about it, she was also fair
about Marigold's having time to herself. If her mom
were here, she'd get that Marigold had been with Zinnie for like a million hours straight at this point and
would let her have her space. But Marigold could tell
that Aunt Sunny wasn't going to budge.

"I think your parents would be disappointed in me
if I let you miss it," Aunt Sunny said, as if reading
Marigold's mind. "A clambake is an essential part of a
New England summer."

"What's a clambake?" Lily asked.

"A bunch of us gather on the beach and dig out a
hole in the sand and make an oven out of hot rocks,
seaweed, and tarps. And then we cook all kinds of
wonderful things in there: lobsters, clams, sausage,
corn on the cob, potatoes. It's just delicious. And"—she
continued as she pulled a dozen eggs and some butter
from the refrigerator and placed them on the counter—
"the beach where we have our clambake is my absolute
favorite. There are big dunes for climbing, magnificent

waves for body surfing, and a pond with a swiftly flowing estuary. You can float on your back and ride the current all the way to the ocean. It's great fun. I've never met someone who doesn't love it."

Marigold glanced at Lily, who was pale with fear from all this ocean talk, and said under her breath, "You might today."

"I think that sounds cool," Zinnie said.

"I don't go to the ocean," Lily said. "Remember?"

"Once you get there, you'll love it," Aunt Sunny said, and disappeared into the pantry.

Marigold and Zinnie exchanged a look. Aunt Sunny didn't get just how much Lily hated the ocean.

"Lily never goes to the beach," Marigold said. "She's scared of the water." Lily nodded.

"Maybe it's time to not be scared," Aunt Sunny said, and returned from the pantry, her arms full of ingredients. "Let's not dwell on it now; let's get cooking." She set the items on the table: flour, sugar, two kinds of chocolate, and vanilla.

"Why don't you use a mix?" Marigold asked. She'd made brownies enough times to know that all you had to do was add oil and a couple of eggs to the brown powder in the box and voilà . . . brownies.

"Blasphemy!" Aunt Sunny said, and shook a wooden spoon at the sky. Lily and Zinnie giggled. Aunt Sunny opened a drawer and took out a set of measuring cups and spoons. "Do you think they would be my famous brownies if I made them from a mix?"

Marigold shrugged. Aunt Sunny filled one pan with water, then put another pan inside it. She put the chocolate and the butter inside the top pan.

"I want to see the chocolate," Lily said, and Aunt Sunny pulled a chair up to the stove so that Lily could watch the butter melt. She handed her a wooden spoon. "Here, Lily, stir this very gently." She gave a mixing bowl to Zinnie. "Zinnie and Marigold, you can crack the eggs into the bowl. Shells go in the compost," she added, nodding to the compost container next to the sink. "And when you've done that, add four cups of sugar and four tablespoons of vanilla."

"Four cups?" Marigold asked.

"I said they were surprise brownies, not health brownies," Aunt Sunny said.

"Why are they called surprise brownies?" Zinnie asked.

"Because every time I make them, I get a surprise."

"Like what?" Marigold asked as she cracked an egg against the side of the bowl.

"The very first time I made them for the community bake sale, this short, handsome newcomer to town named Ham asked me out on a date," Aunt Sunny said.

"I thought all handsome strangers were tall," Marigold said.

"Well, this one was short. And he was the handsomest

man I'd ever met," Aunt Sunny said as she measured and sifted flour into yet another mixing bowl.

"Did you kiss on the first date?" Marigold asked.

"You betcha," Aunt Sunny said with a smile, and added three pinches of salt to her bowl.

*"Ooh-la-la,"* said Zinnie.

*"Ooh-la-la* is right," Aunt Sunny said, dusting off her hands. "And the next time I made the surprise brownies, he proposed marriage. After knowing me for only a month. Let me tell you, it was a great surprise. My heart almost stopped."

"I think these are love brownies," Zinnie said. "You eat them, and it makes people fall in love."

"Kissy kissy," Lily said, and waggled her hips. Zinnie and Aunt Sunny laughed.

"Well, I thought that myself," Aunt Sunny said. "Until I made them the next time and I got a different sort of surprise."

"Was it a bad surprise?" Marigold asked as she added the sugar and vanilla.

"Depends how you look at it," Aunt Sunny said. "Oh, you've done a good job, Lily. That chocolate has melted perfectly. Now we're going to combine your efforts." She turned off the stove and poured the chocolate mixture into the egg mixture.

"What was the third surprise?" Marigold asked.

"Ham lost his job," Aunt Sunny said.

"Oh, no," Zinnie said.

"A bad surprise," Marigold said. "I knew it."

"Well, not exactly," Aunt Sunny said, and handed the spoon to Marigold to stir. "It was also the very same night he decided he would start his own business. A boatbuilding business."

"It was a good surprise hiding in a bad one," Zinnie said.

"That is so well put, Zinnia," Aunt Sunny said. "Now, grab the peppermint extract for me off the shelf, won't you, Marigold?"

"Uh . . . why?" Marigold asked.

"For the brownies, of course," Aunt Sunny said, and poured some into the mixture. "It's the secret ingredient that sets the surprises in motion."

"I wonder what surprise will happen today," Lily said.

"We'll just have to wait and see," Aunt Sunny said. Marigold rolled her eyes.

# 25 · Over the Dune

Zinnie climbed into the backseat of Aunt Sunny's station wagon, which had wide cloth seats and smelled vaguely like doughnuts. It was much lower to the ground than her mother's car, and a bumpier ride too. Also, she had to turn a crank to lower and raise the windows. But just like at home, Marigold sat in the front seat and Lily and Zinnie sat in the back, and as soon as Aunt Sunny started the car, Marigold turned on the radio. Amanda Mills's new hit single, "Kiss Me to Crazytown," was playing.

"This is my favorite song," Marigold said, and started to sing along while gazing glumly out the window. "It reminds me of home."

"It's my favorite song, too," Zinnie said. She sang along as well, even though she only knew the chorus and had to hum though the verses.

Marigold turned around. "Just because it's my favorite song doesn't mean it has to be yours, too," she said. "You need to have your own favorite song."

"Whatever," Zinnie said. She held her breath. When Marigold's voice was sharp like that, it could bring Zinnie to the brink of tears in a flash.

Aunt Sunny turned the radio off. "Let's listen to the birds instead," she said, and rolled her window down. Marigold huffed. They turned onto a narrow little dirt road that ran through a field.

"Check out that place!" Marigold said from the front seat. Zinnie looked up to see Marigold pointing to a mansion ahead of them. It really stood out because there were only a few other houses around, and they all were small like Aunt Sunny's.

"Oh, it's a monstrosity!" Aunt Sunny said. "Four floors, twelve bedrooms, ten bathrooms, two swimming pools, and a screening room. The man who built that house ruined the view for these folks, not to mention one of the best spots for piping plovers, those darling birds, to nest. Darling endangered birds, I should add. I did all that I could to stop him. I established the Piping Plover Society and everything. And to think, he lives here only two weeks a year."

"It looks like an awesome house to me," Marigold said.

"You might feel differently if it ruined your view," Aunt Sunny said.

"Or if you were a piping plover," Lily said.

"Exactly," Aunt Sunny said.

"So were you in a fight with him?" Zinnie asked.

"Whoo boy! Was I ever," Aunt Sunny said as they continued down the dirt road. Zinnie tried to imagine Aunt Sunny in a fight. "Well, with his lawyers anyway. He didn't even bother to show his face."

"Who won?" Marigold asked.

"He did, I suppose, because the house is there. But it took a team of fancy California lawyers to take me down."

"We're from California," Lily said.

"That's right," Aunt Sunny said. They stopped at a low, wide gate, and Aunt Sunny handed Marigold a key. "Marigold, as the front seat passenger, it's your job to unlock the gate while I drive through, then lock it up again when we're on the other side."

"Why does a beach need a gate?" Marigold asked.

"You'll see," Aunt Sunny said.

Marigold grumbled and climbed out of the car.

"She needs to lose the attitude," Lily said, repeating what her mother said to Marigold whenever she was rude. Aunt Sunny laughed. Then Marigold opened the gate, and they drove through.

"Do they have the gate to keep people out?" Zinnie asked, turning to watch Marigold close the gate and lock it behind her.

"Actually, it's more about keeping them in," Aunt

Sunny said. Marigold locked the gate and then, realizing she had locked herself out, climbed over it and jumped to the ground. Zinnie wanted to ride in the front seat next time so that she could be the one to unlock and lock the gate.

"Who?" Zinnie asked, turning back around to see who Aunt Sunny was talking about.

"Them," Aunt Sunny said, pointing to a couple of cows with long, shaggy hair.

"A hairy cow!" Lily said as Marigold hopped back into the car.

"Where?" Marigold asked.

"There! That one has horns," Zinnie said, and rolled up the window. That's when she noticed that these weren't just a couple of cows, but a whole bunch of them. Maybe twenty or so, spread out through the pasture, munching on grass.

"I could've been trampled," Marigold said.

"Those are Highland cattle," Aunt Sunny said as the little car bumped down the narrow sandy road. "This is where they live in the summer. And they aren't dangerous."

"They're all looking at us," Lily said.

"Well, they've never seen you before," Aunt Sunny said, slowing the car so one of them could cross the road. "You should introduce yourself."

"Hello, cow," Lily said. One mooed in response, and Aunt Sunny drove on.

A few minutes later, after they had parked the car, they climbed a big dune single file: Aunt Sunny with the brownies, Zinnie with a bagful of beach towels, and Marigold with Lily on her back, because Lily would not climb the dune on her own two feet.

When they reached the top, Zinnie looked around. In front of her was a stretch of sandy beach and the vast, glimmering ocean. Big waves curled and rolled onto the beach, then retreated back to sea, leaving lacy trails. Over to the right was a big pond, which flowed in a narrow river out to the sea. She realized that must be the estuary. And down the beach to the left was a group of people standing around what looked like a steaming pile of old blankets.

"Is that the clambake?" Zinnie asked, but Aunt Sunny was studying the sky.

"That's a ominous nimbostratus if I ever saw one," Aunt Sunny said.

"Huh?" Zinnie asked, and then remembered that Aunt Sunny used to be a science teacher.

"A serious rain cloud," Aunt Sunny said.

"Oh, yeah," Zinnie said. She should've known that; she'd studied weather in science last year. She saw the flat, dark cloud in the distance. It was moving in their direction.

"It's going to rain?" Marigold asked, out of breath from carrying Lily all the way up the dune. She tried to put Lily down, but Lily wasn't making it easy. She'd wrapped her legs around Marigold tightly and was gripping her neck.

"Probably," Aunt Sunny said.

"Then we should go home," Lily said as she clung to Marigold.

"Yeah, let's just go to the movies," Marigold said.

"No, no," Aunt Sunny said. "We'll make the most of the afternoon and hope it stays out at sea."

Aunt Sunny started down the dune, toward the ocean. Zinnie and Marigold followed. Lily was clinging to Marigold, but as soon as she began to descend the dune, Lily jumped from Marigold's back and planted her feet in the sand.

"I won't go, I won't go," she said, crossing her arms. "I'm staying right here."

"Lily, come now, you don't want to miss out," Aunt Sunny said, but Lily sat down and shook her head.

"I don't want to go near the ocean!" Lily said.

"She won't budge," Zinnie says. "Lily does only what Lily wants. Trust me. That's why we need Berta."

"Zinnia and Marigold, can I have a word?" Aunt Sunny said, taking Marigold and Zinnie aside.

"You may not know this," Aunt Sunny said, "but I'm the youngest of three girls as well, so I know how much she looks up to you two. She'll listen to you like no one else." Zinnie and Marigold nodded. "Show her how fun it is to be here at the beach. Show her that she doesn't have to be afraid."

"I have an idea," Zinnie said. She handed Aunt Sunny the canvas bag. Then she backed up, made a running start, and flew down the dune, her arms flung wide.

"*Woo-hoo!*" Zinnie called as she tumbled at the bottom, landing on her butt in the sand. Lily watched with curiosity.

"Marigold's turn," Aunt Sunny said, winking at her.

Marigold ran down the hill, smiling. "Come on, Lily," she said when she reached the bottom. "You try it!"

Lily shook her head

"Okay, looks like it's my turn!" Aunt Sunny said, and walked down the dune. She couldn't run because her arms were loaded up with stuff. Aunt Sunny, Marigold, and Zinnie waved to Lily from the beach.

"Come on, Lily," Marigold said. "It's not scary."

"Look," Zinnie said. "The waves can't get me from here. They're far away!"

"Sit down, close your eyes, and scoot!" Aunt Sunny said. "We'll meet you at the bottom."

"You can do it!" Zinnie chanted.

"Your mother used to love to run down this dune!" Aunt Sunny said. "I remember one summer when she wasn't much older than you. Up and down, up and down, she went. All day long!" Aunt Sunny said.

"All day long?" Lily asked.

"Lily, you should do it too, so you can tell Mom about it," Zinnie said.

Lily considered.

"I'll let you do my hair," Marigold said.

"For real?" Lily asked.

"For real," Marigold said.

That did it. To everyone's amazement, Lily sat down, covered her eyes with her hands, and started to scoot. When she reached the bottom, Lily peeked through her fingers while Aunt Sunny, Marigold, and Zinnie clapped and cheered. Lily wouldn't remove her hands from her face for at least a minute, but they all saw the smile pushing against her palms.

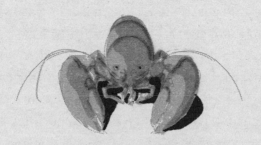

# 26 · Clambake

Zinnie couldn't help going back for seconds, even though she was stuffed. There were red baby potatoes and corn on the cob wrapped in little packages of tinfoil. There was spicy sausage and lobster, which Aunt Sunny showed them how to crack open and use a little fork to get the meat out of. Lily, who had never had lobster before, ate two whole claws. There were clams and mussels, neither of which Marigold would eat, claiming they could give you diseases, but which Zinnie loved. There were jars full of melted butter for dipping and pouring. And it had all been cooked right there on the beach, on a bunch of rocks and a pile of stinky seaweed. Now that she had tried everything, she knew what to get more of. Clams! Salty, buttery clams! Zinnie couldn't believe it, but she preferred clambakes to taco trucks.

She stood up from the picnic blanket where she,

Marigold, and Lily were sitting. Marigold was letting Lily "do her hair" as she read to her from the *Night Sprites* book. This meant that Lily was using the handful of hair elastics she found in Marigold's purse to put a bunch of weird uneven braids and ponytails in Marigold's hair. Normally, Marigold didn't let anyone but a professional touch her perfect golden locks, but she couldn't go back on her promise to Lily. Besides, there was no one here she cared about seeing her, so what did it matter?

Zinnie walked back to the group gathered around the clambake. There were about fifteen people from four different families, but none of them had kids their ages. The only "kids" here were college students, who were laughing together and running behind the dunes. The grown-ups asked the sisters the usual questions like "What grade are you in?" and "How old are you?" Zinnie thought that if you knew the answer to one of those questions, you really didn't need to ask the other, but she was politer than Marigold and more outgoing than Lily, so she answered with a smile for all three of them.

Every time someone learned they were Aunt Sunny's nieces, that person would exclaim: "She's my best friend!" Or "Aren't you lucky?" Or "Isn't she a firecracker?" Or "You mean the sage of Pruet?" And their faces would open into big, laughing smiles. As for Aunt Sunny herself, Zinnie hadn't seen her sit down once the whole time. She was laughing and chatting, flitting around the clambake like a hummingbird in a field of wildflowers.

The tall man with a sunburned nose and white hair who had done most of the cooking, Tony, smiled so much when he talked about Aunt Sunny that Zinnie thought his face might break.

"I'd like more clams, please," Zinnie said to him when she went back for seconds.

"You take after your aunt," he said, and piled clams onto her plate. "These littlenecks are her favorite. She eats 'em like candy. Maybe if you eat enough of these, you'll be as smart as she is. She's the smartest woman I know. Did you know that she once explained hydro-dynamics over a coffee cake at Sue's Café?" Zinnie shook her head. He paused for a moment and added, "Yep, she's one of kind. And pretty as a peach."

*Pretty as a peach?* Though Aunt Sunny did have a nice, friendly sort of face, Zinnie had never thought of her as pretty. She wore her gray hair short and had old-fashioned-looking glasses and never dressed up or wore makeup. She also had kind of yellow teeth.

"I see you've met Zinnia," Aunt Sunny said, and put a hand on Tony's shoulder. Aunt Sunny was pretty short, so in order to touch his shoulder, she had to reach her hand up past her head. Tony turned as red as a fire engine.

"Why, your ears must've been burning up," he said.

"We were just talking about you."

*You're the one who's burning up,* thought Zinnie.

"You're not telling her how we locals like to whoop it up at the Clam Shack, are you?" she asked.

"Nope," Tony said, and laughed.

"Well, that's good. I'm a role model, you know." Then she squinted, looking at something in the distance. "Well, I'll be darned. They decided to join us, despite the impending weather," Aunt Sunny said. Zinny dug into her clams. She ate two, and Aunt Sunny took one off her plate, claiming it was "the aunt tax." Zinnie wasn't missing the town beach at all. In fact, as she devoured another buttery clam, she wished there were a clambake every day. Aunt Sunny waved to someone behind Zinnie. "So glad to see you, Jean, and you've brought our champion sailor."

"We're a little late because of a birthday party, but we couldn't wait to get here," a lady said.

"I'm so pleased for you to meet my niece. This is Zinnia Silver."

"It's so nice to—" Zinnie turned around, ready to shake hands for the zillionth time that day. But her fingers went limp, and she felt her cheeks get as hot as the rocks that had cooked the clams. She had no idea how to finish the sentence she'd started, for she was face-to-face with Peter Pasque, who knew her by an entirely different name.

# 27 · It's Raining Cows

In a matter of seconds the raindrops started to really come down, but Marigold was the only one who seemed to care. She ducked against the rain and shoved her *Night Sprites* book deep into her purse. *These people are nuts,* she thought, noticing that almost all of them were laughing as they collected the trash and loaded their arms with beach chairs, towels, pots of seafood, and baskets of rolls. They were smiling as they covered their plates with other plates and shoved their sodas into their beach bags and started to climb back over the dune. As if this were normal! As if it were cool to be stuck on the beach in the rain! As if her leather bag weren't going to be ruined—the second purse in less than a week! Not to mention her brand-new gladiator sandals!

"Come on," Marigold said. She rolled up their towel

and took Lily's hand. She stood up and looked for Zinnie, who would be easy to spot because her hair became so wild and frizzy in the rain, it stood up four inches from her head. Sure enough, she found her in a second. She was helping roll up tarps and talking to a boy. "Zinnie!" Marigold called. "Come on, let's go!"

Zinnie and the boy stopped rolling up the tarp, turned around, and looked at Marigold. Zinnie's eyes were wide. Oddly wide. Wide with warning. Marigold shrugged a kind of what's-up? shrug. And then she realized who it was: Peter Pasque! The boy she'd told her name was Seraphina Snoopy! The boy who'd seen her topple backward into the water! She was about to run her hands through her hair, something she always did when she was nervous, when she felt Lily's hair-styling creations all over her head. There was one ponytail sticking straight up on top and two more next to her ears. The back of her head was covered in braids. She knew she looked like a total freak, but there was no time to fix it.

"Hey, Lily, I'll race you to the car!" Marigold said, and took off. "Run fast and pretend we're being chased by the hairy cows!"

"You can't catch me, hairy cows!" Lily called. Then, a few seconds later: "Marigold, wait up!"

Marigold paused for a moment, giving Lily a chance to catch up, then grabbed her arm and sped up again, practically pulling Lily, who was breathless and giggling, over the dune. "It's raining cows!" Lily sang, laughing in the afternoon shower.

"And the cows are mad and they're after us," Marigold said, hoping to get Lily to hurry up, but instead, Lily sat down and stuck her tongue out, claiming that she was thirsty. Marigold scooped Lily into her arms and raced down the dune and dropped her sister into the backseat of Aunt Sunny's station wagon. She hopped in front and caught her breath as Lily giggled in the back, thrilled by the downpour. Marigold had wanted to see Peter again, but not when she was soaking wet with an insane up-do! And not when she'd be forced to reveal her true identity, which was now inevitable.

At least she hadn't had to see him face-to-face today. *Phew!* She started to remove one of her braids when Lily shrieked. "No, Marigold! Don't! Don't take them out! It looks so beautiful, and I worked so hard!"

Marigold's fingers froze as she watched Lily's face assume a precrying frown. "Okay," Marigold said in her calmest voice. "Don't cry."

"Promise you won't touch it?" Lily asked, her lower lip trembling ominously.

"Promise," Marigold assured her, sinking in her seat on the chance that Peter might walk by the car. "At least not until I go to bed."

"Not even then," Lily insisted as Marigold slid into a strange crouching position below window level. "You need to keep it like this the whole summer."

"But I won't be able to sleep with this—" Marigold began to say, but at that very moment Zinnie opened the car door and climbed into the backseat, along with Peter Pasque.

"I told him our real names," Zinnie said, dripping with rain. "I had to. Aunt Sunny introduced me. I guess this was the surprise from the surprise brownies."

Peter grinned. "Why do you look so miserable, Marigold? Did the rain ruin your hair?"

## 28 · The Surprise

"Now my shoes are destroyed," Marigold said, trying to stay calm as she buckled her seat belt over herself and Lily, who was seated on her lap. Being cool was not easy with her hair done up in these silly braids. And to make matters worse, she had been demoted to the backseat. Aunt Sunny was giving Peter and his mother, Jean, a ride home because they had walked here. Jean, as an adult, automatically got shotgun. "Another pair ruined! The first pair—" She stopped herself.

"You mean your wedges, Marigold?" Peter asked with a devilish grin. Marigold had never heard her name pronounced the way Peter did, *Maah-ri-gold*. She wasn't at all sure that she was okay with it.

"Peter, how do you know about wedges?" Jean asked with a laugh, turning in her seat to face him. Then she noticed the book peeking out of Marigold's bag. "Oh, are you reading the *Night Sprites* series?" Jean asked.

"Yes," the three sisters answered at once.

"Do you know that they're making a movie of this?" Jean asked. "Directed by Philip Rathbone?"

"Yes," Marigold said. Did she know? Of course she knew! It was all she thought about. Day and night. At the town beach. In her boat bed. While eating plain yogurt at the breakfast table.

"And I suppose you know where Philip Rathbone spends two weeks every July?"

"No, I don't," Marigold said, leaning forward.

"Right there," Jean said, and pointed to the mansion on the hill, tapping her fingernail on the window.

"The monstrosity!" Lily said.

Aunt Sunny laughed and added, "The piping plover–destroying monstrosity!"

Marigold gazed up at the mansion in awe. Zinnie had been wrong, she thought. This was the surprise from the surprise brownies. She and Zinnie locked eyes and smiled. It started to rain bullets. It started to rain so hard that a wall of water fell on the station wagon and Aunt Sunny had to pull over. But Marigold didn't mind the pounding rain or clouds that darkened the sky. Inside her mind the sun was shining.

## 29 · Lights-Out

After a dinner of granola and blueberries because they all were so stuffed from the clambake, they gathered in the living room. The rain was drumming the windows. Marigold, whose mood that afternoon had been as bright as the flower for which she was named, was sitting at Aunt Sunny's ancient computer, practically sweating with exasperation. It had taken the stupid old thing nearly ten minutes to turn on and crank to life. Now she was attempting to get online to search for information about Philip Rathbone. Who lived—it made her giddy each time she thought it—right here in Pruet!

She was just beginning to think it would be faster to get this information if she flew back to their home in Los Angeles, where they had Wi-Fi and computers from this century, when the Google home page finished loading. She typed in "Philip Rathbone" and "Pruet," hoping to dig up some clues to where he spent his time in this dinky podunk town so that she could run into him. Marigold hit Search, and the computer moaned from the strain. This was going to take all night, but she was determined. She grumbled in frustration and waited. And waited. And waited. She looked at her sisters.

Zinnie was on the sofa under the big bay window that looked out into the garden. She was reading a *Night Sprites* book by the light of a lamp whose slightly dusty shade was decorated with, of course, a sailboat. Zinnie leaned against the wool blanket that rested on the back of the sofa. It was the *Night Sprites* book that Marigold had finished last night, and she could see that Zinnie was almost at the end. She was probably reading the part that took place in the haunted forest, where Seraphina and Xiomara had only until first light of dawn to rescue the amethyst amulet, and the demon ravens were hot on their trail, so they put on a musical performance to charm them. There was a clap of thunder, and Zinnie jumped. She gasped silently and touched her heart for a moment before she caught her breath and turned the page.

Lily was sitting on the knotty mermaid rug, gluing buttons to an old hatbox. Aunt Sunny had found the buttons in the attic last winter and said that she'd known they would come in handy one day, even if her more sensible self had told her to throw them out. Lily was creating a bed for Benny, the bunny, who Lily had always insisted enjoyed sleeping in boxes, especially fancy round ones covered with buttons of every conceivable shape and size: big, sturdy black buttons; tiny, pearly white buttons; triangle-shaped hot-pink buttons; and even tiger-striped buttons.

"I'm so glad I didn't throw those away," Aunt Sunny said, pausing in her newspaper reading for a moment to check the progress of Lily's project. She laid the *Buzzard's Bay Bugle* on her lap and peered over her glasses to take a closer look. "That's a nice pattern you've made, Lily. Benny will be so happy to have such an ornate bed."

Just then the rain picked up and thunder shook the house.

"This is one heck of a low-pressure system," Aunt Sunny said.

"It's like a freaky haunted house," Marigold said as three bright veins of lightning cracked the sky.

"The raven lord must be angry!" Zinnie said as wind rattled a window. Marigold knew that was a line she'd just read. *Boom,* another roll of thunder.

"I think the hairy cows are running on the roof," Lily said, sending everyone into a fit of laughter.

But the laughter turned to a collective gasp as the room went totally dark.

"Looks like we've lost power," Aunt Sunny said.

"Stay where you are. We don't need any cracked skulls. I'll grab the lanterns. They're in the closet next to the whistle hole. Or are they above the icebox?"

The girls heard her get up and move around the room she knew so well.

"Where's the whistle hole?" Marigold asked.

"Who knows?" said Zinnie. "What's an icebox?"

Then all three sisters jumped as lightning illuminated the room in a flash. Marigold leaped onto the sofa next to Zinnie and surprised herself by clinging to her. It wasn't a half second later that Lily was on the sofa too, squeezed in the middle, with an arm around each sister.

# 30 · By the Firelight

"I just love a roaring fire in the middle of a storm," Aunt Sunny said, and poked at a glowing log in the fireplace with a long metal stick. They were seated around the fireplace. Aunt Sunny was in an armchair, Zinnie and Marigold were on the rug, and Lily sat in a small rocking chair.

Zinnie was transfixed as flames twisted into the air. Aunt Sunny had made the fire with a few of the logs that were stored under the stairs and some kindling from a brass bucket by the fireplace and an old copy of the *Buzzard's Bay Buyle*. They had a fireplace back home, but it turned on by remote control. Zinnie couldn't remember the last time they'd used it. This fire was alive and jumping, and the glow it cast on their faces made them all look a little magical. As

Zinnie watched orange sparks leap up the chimney, she imagined the tiny lights were Night Sprites, dancing away from danger. She hadn't been able to finish her chapter because the lights had gone out, and her imagination was still going.

"This rocking chair is perfect for me," Lily said. It was true. Her sturdy little feet touched the ground.

"It is," Aunt Sunny said. "Ham made it for me."

"But you're too big," Lily said, rocking a few times to demonstrate how well it suited her.

"Yes," Aunt Sunny said, and Zinnie saw sadness pass across Aunt Sunny's face and settle in the corners of her mouth. Her voice softened to a near whisper. "We always thought we were going to have children." She leaned over and poked at the fire again, even though it was going strong. It was quiet for a few moments, except for the snapping fire.

"Do you think we should get the ice cream?" Zinnie asked. She knew there was coffee ice cream in the freezer, and Aunt Sunny had said it was one of her top five favorite things in this world. "Since it might melt anyway if the power is out?"

"That's a great idea," Aunt Sunny said. Zinnie stood up, turned on her flashlight, and headed into the kitchen. "It's in the back of the icebox. And let's not bother with the bowls. Just four spoons," Aunt Sunny called from the living room.

"So if the icebox is the freezer, what's the whistle

hole?" Zinnie asked, returning to her spot on the rug with the carton of ice cream and four spoons.

"It's the toilet," Aunt Sunny said with a smile. Lily giggled.

"What?" Marigold asked.

"Why do you call it the whistle hole?" Zinnie asked.

"I'll tell you. But first I need a bite of ice cream." Zinnie handed Aunt Sunny the ice cream, and Aunt Sunny took a big spoonful before sending the carton along to Marigold. "So, back in '78, Mr. and Mrs. William P. Winthrop, summer residents who made a vast fortune on Wall Street, decided to sail around the world."

"The whole world?" Lily asked.

"That's right," Aunt Sunny said. "And they set out on their journey from right here in Pruet on a schooner called *Elizabeth*. In preparing for their trip, they'd gotten to know Ham, who had done some repairs for them. Ham could charm the pants off just about anyone, even New York millionaires. You can imagine our delight when we received a letter from South America, inviting us to join them on the journey from Greece to Germany."

"Did you go?" Zinnie asked, her mouth full of ice cream.

"You bet your bippy! My father, your great-grandfather, taught me to never refuse a generous invitation. A bit of advice that I'm now passing on to you. We booked a flight and met them in Greece. What an adventure we had!"

"But what about the whistle hole?" Lily asked.

"Oh, yes, well, on the *Elizabeth* there were two heads on the deck. A head is what you call a bathroom on a boat. These heads were like little outhouses, one on the left, or port, and one on the right, or starboard. They were nothing more than four small walls and a hole that dropped right into the sea."

"You went to the bathroom . . . in a hole?" Marigold asked, so disgusted that she passed the ice cream along without taking a bite.

"Yes," Aunt Sunny said. "And the air made a racket in there." She made whistling sounds.

"The whistle hole!" Lily said, satisfied.

"Was it . . . cold to sit on it?" Zinnie asked.

"I'd say it was invigorating," Aunt Sunny answered. "Anyway, we started calling it the whistle hole, and we kept it up when we returned."

"Um, okay, anyway. Aunt Sunny, do you know where Philip Rathbone hangs out?" Marigold asked.

"Are you still thinking of auditioning for that terrible man?" Aunt Sunny asked. "After what I told you about the endangered piping plovers?"

"Um, I feel really, really bad about the birds, but this movie is going to be huge," Marigold said. "It could change my life."

"And the books are awesome," Zinnie added. She

didn't want Aunt Sunny to think poorly of Marigold. This really had been Marigold's dream, before she'd even known that piping plovers existed.

"Well, I suppose being in a movie would be an adventure," Aunt Sunny said.

"Do you think you could give me just one little teensy tiny clue where I might run into him?" Marigold asked.

"You should talk to Jean," Aunt Sunny said.

"Peter's mom?" Lily asked.

"Yep," Aunt Sunny said. "Her husband, Mack, manages the yacht club and she manages the casino, and they might as well be the mayors of Pruet."

"A casino? Like Las Vegas?" Marigold asked.

"No, no. Unless you count bingo on senior night." She laughed a little. "'Casino' is an old word. It used to mean social hall or community center, and around here it still does. It's where they hold town meetings and have the summer dances. Stuff like that. Back in the old days they even had plays there. Professional companies would come up from New York.

"And there's a dance there every summer after the junior sailing team races. You girls will be able to go this year if you like," Aunt Sunny said. She scraped the last bit of ice cream from the bottom of the carton and looked at Marigold. "So that's my advice. Talk to Jean. But I can't have anything to do with that man, and I wouldn't tell him that you know me."

And with that, the lights came back on.

# 31 · A Flash of Brilliance

The idea came to Zinnie after she'd been lying in bed for what felt like hours. The rain had stopped, and the smell of wet grass drifted in the open window. She could hear the ocean in the distance and crickets right outside and a mosquito somewhere in the room. But once the idea hit, she could see and hear only it. She leaped out of bed as quickly as those sparks from the fire had leaped up the chimney.

"Marigold, wake up," she said, and ran to her sister's bedside.

"I'm not asleep," Marigold said.

"We should put on a play," Zinnie said. "We should put on a play at the casino and invite Mr. Rathbone to see it." Marigold sat up. She was very, very still, but Zinnie could tell that she was listening. Her eyes were still focused, and she didn't appear to be breathing.

"I mean, I don't know exactly what the play will be. And I don't know exactly how we'll get him to come see it. And I don't know exactly when we'll do it. But I think . . . I think . . . it could work."

"Zinnie," Marigold said, standing up and taking her sister by the shoulders, "you're a genius. How did you think of this?"

"I don't know," Zinnie said. It had come to her as suddenly as that rain shower at the beach. And then she realized. "I know! The idea came from *Night Sprites*—when Xiomara and Seraphina put on that musical performance, and it totally charms the demon ravens. We'll charm Mr. Rathbone!"

And for the first time in she didn't know how long, without anyone telling her she had to, Marigold hugged her.

# 32 · The Casino

"What a nice surprise!" Jean said the next afternoon when Marigold, Zinnie, and Lily walked through the door of the casino to ask her about putting on a play there. Jean was setting up folding chairs for a town meeting that was taking place that evening. "And just in time. I could really use some help with these chairs. Normally, I'd have done this in advance, but I was out running errands."

They knew that Jean had been running errands because they'd gone to see her right after lunch and had been waiting for her for the rest of the afternoon, taking breaks to find the library, where Zinnie borrowed two new novels despite having discovered a whole bunch of promising books at Aunt Sunny's, to get ice cream at Edith's, and to see Ashley at the town beach. After each trip, they checked to see if Jean was at the casino. Now that she had returned and the moment was here, the girls were feeling unusually shy. Zinnie and Marigold each grabbed a chair. Lily knew the chairs were too heavy for her, so she started wandering around, looking at all the pictures on the walls of people from a long time ago.

As Zinnie unfolded a chair, she glanced up at the stage. It was smaller and plainer than the stage at their school, with no curtains or fancy lights, which was okay with her because she had no idea how to use those fancy lights anyway.

"Now I have a feeling," Jean said when the last chairs were in place, "that as helpful as you've been, you didn't come here to set up chairs."

Zinnie and Marigold exchanged a glance. Then Marigold nodded at Zinnie, and Zinnie knew this meant she wanted her to ask.

"Actualllllly," Zinnie said, stretching out the word, "we were wondering if we could put on a play here in the casino."

Instead of saying "Yes!" right away as Zinnie and Marigold had hoped, Jean said, "Hmm," and bit her lip.

Marigold jumped in. "See, Aunt Sunny told us that there were plays here in the old days, and we thought everyone would like it if we brought that tradition back."

"It's not so simple," Jean said. "The town pays for this casino, and there's a committee that decides who gets to use it and when." She sat down on the stage stairs. "What play were you thinking of doing?"

Zinnie and Marigold looked at each other in a panic. They had just been so excited about having their idea that they hadn't thought it through.

"*The Sound of Music*?" Zinnie said. She had to say something, and who didn't love *The Sound of Music*?

"I don't know, girls," Jean said. "I admire your gumption, but I don't think it's possible to put on a production of *The Sound of Music* in two weeks, even with a team of Broadway experts."

"And I can't sing a note," Marigold said. She sat on one of the folding chairs with her chin in her hands.

"It's true," Zinnie said, feeling really stupid. "All three of us are tone deaf."

"Hey, is this Aunt Sunny?" Lily's voice called from the other side of the casino. She had paused in front of a small photo hanging low to the ground in the back. "She looks so silly!"

"Is she wearing a sailor suit?" Jean asked.

"Yes," Lily said, giggling. "And she's dancing with a man wearing coconuts!"

"That's her," Jean said.

Marigold and Zinnie had to see this. They rushed over to see the picture Lily was looking at. Sure enough, Aunt Sunny was singing and dancing in a sailor's suit. Her arm was linked with Ham's, and not only was he wearing a coconut bikini top, but he was also in a grass skirt!

"They were doing a number from *South Pacific,*" Jean said. "They really stole the show."

"Wait a second," Zinnie said, noticing a banner in the background that read: ANNUAL PRUET TALENT SHOW. "Is there a talent show every year?"

"There used to be. In fact, your uncle Ham was the one who started the whole thing. He and your aunt organized it and got the whole community involved. He thought it was a great way for the town kids and the summer kids to come together. But when he died, well, the talent shows stopped," Jean said.

"Why didn't Aunt Sunny keep it going?" Marigold asked.

"I think it was just too sad for her," Jean said.

"Maybe it's time to bring it back," Zinnie said.

"You know," Jean said, "that's something I could get the town committee to agree on."

"We may not be able to do *The Sound of Music,* but I bet we can get people to sign up for a talent show," Zinnie said.

"And we could do a short play," Marigold said. "Without any musical numbers."

Jean smiled. "Now you're talking."

Jean took a look at her calendar and found there was a free night in a little over two weeks, after the big dance and before the girls were scheduled to return to California. Thinking aloud, Jean decided that fifteen acts would be enough for a solid evening of entertainment. She told them that if they could get fourteen other kids to sign up by the end of the day tomorrow and the town committee approved, they could have their talent show.

They hugged Jean and were halfway down the block when Jean caught up to them and handed the picture of Aunt Sunny to Zinnie. "She should have this."

# 33 · Guess What, Aunt Sunny!

"Like a band of wild horses!" Aunt Sunny said, taking off her gardening gloves and standing up to greet the sisters, who were bounding through the yard, running toward the fence where Aunt Sunny was working, plucking some small plants that were sprouting next to the brigh-pink flowers that bloomed as tall as basketball players. The evening air was alive with crickets and the sweet smell of honeysuckle, and even though there was still plenty of daylight, Zinnie noticed a faint disk of a moon hanging in the sky. Bursting with their news, the girls were just too excited to walk. Even Marigold couldn't resist breaking into a trot. "I was starting to get a little concerned. You left after lunch, and it's almost time for dinner."

"Jean was running errands this afternoon," Marigold explained.

"So we walked all the way to the library, went to Edith's Ice Cream Shop, and visited our friend Ashley at the town beach while we waited for her," Zinnie said.

"Sounds like a nice afternoon," Aunt Sunny said.

"Why are you digging up those plants?" Zinnie asked. She liked the tall flower stalks with their abundant pink and red blooms.

"These are what we call volunteers," Aunt Sunny said, holding up a seedling. "I didn't plant these. They're growing on their own from seeds that the hollyhocks have dropped. But the thing about hollyhocks is that they can't grow too close together. They need their own space or they won't grow properly. Now tell me, did you get a chance to talk to Jean?"

Zinnie nodded.

"And guess what!" Lily said.

"I can't imagine," Aunt Sunny said.

"We found a picture of you!" Lily said.

Zinnie handed the picture to Aunt Sunny and watched as her face lit up. "Wherever did you find this?"

"It was in the casino," Lily said. "Hanging in the very back. You and Ham were funny."

Aunt Sunny ran her hand over the picture. "Yes, we had a lot of fun. My goodness, I haven't thought about the talent show for years and years."

"Then you'll be glad to know that we, your nieces,

are going to bring it back," Marigold said.

"Is that so?" Aunt Sunny asked. "Did Jean say yes?"

"Yup. If we can find fourteen acts by tomorrow," Zinnie said, "and get the approval of the town committee."

"That's terrific!" Aunt Sunny said. "But you'd better get crackin'."

"She's right," Marigold said. "We should start going door to door right now."

Aunt Sunny raised a finger in protest. "Not until after dinner. I have a chicken roasting in the oven, and I need someone to wash the lettuce." She reached into her basket and handed the fresh lettuce to Marigold. "Someone to peel the carrots." She handed carrots to Zinnie. "And Lily, you can husk the corn that's on the kitchen table."

"I'll race you guys," Lily said. The girls took off through the pear orchard and under the brick archway toward the little house, but Zinnie stopped when she realized that Aunt Sunny wasn't following them. She turned around and walked back toward the garden. She peeked around the archway. Aunt Sunny was standing in the garden with the fading sun on her face. The old photograph was in her hand, and she was gazing at it with a soft, still smile. Then she tucked the photo into her apron pocket and walked toward the house. Zinnie waited for her.

"Did you guys win the talent show that year?" Zinnie asked Aunt Sunny as they walked together up the stone pathway.

"No, the talent show was always for the children. We just hosted it. But we were quite a team."

"Would you ever want to be a team with . . . someone new?" Zinnie asked, remembering the way Tony had looked at Aunt Sunny that afternoon at the clambake.

"I'm too old for that," Aunt Sunny said.

"No one is too old for love," Zinnie said. She gestured to the pale sky. "Not even the moon!"

"Oh, do you ever have a way with words, my dear," Aunt Sunny said, and put a hand on her shoulder. "Now tell me, what are you going to do for the talent show?"

"We're going to perform a short play," Zinnie said.

"Fabulous!" Aunt Sunny said. "And where are you going to find this play?"

Zinnie thought for a moment and then said: "I think I'm going to write it."

When the phone rang that evening, all three girls ran toward it. They knew it was their parents making their scheduled conference call, and they all had big news to report. Marigold, whose turn it was to do the dishes, leaped from behind the sink without even bothering to peel the dishwashing gloves from her hands. Zinnie sprang up from the sofa, where she'd been reading a book about a girl detective that she'd discovered on one of Aunt Sunny's bookshelves. But it was Lily, who was sitting on the floor with Aunt Sunny practicing paddling her arms while wearing floaties, who beat her sisters to the phone.

First she told her parents all about the dune she'd so bravely climbed over. Then she described the hairy cows in great detail. Finally she listed everything she'd eaten not only at the clambake but over the past several days. After what seemed like an eternity, she passed the phone off to Marigold.

"I may have the chance to audition for Philip Rathbone after all," Marigold said into the receiver. Zinnie listened as Marigold breathlessly told the story of the clambake and of discovering that Philip Rathbone lived in this town for two weeks every year. Aunt Sunny shook her head as Marigold added, "And he lives in the most beautiful mansion." But Zinnie beamed when Marigold told them, "And Zinnie had the idea to put on a show, and we think we can actually make it happen."

"It sounds like you're having a great time," Mom said when it was at last Zinnie's turn to talk to her parents. "Tell me about this talent show."

"I'm going to write a play," Zinnie said, feeling

herself grow at least a quarter of an inch.

"That's great, Zinnie!" Mom and Dad said at the same time, and even though they were thousands of miles away, she could hear them smiling.

# 34 · A Powerful Hat

"Oh, no," Peter said when he saw Marigold approaching him. He was filling a wheelbarrow with bags of ice from the ice machine. "I'm not going to be in your talent show," he said. Then he took off with that wheelbarrow down the dock.

"Hey, wait up," Marigold said, and hustled after him. In order to get fourteen other people to sign up, she and Zinnie had split up for the morning. Marigold had taken the yacht club, and Zinnie was at the town beach. They were going to meet up at Edith's Ice Cream Shop at noon and see how many people they had come up with. Aunt Sunny was taking Lily to the local YMCA for a swimming lesson. The classes were all filled up, so she couldn't enroll Lily in any official swimming lessons. Instead, Aunt Sunny said she'd teach Lily herself during free swim.

Marigold was thinking that she and Zinnie ought to take a swimming break today. It was hot even with a breeze. She could feel a trickle of sweat running down her back as she chased after Peter. And once again, Marigold regretted her shoe choice. Her sparkly flats didn't allow her to catch up to Peter as quickly as she wanted to. What was it about this town that made ugly tennis shoes the best thing to wear?

Finally she caught up to him when he stopped in front of a big boat called *Sweet Caroline*. She waited as he handed the bags of ice to a sunburned man on the boat.

"Have fun on the Vineyard," Peter said to the man, and the man gave him some folded-up money. Peter stepped away from the boat and counted the money.

"Won't you at least think about it?" Marigold asked as Peter shoved the money into his pocket.

"No," he said. He removed his baseball hat to wipe some sweat from his brow, then put it back on, picked up the wheelbarrow, and headed back toward the club-house. "I don't like getting up in front of people."

"But your mom said you were really good on the guitar," Marigold said.

"She's my mom," Peter replied. "Of course she said I'm good. I can only play like four songs."

Marigold jumped in front of the wheelbarrow, blocking his path. "Come on, Peter, why not?"

"Why not? It's more like . . . why?" He shook his

head when he looked at her. "Why are you always dressed like you're going to a party?" When Peter said "party," it sounded like *pah-ty*.

"It's called having style," Marigold said. "And it isn't a crime. Not even here." It was true that Marigold had dressed up a little more than usual today. She was wearing a yellow dress with daisies embroidered on it and silver flats, and she had her hair done up in a topknot. She had wanted to look her best in order to convince people to be in the show. "I could ask you why you're always wearing that nasty hat." She pointed to the tattered, faded baseball hat on Peter's head. "You should wash that thing. It's probably carrying diseases."

"Marigold, if I wash this hat, the Red Sox will have bad luck. Now, would you mind stepping out of the way?"

"Do you really believe that the Red Sox's winning has anything to do with some kid wearing that hat?" Marigold said, not moving an inch.

"I'm not just some kid," Peter said. "And for your information, I was wearing this hat when I caught a fly ball in Fenway."

"What's Fenway?" Marigold asked.

*"What's Fenway?"* Peter asked.

Marigold wondered if it was a really important country that she should know about. "Wait. Is it the capital of New Hampshire?" she asked.

"What's wrong with you?" he asked. "Fenway is where the Red Sox play baseball. You know? Baseball?" He dropped the wheelbarrow and mimed holding a bat and taking a swing. Then he lowered his voice. "I wouldn't tell anyone else around here that you don't know what Fenway is. And just so you know, catching a fly ball at a Red Sox game is a pretty huge deal. Like, it might be the biggest thing that ever happens to me in my life. I was on TV and everything." He picked up the wheelbarrow and moved right past her. "I'm practically famous around here."

"I've been on TV too, you know," Marigold said.

"I know," Peter said.

"I'm just saying," she said, "if you want to be on TV again, maybe my talent show can help. Come on. I'll be your best friend."

"Why would I want a girl as a best friend?" Peter asked. He returned the wheelbarrow to its place by the ice machine, took out a scoop of ice, and ran a piece over his neck.

"Because girls are the best. We can do anything we set our minds to," Marigold said, picking out a piece of ice and rubbing it along her wrists like it was perfume.

Peter smiled. "Oh, yeah. Can you sail out to that buoy?" He pointed. Marigold peered out to the thing sticking out of the water that wasn't a rock. It really wasn't all that far away. In fact, she thought that she could probably swim out there if she had to. And it wasn't as if she'd never been sailing before. She'd done it once for Girl Scouts. Sure, it had been four years ago, and there was a counselor with her the whole time, but it hadn't been that hard. And she had remembered how to tie that knot without any trouble at all.

"Yeah," Marigold said. "If I wanted to. But I don't really want to. I'm way too busy."

"Maybe I'm too busy to enter a talent show," Peter said. "Ever think of that?"

"I think you're scared," Marigold said.

"Nah," Peter said. He squinted into the sun. "I just don't want to."

Marigold put a hand on her hip. She couldn't show up at Edith's without even getting Peter's name on the list. Also, she had the feeling that he was beating her at something. If there was one thing Marigold couldn't stand, it was losing. "If I did sail out there, would you be in the show?"

"Like, if you sailed out there right now?" Peter asked.

"Right now," Marigold said.

"Is this a bet?" Peter asked.

"Yep," Marigold said, and held out her hand.

"Wait a second," Peter said. "What if you lose? I gotta get something." A smile spread across his face as slow as molasses. "You have to wear my hat. And you can't wash it."

"*Ew*," Marigold said, then, figuring she could just wear it around the house in the dark, added, "Whatever."

"To the dance," Peter said.

Marigold gasped. "But I don't wear any sort of hat—"

"Final offer," Peter said, grinning.

"Fine," she said, and they shook on it.

# 35 · A Very Expensive Announcement

"Don't tell me—you want a red ice pop," Ashley said as soon as she saw Zinnie sidle up to the snack bar.

"Yes," Zinnie said. "I'd love one."

"Do I know my customers, or what?" Ashley said. She handed Zinnie an ice pop and then fluffed her bangs in the reflection of the snack bar window. "Where's your sister? The one with her nose in the air?"

"At the yacht club," Zinnie said.

"Figures," Ashley said. "Don't you have a little sister, too?"

"Yep," Zinnie said.

"You've got sisters coming out of your ears," Ashley said. *Sistahs comin' out of yah ee-yahs.* Zinnie loved how people talked around here.

Zinnie slurped her ice pop and studied Ashley, wondering what the best way would be to make her say yes to being in the talent show.

"You're lookin' at me weird," Ashley said.

"I have something to ask you," Zinnie said. "It's sort of a strange question."

"It's not the facts of life, is it?" Ashley asked.

"No." Zinnie laughed.

"Good, 'cause I was about to say, talk to your mother about that. I just sell ice pops." Ashley wiped down the counter and shook her head.

Zinnie laughed again. "No, no. It's just my sisters and I are trying to put on a talent show, and I remembered what a nice singing voice you have."

Ashley blushed. "Are you serious? You remembered?"

"Yes. I think you have a great voice. And I think you should enter the talent show," Zinnie said.

"Okay," Ashley said as she wiped down the counter. Well, that was easy. Zinnie whipped out her notebook and wrote Ashley's name.

"What song are you going to sing?" Zinnie asked.

"'Ave Maria,'" Ashley answered, as if she'd been waiting for someone to ask her this question all day.

"What's that?" Zinnie asked.

"Seriously? You don't know 'Ave Maria'?" Ashley asked as she unpacked a box of soda cans and put them in the refrigerator. "It's like the most famous song in the world. It's so beautiful it will make you cry like a baby. You should see my nana when she hears the song. Waterworks. You hear it a lot at Christmas."

"My dad's Jewish," Zinnie said. "And my mom isn't anything, so we don't go to church."

"Guess that would explain it," Ashley said.

"Yep," Zinnie said, and looked out at the beach. There were probably twenty kids in her line of vision alone. Was she supposed to just go up to all of them and ask if they wanted to be in the show? She suddenly felt a little shy.

"Uh-oh, you're quiet," Ashley said. "And you're nevah quiet. What's wrong?"

"I need to get a lot of people to sign up, and I don't know how I'm going to do it," Zinnie confessed.

"Is there a prize if you win?" Ashley asked.

Zinnie frowned. She hadn't thought of that.

"You gotta have a prize," Ashley said.

"I have a hundred dollars of allowance money saved up," Zinnie said.

"Perfect," Ashley said. Before Zinnie could protest, she picked up a bullhorn from behind the snack bar. When Ashley turned it on, it screeched for a second. "Listen up, everybody," Ashley said into the microphone. The lifeguards turned around. Kids who were building sand castles paused and looked up. Teenagers stopped texting and waited for Ashley to speak. "There's going to be a talent show at the casino in two weeks. A wicked-awesome talent show! Maybe you'll be discovered and be a star. You'll never know unless you try. First prize is a hundred bucks cash. Come to the snack bar and sign up. Quick, quick before all the spots are taken! Don't miss the opportunity of a lifetime!"

"Hey, you're good at that," Zinnie said.

"My dad owns Peretti Toyota out on Route Six. I watch him do his commercials," Ashley said.

Soon there was a bunch of kids surrounding Zinnie. Kara and Tara, twins from Boston, wanted to do a gymnastics routine. Derek, a boy from Ashley's class, wanted to do a comedy act, and his younger brother, Cody, wanted to do his animal impressions. McKenzie, a girl Zinnie's age, was going to do magic tricks.

As Zinnie wrote down everyone's name, Ashley started practicing her scales from behind the snack bar. Zinnie was excited that the talent show was becoming real, but she also couldn't help feeling a sharp pang as she envisioned giving away her life's savings, which were tucked neatly inside a pink envelope. She'd written her name on it in her best, most careful calligraphy.

# 36 · Jibe Ho!

"It's what they call a Cape Cod catboat," Peter said as he rowed them toward the little sailboat. "But you probably knew that already. My dad and I fixed it up last year. We haven't thought of a name, though."

"Cool," Marigold said, and she gulped. Marigold wasn't sure why they had to take a rowboat, which Peter called a dinghy, to get to another boat. Why not keep the sailboat tied to the dock so he could just walk right to it? As she looked around the harbor, she noticed that there were a lot of sailboats floating out there, tied to what looked like big volleyballs, some of them white, some of them colored, some of them with a stripe. She guessed there wasn't enough room at the docks for all the boats, but what exactly were these volleyball thingies and how did they keep the boats from drifting away? She was afraid to ask Peter any questions that might reveal her ignorance. She didn't want to let on that she knew almost nothing about boats or sailing. In fact, with each stroke of the oars that brought them closer to the little sailboat, she was regretting this bet more.

"Hop aboard while I tie the dinghy to the mooring," Peter said as he rowed them right next to a small sailboat. *Okay, so those volleyball things are called moorings*, she thought, as Peter pulled an oar inside the dinghy and held the boats together with his arm. Marigold stepped out of the rowboat and into the sailboat. *Whoa*, she thought as the sailboat rocked. She caught her balance and took a deep breath, suddenly a bit nauseous. She thought it would be best if she just sat down. In fact, she needed to sit down. There were no seats or anything, so she plopped right down on the floor of the boat. She could feel some water seep into her yellow dress, and she wondered what she had gotten herself into. From far away the small sailboat had looked like a toy that anyone could sail, but up close it was a real thing—a real thing that she was supposed to get from one place to another!

Peter hopped aboard and looked at Marigold. "You okay?" he asked.

She nodded. *Don't freak out*, she thought. *Don't let him know that you're scared.* She was determined to win this bet, but it wasn't going to be as easy as she'd hoped.

He smiled. "I'll get you started." He lifted a piece of wood from the middle of the boat and lowered it on the back of the boat, and then he put another piece of wood down the middle. He untied a few ropes, halyards he called them, and pulled on them so that the sail rose up. It flapped in the breeze.

"Time to cast off," he said.

"Okay," Marigold said, but she didn't move. Her first problem was that she had no idea what "cast off" meant. Her second problem was her stomach, which felt like it was turning over. She wasn't sure if she was seasick or just dreading telling Peter that she had no idea how to sail. Nothing from Girl Scouts was coming back to her. It was just a freak thing that she had remembered that one stupid knot!

"All right. You take the tiller, and I'll cast off," he said. He pointed a long, smooth piece of wood at her, and she took it in her hand. *The tiller*, she thought. Like magic, something did come back to her. She remembered that this was what steered the boat. She also remembered that the boat would go the opposite way of whatever direction she pulled it. She felt a cool breeze on her face, and the gripping in her stomach loosened. *I can do this,* she thought.

"We're free," Peter said, and the boat started to drift backward. "Grab the sheet."

"Huh?" she asked.

He sat down next to her and handed her a rope.

*This rope is called a sheet,* she thought, and mentally added "sheet" to her rapidly growing sailing vocabulary. Holding the tiller steady, she took the sheet in her hand and felt the wind push the sail over to one the side of the boat.

"Trim it," Peter said, making a jerking motion with his hand. She instinctively pulled the sheet toward her, and the sail tightened. "Not too much. There you go."

Marigold smiled. It was like he was speaking a foreign language, but one that she could almost make out. This boat was moving, and she was doing it. The sun was on her face, the wind was in her hair, and she was sailing.

Peter leaned in close. "Okay. You're headed right for the beach. You're going to have to tack."

"Tack?" Marigold asked.

"Just aim for the buoy," he said, pointing to the metal thing bobbing up and down in the water, "and trim the sail." She used the tiller to aim the boat, and it turned a little. She felt a kick of happiness. "That's it," Peter said. "Now aim for that rock." He pointed to a bunch of rocks with a flock of seagulls on them. A gust blew and filled the sail like a wing. Marigold pressed her feet to the boat and leaned back, holding the sheet. The boat tilted on its side so high that some water spilled into the boat. She screamed with delight. They were flying! She was going to make it to the buoy!

"Leave it to port," Peter said.

"Speak English!" Marigold said.

"To your left," Peter said, gesturing for her to aim to the right of the buoy.

"Whatever you say," she said, laughing. They sailed for several minutes with only smiles, no words, passing between them. When the little boat passed the buoy, Marigold whooped. *"Whoo-hoo!"*

"So I won the bet," she said, trying to hide the question in her voice, because she certainly couldn't have done it without Peter's help.

"I think we both won," Peter said. "Want to take a tour?"

"Yes!" she said, feeling as bright as the high white sun above them. Her skin was tingling from the salt wind, and all around her the water was sparkling.

"Then it's time for a flying jibe," he said. "Duck!" He took the tiller and the sheet from Marigold. "Jibe ho!" he called, pulling the tiller toward him and letting the sail out. "Watch out for the boom!" he said. Marigold ducked down even more as the beam of wood that held the bottom part of the sail flew clear across the boat to the other side. Water sprayed Peter and Marigold as they scurried to the other side of the boat.

"Now I can really show you Pruet," Peter said, beaming. He brought them in close along the shore of a small private beach. He took her under a bridge where the air was cool and their voices echoed. He pointed out Martha's Vineyard and some closer, smaller islands. He even showed her one where there used to be a leper colony. When they returned to the harbor, he made sure to sail by what he told her was his favorite boat. It had a green sail cover, a thin stripe on its side, a star painted on the front, and a crescent moon at the back. It had never occurred to Marigold to have a favorite boat.

By the time they tied up the sailboat to the mooring and rowed back to the dock, Marigold was already fifteen minutes late to meet Zinnie at Edith's Ice Cream Shop. "I gotta go," Marigold said. Then she remembered the point of this whole excursion. "So I guess you're going to be in the talent show," she said.

"If you wear my hat to the dance," he said.

She had no time to think this over. Zinnie was going to be mad at her for being late.

"Okay, fine," she said. "See you later." It wasn't until she had run halfway up the dock that she started to wonder: If she wore his hat, did that make her his date?

# 37 · Edith's Ice Cream Shop

"You only got one name?" Zinnie asked, her mouth full of vanilla-chocolate swirl soft-serve ice cream. They were sitting in one of the booths at Edith's. Zinnie had been waiting for Marigold for almost a half hour, during which time she felt really stupid sitting all by herself, looking as if she had been forgotten, though it had given her a chance to talk to Edith and meet her dachshund, Mocha Chip. Edith had even let her choose a few songs to play on the jukebox for free.

"Peter's name! I had to sail a boat to get it!" Marigold said, stealing a spoonful of Zinnie's ice cream. Zinnie pulled her dish closer to herself and guarded it with her hand. Marigold didn't seem to notice. She was smiling more than Zinnie had ever seen her. "It was actually really fun. We were going so fast and it felt like the boat was going to tip over and then Peter showed me this secret little beach and took me under a bridge—"

"I got nine names," Zinnie said, and held up her notebook. "Nine!" She held up nine fingers to drive the point home.

"It was not easy to get Peter to sign up," Marigold said. "I've only ever sailed once before in my life, but today I made it all the way out to the buoy with hardly any help."

"And I had to give up all of my saved allowance," Zinnie said.

"What?" Marigold asked, sneaking another bite from Zinnie's bowl.

"For a prize! I needed a prize to get people to sign up," Zinnie said, pulling her ice cream toward her again.

"Oh, good idea," Marigold said.

"And while I was waiting for you, I convinced Edith to give us a gift certificate for four ice cream cones. So we have a second-place prize, too."

"Doesn't seem quite fair to me that you should have to give up all of your savings," Edith said as she wiped the counter. "I'm sure you can talk someone else into making a donation. It's not like you don't have the gift of gab, Zinnie. You could sell ice to an Eskimo. You almost convinced me to make pickle ice cream." Edith shook her head.

"*Ew!*" Marigold said.

"I know, disgusting, right?" Edith said.

"What? I love pickles and I love ice cream," Zinnie said. "Why not put them together?"

"I'm telling you," Edith said with her hand on her hip, "it was starting to sound like a good idea. You're going places, kid."

"Let's see what people are doing." Marigold said, and snatched up Zinnie's notebook. She read the list

1. Marigold, Lily, and Zinnie—Zinnie's play
2. Ashley—singing "Ave Maria"
3. Derek—stand-up comedy
4. Kara and Tara—gymnastics
5. Jake—break dancing
6. Katie—the song from *The Little Mermaid*
7. Daniel—karate
8. Grace—recorder
9. McKenzie—magic tricks
10. Cody—animal impressions

Marigold added: "11. Peter—guitar song." The bell that hung over the door rang, signaling a new customer.

"Hiya, Tony," Edith said. "Let me guess. Iced coffee with a scoop of vanilla."

"You know me," Tony said. "That stuff is my kryptonite."

Zinnie and Marigold waved.

"Oh, hey there," Tony said. "You girls look like you're planning something big."

"We are," Zinnie said. "We're planning a talent show. And we need four more acts or we might not be able to do it."

"You're bringing the talent show back?" Tony asked as Edith handed him his iced coffee topped with vanilla ice cream. "That's great. My girls won that two years with their ballet."

"Do you think they'd want to be in it this year?" Marigold asked.

Tony laughed. "They're thirty-five and thirty-seven years old now, and my youngest is pregnant with twins. But you should stop by Miss Melody's School of Dance. That's where my girls used to practice. Their whole class used to participate. When is the talent show?"

"In less than two weeks," Marigold said, "the day after the dance."

"If we can get enough people to sign up," Zinnie added. "We're on a mission."

"Get on over to Miss Melody's," Tony said. "It's right up the road."

"Let's go," Zinnie said, finishing the last bite of ice cream.

"Say, are you girls coming to the dance?" Tony asked them just as they were about to leave.

"Yes," Marigold answered.

"I hope that means your aunt Sunny is coming too?" Tony asked. "My band is playing."

"You have a band?" Marigold asked.

"Tony and the Contractors," Edith said with a smile. "They always get me on the dance floor." She bit her lip and danced a little twist.

"We do the Beach Boys, the Beatles; we really rock out," Tony said. "I play the guitar myself."

"And he does all the vocals," Edith said, and leaned into her broom to croon a little Elvis. Mocha Chip howled in tune.

"Give my best to Sunny," Tony said, his face turning just the slightest bit pink as he spoke her name.

Zinnie and Marigold walked all the way to Miss Melody's School of Dance. Tony was right. They got the extra four acts in no time. Two girls signed up for solo routines. One boy signed up for a Broadway song, and a whole class of ten- to twelve-year-olds signed up for a zombie dance number.

"That's fifteen acts," Zinnie said to Marigold. "We did it!"

"Come on," Marigold said, watching herself in the mirror as she turned a lively pirouette. "Let's go find Jean!"

# 38 · Ask a Tree

A few days later Zinnie sat in Aunt Sunny's study and gathered her materials. Pencils. Erasers. Paper. They'd handed over their list of fifteen acts, the town committee had approved, and Jean had officially put the talent show on the calendar. Now all Zinnie had to do was write a play.

"Are you sure you don't want to come to the beach with us?" Aunt Sunny asked Zinnie. She was standing in the doorway of the office with a white stripe of zinc oxide across her nose, a big, floppy hat on her head, and a canvas bag filled with roast beef sandwiches, lemonade, and oatmeal–chocolate chip cookies.

"Of course I want to go," Zinnie said. "But I have a whole play to write."

"She does need to write our play," Marigold said as she passed by the open door in a purple bikini and the sarong their mom had brought back from a trip to Mexico. "I need to get started on my lines."

"I shan't keep an artist from her work," Aunt Sunny said, fiddling with her keys. "The list of phone numbers is on the fridge. You've met all the neighbors. Holler if you need something. I'll have Jean stop by for lunch. Oh, and there's some leftover blueberry pie in the fridge. Make sure to offer Jean a slice."

"Okay," Zinnie said. She lined up her paper and placed an eraser next to her neat pile.

"Benny needs a babysitter," Lily said, and sat her beloved bunny on the desk. She whispered to Zinnie: "He likes to have peanut butter on crackers after his nap. And don't let him sleep too long or he'll never go to bed tonight."

"No problem," Zinnie said, patted her little sister on the head, and pushed her out the door.

"The writer must be left in peace, girls," Aunt Sunny said to Marigold and Lily, and shut the door behind them.

But as soon as she heard Aunt Sunny's station wagon rumble out of the driveway, Zinnie started to panic. She couldn't think of a single thing to write. The house was too quiet; the minutes were too long; the piece of paper was too blank. She needed help. She paced around the too-empty house for a good fifteen minutes and then left a desperate message on her father's voice mail.

When the phone rang, she answered it right away. "Hello?"

"Zinnia, I got your message," Dad said. "And I'm extremely worried. What's the emergency?"

"It's a creative emergency, Dad," Zinnie said, holding the heavy, old-fashioned phone receiver to her ear. She felt her whole body relax at the sound of Dad's voice. "I'm writing a play, and I need your help."

"Jeez," Dad said, "you nearly gave me a heart attack."

"Sorry," Zinnie said. She explained all the latest developments. "The talent show is on. It's actually happening, and it's only ten days away. But I can't think of any good ideas, and I don't have much time, and Marigold is depending on me. So can you tell me what to write about?"

"Sorry, Zin," Dad said. "Part of being a writer is figuring out what to write."

"But you have a zillion ideas, Dad. Can't you just give me one of them? Or if I give you a list, can you just say yes or no? Like, should I write about horses? Dragons? Dogs?" Zinnie could hear herself whining. "I don't know where to start."

"Well, I can tell you that I usually start with something that's bugging me," Dad said. "Is there anything on your mind these days?"

"I guess the fact that there are wars and global warming stuff," she said, though she was really just saying what she thought a responsible girl who was going into the sixth grade at Miss Hadley's should say. She knitted her brow and twirled the old-fashioned phone cord around her finger.

"Hmm," Dad said. "Can you think about something more personal? Something in your life? What bugs you on a day-to-day basis?"

"Duh. Marigold," Zinnie said.

"Why?" Dad asked.

"She thinks she's so awesome. Like, I had to give up my whole life savings for the talent show prize, but because she's, you know, Marigold, she didn't even offer to chip in. But she still expected me to do it. And no one would expect Lily to give up her allowance because she's so little and cute."

"That's pretty rough," Dad said. "How much savings do you have?"

"A hundred dollars," Zinnie said.

"That's a lot. I'll talk to Mom about that. You shouldn't have to give up your savings, honey. Together we'll work something out. But I only have a few minutes here, so tell me, why do you think that happened with Marigold?"

"Because she's the automatic boss," Zinnie said. "It's like Marigold is the queen of the world and Lily is so adorable and I'm just . . . blah. In the middle."

"For the record, there is nothing blah about you. But there's your idea," Dad said. "Write about being in the middle."

"How?" Zinnie asked.

"I don't know, Zin," Dad said. "There's no one right answer. Just remember that your main character needs a specific problem to solve, and there has to be a beginning, a middle, and an end. Oh, and something needs to happen!"

Zinnie sighed. She'd learned all this in English class. "Can you at least tell me how long it should be?"

"A play is about a page a minute. So if you want it to be about five minutes, write about five pages," Dad said.

"Five whole pages?" Zinnie asked. With the exception of her report on gray wolves, which had included several pictures, Zinnie hadn't ever written anything that long.

"I need to go, sweetie. I have to get back to the team. They're measuring today, and they think we've got a winner. The tallest living thing on earth," Dad said. "Oh, and here's one last piece of advice: If you get stuck, ask a tree."

"Ask a tree?" Zinnie pulled on her curls in exasperation.

"I've been talking to this tree for weeks, and I've never felt so inspired in my life. And besides, we're from California," Dad said, and laughed. "We've come from a tradition of nature lovers and tree huggers. Try talking to a tree. You might be surprised."

# 39 · California Wildflowers

A half hour later, after eating a piece and a half of blueberry pie, clipping her toenails, and straightening the pictures on the wall, Zinnie sat back down at the desk. She placed a fresh piece of paper in front of her and decided to just write the first thing that came to her.

"Being in the middle isn't as easy as it looks," she wrote. "You might get squished." But then she had no idea what to put after that. She crumpled the paper and threw it in the trash. She took a deep breath and tried again, this time starting with a character. Zora? No, too fancy sounding. Alejandra? No, too long. How about Justine? Oh, yes. She liked Justine. "Justine: I'm a poor girl and everyone makes fun of my tattered clothes. Tonight I shall run away to join a traveling circus. As a middle girl, will anyone even notice I'm missing?"

Zinnie read it over. She liked the circus part, and Marigold would make a perfect Justine, but would that mean that Lily and she would have to play all the characters at the circus? She crumpled the paper. Maybe she wasn't any better at writing than at acting. Maybe she wasn't going to ever be good at anything. Maybe she really was just a . . . blah. A short, frizzy-haired, stuck-in-the-middle blah.

All this thinking had made her tired. She remembered that Mr. Herrera, who was probably the best fifth-grade teacher in the whole world, did yoga every morning before school and said that headstands were good for coming up with ideas because they made all the blood go to your brain. She decided to try a headstand right there in Aunt Sunny's study. She was desperate. When she was upside down, she found herself face-to-face with Aunt Sunny's bookshelf. It was packed with books about trees and plants, probably from her days as a science teacher. The bottom shelf, the one she was eye level with, was stacked with books about flowers.

When she saw *A Guide to California Wildflowers* written on the spine of the biggest book on the shelf, she somersaulted to a sitting position and opened it up. It was filled with photographs and illustrations of wildflowers that grew in California, as well as stories of how they got their names. She flipped to the index to search for zinnia. "Zinnias thrive in rugged terrain and are favored by butterflies." She smiled at the idea that her flower was the favorite of butterflies. "Zinnias symbolize constancy." Constancy? She had an idea what it meant but decided to look it up in the dictionary to be safe. "The quality of staying the same: lack of change." *Well, that's a boring thing to symbolize,* she thought, and looked up her sister's name.

"Marigold" meant "beautiful, golden daisy." *Of course*, Zinnie thought, and rolled her eyes. However, she also read that marigolds also symbolized jealousy. *Interesting*, Zinnie thought, *very interesting*.

She looked up lily. There were about a million different kinds of lilies. There was the alpine lily, the meadow lily, the swamp lily, the tiger lily, the morning star lily, the trout lily, the snake lily, and, Zinnie's personal favorite, the liver lily. They symbolized sweetness and youth. That made perfect sense.

Then she read about other wildflowers with crazy names, names that had stories in them: jack-in-the-pulpit, ragged sailor, ghost flower. Some wildflowers sounded like a fairy language: maypop, chicory, trillium. And then there were the ones that read like the ingredients of a witch's spell: toadflax, soapwort, bloodroot.

Stories. Fairies. Witches. Zinnie felt she was on to something. Even though she couldn't quite get a grip on an idea, she was filled with energy. Maybe it was time to ask a tree. As she walked into the yard, she thought about how maybe she could use the names of the flowers in her play. What if instead of Night Sprites she wrote about flower fairies? This would make her play close enough to Night Sprites that Mr. Rathbone would think that the sisters would be perfect for the movie, but she wouldn't be copying.

Zinnie broke into a skip, thinking that her idea might be even better than the Night Sprites. After all, sprites were made-up things, but flowers were real in a way that one could touch and smell and see. What if flowers had secret lives that no one knew about? What if the moment they were cut was the moment their souls had only a few hours left to fulfill a mission from the butterflies? Ideas were coming all at once. How was Zinnie ever going to decide which was the right one?

At the far end of Aunt Sunny's yard, through the archway, past the pear orchard and the vegetable garden, and beyond the shed, was a big beech tree with a zillion leaves. If there ever was a tree with answers, this was it. Zinnie walked beneath its branches and stared up.

"Hello," Zinnie said. "Dad said that you could help me write my play. And I finally have a good idea, but where should I start?" Zinnie listened. A breeze blew. Leaves rustled. Maybe she was talking to the wrong side of the tree. She decided to do a little dance around it. "Help me with my play, great tree!" she chanted as she skipped around its trunk.

"Zinnia?" A voice startled Zinnie out of her trance. "You okay?" Zinnie turned around to see Jean, standing at the edge of the driveway with a hand on her hip and an expression of concern. "Whatcha doin'?"

"Um," Zinnie said. "Just . . . talking . . . to myself."

"Hmm. Okay, well, I brought over some chicken salad," Jean said. "How about you wash your hands and join me in the kitchen?"

"Okay, one sec." She waited for Jean to walk up the driveway, and then she turned back to the tree and pleaded. "Please, I need a main character with a specific problem," Zinnie whispered. "Oh, and a beginning, middle, and end. Thanks."

"You coming?" Jean called from the back door.

"Yep," Zinnie said, and started toward the house. Just then she spotted a cluster of small blue flowers growing near the shed. She'd never noticed them before. But why would she? There wasn't anything special about them. In fact, they were kind of ordinary looking. She walked past them. But seconds later something inside her made her turn around. She needed to see them up close. She needed to pick them. It was as if they were calling her name.

Zinnie ate her chicken salad sandwich and served Jean a piece of blueberry pie. After Jean left, Zinnie placed the blue flowers in a drinking glass. She filled it with water and carried it into the office, where she set about identifying the flowers with Aunt Sunny's books. It took only a few minutes to discover that they were forget-me-nots and that they were as common in Massachusetts as they were in California. She wrote "forget-me-not" on a fresh piece of paper and circled it. There was a name with a story in it. The tree had given her an answer! Forget-Me-Not would be her main flower fairy character. Her dad had said that the main character needed a problem to solve, and Forget-Me-Not's was right there in her name. Zinnie sharpened her pencil and began.

## 40 · Where the Ocean Meets the Sand

**M**eanwhile, Aunt Sunny, Marigold, and Lily went to the big beach where they'd had the clambake. Aunt Sunny was meeting her friends for what she called a sea chat. A sea chat, Aunt Sunny had explained, was sitting in the water and chitchatting for as long as they pleased. Marigold was going to babysit Lily on the beach while Aunt Sunny talked to her friends in the water.

As soon as Aunt Sunny, Marigold, and Lily climbed over the dune, they saw Peter. He was walking along the beach with his Red Sox cap on and a towel draped over his shoulders, eating a sandwich.

"Hello, Peter," Aunt Sunny called.

Peter looked up, smiled, and practically ran over to them.

"Hi," Marigold said, a little breathless from giving

Lily yet another piggyback.

"Hey," Peter said, stuffing the last of his sandwich into his mouth.

Marigold put Lily down and raised her sunglasses to the top of her head, where they held back her hair like a headband. She smiled at Peter and couldn't help noticing that his cheeks turned pink, like she'd given him an instant sunburn.

"What are you up to this fine day?" Aunt Sunny asked.

"I'm here with my dad," he said. "He's surf casting." He nodded toward a man standing out in the water, holding a long fishing pole. He seemed very far away, and yet the water only came up to his knees.

"What's he hoping to catch?" Aunt Sunny asked.

"Blues," Peter said. Aunt Sunny nodded. He turned to Marigold. "I'm about to go ride the current. It's fast today. Want to come? We can start at the pond, then float right out to the ocean. But you have to be a really good swimmer or it can carry you pretty far out."

"Sounds fun," Marigold said.

"Marigold," Lily said, and tugged on her sister's sarong, "you said you were going to stay with me, remember?"

"Oh, right," Marigold said. She looked at Peter. "Lily's afraid of the ocean. We gotta stay on the sand."

"You're welcome to join me for my sea chat, Lily," Aunt Sunny said, "especially since you've done such a terrific job at the YMCA. Why, just yesterday you were floating like a champ all by yourself."

Lily shook her head. "That's different. That's in a pool."

"It's okay," Marigold said to Aunt Sunny. "I'll stay with Lily."

"I'm counting on you to keep a close eye on her," Aunt Sunny said to Marigold. Then she waved to her friends, three ladies in bathing caps standing at the water's edge.

"Don't worry, I got it," Marigold said.

"Yeah," Peter said to Aunt Sunny. "We got it."

"Good," Aunt Sunny said, tucking the ends of her hair into her cap, and went to join her friends.

"I used to be scared of the ocean, too," Peter said to Lily.

"You were?" Lily asked.

"Sure," he said, and knelt so that he was eye level with her. "All those big waves. And who knows what's under the water when you can't even see the bottom, right?"

"Right," Lily said.

"Hey, maybe you can help me," Peter said. "I have a sea glass collection, and I'm looking for a new piece."

"What's sea glass?" Lily asked.

"It's a piece of glass that's been in the water so long that it's gotten really smooth and kind of frosty look- ing. I used to search for pieces when we came to the beach and I didn't want to go swimming."

"Cool. What colors do you have?" Marigold asked.

"I have a lot of green, and some blue, and some clear," Peter said, squinting up at Marigold. Then he turned back to Lily. "But I've always wanted a red piece. They're very rare, but they're the coolest ones of all. If I found one, my collection would be complete."

"Let's find one," Lily said.

"Okay," Peter said, "but you've got to get your feet wet. The best ones are right at the ocean's edge."

Lily shook her head.

"We'll be right next to you," Marigold said, "the whole time."

"If a wave comes, I'll rescue you," Peter said.

"How strong are you?" Lily asked. Marigold laughed.

"Superman strong," Peter said, and flexed his muscles. They were small muscles, but still, they were there, and Marigold noticed.

"And how fast can you swim?" Lily asked.

"As fast as a sailfish," Peter said. "And they're the fastest. Now let's see what you've got, Lily." Lily flexed her muscles and puffed up her chest. "Wow," Peter said. "You could probably beat me up."

"I would never beat you up," Lily said.

"What about me?" Marigold asked.

"That depends on your attitude," Lily said, snapping her fingers and striking a pose.

Peter laughed pretty hard at this.

"Thanks a lot," Marigold said, but Peter's laughter was contagious, and soon she was laughing, too. "So what do you think, Lily?" Marigold asked. "Are you ready to put your toes in the water if Peter is holding your hand?"

"Okay," Lily said, and grabbed Peter's hand.

"I think she likes you," Marigold whispered in Peter's ear. With the exception of Martin Goldblatt, she had never been so close to a boy before. If she'd been any closer, she'd be kissing him. He smelled like laundry detergent. In a good way.

Together the three of them walked toward the water's edge. Lily was gripping her hand tightly as the cool, frothy water washed over their toes. Marigold and Peter lifted her up. "Upsy daisy!" Marigold said as they swung her between them. Lily laughed as they put her back down. Marigold couldn't believe it. Lily was up to her ankles in the ocean and laughing!

Then Peter stopped to picked up a rock that was shiny and black with two pinkish stripes that went all the way around it. He rinsed it off in the ocean.

"For you," he said, and handed it to Lily. "To keep you safe, always." Lily smiled up at Peter, who in turn smiled up at Marigold.

# 41 · Big News

That night, before dinner but after Lily had recounted how brave she'd been, Zinnie showed Marigold the play. They were sitting at the kitchen table, where Aunt Sunny had asked Zinnie to shell peas and Marigold to shuck corn. Aunt Sunny was placing a pot of boiling water on the stove, checking the chicken that was roasting in the oven, and humming. She said that a sea chat always put her in a glorious mood. Lily was playing with Benny on the mermaid rug. Zinnie handed Marigold her play, which was five handwritten pages held together with a blue paper clip, complete with a title page on which Zinnie had drawn a border of flowers.

"*How Forget-Me-Not Remembered,*" Marigold said. She looked up. "Am I Forget-Me-Not?"

"Of course," Zinnie said.

Marigold nodded and turned the page. Zinnie held her breath as she watched Marigold read. When she turned to page two, Marigold smiled. Zinnie wanted to ask her what line exactly was making her smile, but more than that, she wanted her to keep reading.

The story Zinnie had come up with was personal, just as Dad had suggested. Forget-Me-Not was a flower growing smack-dab in the middle of a field of wildflowers. She was an ordinary flower. At least, she seemed so. She was simple and blue. She wasn't ugly enough to be named Goatsbeard, like the flowers to her right. Nor was she beautiful enough to be called Ladies' Tresses, like the flowers to her left. In fact, she was so ordinary that no one had ever bothered to name her.

But then something happened. A butterfly told the flowers that their flower field was going to be paved over to build a supermarket. The flowers decided that one of them needed to volunteer to be cut by their friend the hummingbird, for when flowers were cut, they turned into fairies and were granted the powers of flight and human language. Some flowers needed to fly away, find people with hearts and imaginations, and explain that if their field was demolished and paved over, all the flowers would die. The problem was that once flowers became fairies, they could never go back to being flowers. The Ladies' Tresses said that they were too beautiful and important to be cut down. The Goatsbeards were having too much fun to volunteer.

Forget-Me-Not was the perfect candidate because no one would miss her if she were gone. So she volunteered to be cut down by the hummingbird. She sprouted her fairy wings and soared up into the blue, blue sky. She went on a great adventure. First she met a hilarious chicken named Gus. He was hoping to charm the supermarket owners into going vegan with his amazing dance moves. Along their journey, Gus made Forget-Me-Not laugh as he boogied his way into town. Finally Forget-Me-Not found a girl named Hope (this part would be played by Lily), whose parents were building the supermarket.

With her newly acquired ability to speak the language of people, Forget-Me-Not persuaded Hope to come see how pretty the flowers were. Once Hope had set her eyes on the glorious field of wildflowers in full bloom, she convinced her parents not to raze it to build the supermarket. When Forget-Me-Not returned to the wildflowers to tell them all the good news, she also told them her stories about everything she'd seen. Even though Hope didn't live very far away, Forget-Me-Not was still the only flower that had traveled beyond their patch of soil, and she regaled them with tales of the wider world. But of course the best part of the story was Gus.

The other flowers couldn't believe how funny that dancing chicken was or how entertaining Forget-Me-Not had turned out to be. "You are extraordinary," they all said to Forget-Me-Not. "Why didn't you tell us you were such a hot tamale?" the Ladies' Tresses asked. "We'll never be able to forget you now because you saved us!" the Goatsbeards added. Forget-Me-Not responded by telling them that she had always been like this. "You can call me and all the flowers who look like me Forget-Me-Not," she said, "so that when you say the name, you'll remember that everyone has something unforgettable inside."

Zinnie watched as her sister turned back to the cover page and read the play again. Zinnie had to sit on her hands, she was so excited. When Marigold finished reading it a second time, she sat up straight and took a deep breath. "I'm going to start memorizing my lines."

Marigold liked it!

Just then there was a knock at the door. "Heavens, I wonder who that is," Aunt Sunny said. "My hair's a fright. Always is after a sea chat." She combed her hair with her fingers, took off her apron, and went to answer the door. "Oh, well, if whoever it is thinks I've got bats in the attic, so be it."

"There are bats in the attic?" Lily asked, but Aunt Sunny had already turned the corner into the living room and was headed toward the front door.

"It's an expression," Zinnie explained.

"Girls," Aunt Sunny called from the hallway, "Jean is here, and she has some news for you."

Marigold, Zinnie, and Lily ran to the door. Jean was standing in the doorway, looking like she was about to jump ten feet in the air.

"I could've called, but I couldn't stand it—I had to tell you in person," Jean said, and bit her knuckle out of excitement.

"What?" Zinnie asked. Jean looked like she was going to explode.

"Mr. Rathbone is going to judge our contest," she said, raising her hands in triumph.

Marigold squealed. Lily clapped, though she wasn't sure exactly what was happening. Zinnie stopped breathing. Philip Rathbone, the famous director, was going to personally see her play! Maybe he would want to make her play into a movie, too!

"And . . . ," Jean said.

"There's an and?" Marigold asked, flapping her hands like little wings.

"And he's going to be filming a portion of *Night Sprites* right here in Pruet! He said he would let the winner have a walk-on role." The sisters grabbed hands and started jumping up and down. Jean turned to Aunt Sunny, who didn't look nearly as happy as her nieces. "This is good for the local economy, Sunny. There're going to be jobs, not to mention the tourism it will inspire. And my goodness, could we ever use a large donor to help us repair the casino. That roof is a liability."

"Does he have the correct permits?" Aunt Sunny asked.

"Yes," Jean said. "He crossed all of his *t*s and dotted his *i*s. In fact, he said he would judge the contest so that he could get to know this community better. He understands he's not that popular with all the natives."

"Is that what he called us?" Aunt Sunny asked, a hand on her hip. "The natives?"

"That's what I called us," Jean said. She linked arms with her old friend and gazed at the sisters, who were still jumping up and down like popcorn in a bag. "Would you look at these three?" Aunt Sunny couldn't help smiling.

The oven timer went off.

"Come on, girls," Aunt Sunny said. "Even Hollywood starlets must eat. Jean, won't you join us? The silver queen corn is sweet as candy this year."

# 42 · Ceiling Stairs and Doll Tears

Rehearsals began the very next day at Miss Melody's School of Dance. As a *Night Sprites* fan herself, Miss Melody was happy to volunteer her studio. But they had to take the day off a few days later when a heat wave started. It was just too hot to do much of anything. Neither Miss Melody nor Aunt Sunny had air conditioning; hardly anyone in Pruet did. Aunt Sunny's house seemed particularly hot. Even with all the fans in the house whirring like propellers, it seemed impossible to cool down, especially for someone with a wild head of hair like Zinnie's, which she was certain trapped extra heat around her head. It got hot in Los Angeles, but it always cooled down at night. Not here. This was a different kind of heat: thick and sticky, even after the sun had set. Aunt Sunny hadn't even bothered cooking dinner. It was too hot to turn on the oven, she said, so they ate tuna fish sandwiches and fruit salad. Now Marigold was doing the dishes (it was her turn), and Zinnie, Lily, and Aunt Sunny were finishing up their ice cream.

"Where do you think I can find costumes for my play?" Zinnie asked Aunt Sunny.

"I have lots of stuff up in the attic," Aunt Sunny said, pointing to the ceiling. "Old clothes, some ancient toys, relics from the past, all kinds of good things."

"Toys?" Lily asked as she picked up her bowl to lick it.

"Can we go up right now?" Zinnie asked, placing her cold ice cream spoon on her warm forehead.

"It'll be hotter than hades!" Aunt Sunny said.

"We'll only stay ten minutes," Zinnie said. "I promise. Please? Costumes really help the actors get into character."

"Ten minutes," Aunt Sunny said. "I don't want us to get heatstroke."

Three whole days had passed since Jean's big announcement about Mr. Rathbone, and Zinnie had been thinking about her play pretty much nonstop. She thought about the play when she went to the town beach in the morning and to the library in the afternoon before rehearsal started. And she planned every rehearsal down to the minute. Zinnie had checked out a book about how to put on a play titled *Seven Steps to Putting on a Play*. The librarian had told her the book was meant for high school kids, but Zinnie assured her that she was an advanced reader and found a quiet table to do her research. Marigold didn't mind hanging out at the library. For one thing, it was one of the only places in town that were air-conditioned. And for another, the girls had finally discovered the nook in the back that had computers with actual, modern, twenty-first-century Wi-Fi.

They both wrote their parents emails full of updates about the play and Lily and her swimming lessons. Marigold had even emailed Jill Dreyfus about Mr. Rathbone, but when she received a quick reply stating that while she loved Marigold's enthusiasm, the casting director for *Night Sprites* was "no longer auditioning young actresses" and to "have fun on vacation" and to "call when you're back in town," Marigold decided not to be too pushy. She didn't want to mess up her relationship with her new agent. Besides, once Mr. Rathbone saw her onstage in Zinnie's play, he'd find a part for her. She was sure.

While Marigold emailed Pilar, telling her about her sailing adventures and how she was going to perform for Philip Rathbone, Zinnie studied her book. With the play only a week away, she wanted to see the big picture of what was ahead of her, so she decided that for now she would just read the chapter headings. She could check the book out and read the rest of it back at Aunt Sunny's. According to the book, step one was finding a play. Step two was hiring a director. And step three was securing a date and location for the performance. Zinnie felt a jolt of confidence. She'd already taken care of the three first steps! The fourth step was choosing the actors, and she was almost done with that as well.

Zinnie had cast herself as the narrator. She decided she would be dressed in black and read her lines from a stool off to the side. She had seen a production at the high school done this way and thought it had been very dramatic and effective. And of course Marigold was Forget-Me-Not. Lily played Hope. She had only two lines: "Greetings, fairy," and "Mama and Papa, you must not build that supermarket or the enchanting flowers shall die!" Zinnie was a little worried about Lily's being able to remember all that, but Aunt Sunny told her that she was just going to have to have faith.

Luckily, Zinnie had convinced Miss Melody's modern dance class to be the chorus of wildflowers, letting them flip coins for who got to be the Ladies' Tresses, Hollyhocks, and Morning Glories and who got to be Goatsbeards. They had only a few lines, which she gave to the two bossiest girls, who were both named Sophie. Zinnie figured that it was important to have the bossy girls in her corner.

The only problem was trying to find someone to play Gus, the dancing chicken, a role Zinnie was convinced was going to be a star maker. Marigold couldn't do it because (a) she wouldn't be caught dead playing a chicken onstage, let alone a dancing one, and (b) she was onstage at the same time as Gus, so it would be physically impossible. Lily could barely handle one role, let alone two. And none of the dancers would even consider it. Zinnie had asked every single one of them during rehearsals. They thought it was a funny part, but they had no interest in dancing for laughs. They danced only for applause. "If anyone's going to do it," tall Sophie said, "it's going to be a boy." Zinnie knew only one boy in Pruet, and that was Peter. She didn't have a good feeling about his saying yes, so she'd sort of put casting Gus on hold while she'd moved on to step five, finding costumes. Step six was rehearsing the play, and step seven was performing it. She couldn't exactly check those off her list in advance.

"Stand clear!" Aunt Sunny said as she climbed up a step stool. Zinnie, Marigold, and Lily stepped back and watched as Aunt Sunny pulled a latch on the ceiling and lowered a set of stairs to the floor below. When Zinnie had begged Aunt Sunny for a trip to the attic just moments before, she hadn't anticipated a secret ceiling staircase.

"It's like something from a book," Zinnie said as she climbed the stairs to the attic, where the temperature was definitely warmer. She felt her hair expand an extra inch in the attic heat as she wondered what other clandestine features Aunt Sunny's house might have. Was there a passageway behind a painting? A trapdoor in the kitchen? A tunnel under the vegetable garden?

"Where are the old clothes?" Marigold asked as she stepped into the attic. "Do you have any cool vintage stuff?"

"Are there any bats up there?" Lily asked, before she followed them up.

"No bats. Watch your heads now," Aunt Sunny said as she pulled a string to turn on a light and the girls filed past her into the small attic room. There were two tiny windows, one at each end, and Aunt Sunny promptly opened them both. The ceilings were so low and slanted that Aunt Sunny and Marigold could stand up straight only if they were in the middle of the room, where the ceiling peaked. Lily quickly spotted an old-fashioned doll with an elaborate dress, a porcelain face, and blond ringlets.

"That was my mother's," Aunt Sunny said. "You may play with her if you like, but she's very old, so you must be careful."

"I'll be careful," Lily said, cradling the doll in her arms. "Her hair is like mine."

"So it is," Aunt Sunny said. "Marigold, why don't you start with that wardrobe?"

Marigold opened an old armoire and began to look through it.

"She looks sad," Lily said, staring at the doll. "I think she misses someone."

Zinnie thought the doll was more scary than sad with its unsmiling painted-on lips and jowly cheeks, but Lily wasn't frightened. She began crooning one of Berta's Spanish lullabies into her ear.

"Aha," Aunt Sunny said, lifting an old hatbox off a shelf. "These may come in handy. They're from the days when teachers actually dressed up for work."

Zinnie opened the box to discover a collection of silk scarves. Immediately she knew they would make perfect costumes for the chorus of wildflowers. The Ladies' Tresses, Hollyhocks, and Morning Glories could wear the pink and purple and red ones, and the Goatsbeards could wear the brown and gray and green ones. She wasn't sure who would wear the mustard-yellow ones, of which Aunt Sunny seemed to have a surprising number.

"Um, this is full of winter clothes," Marigold said, holding up an old coat.

"Check the drawers," Aunt Sunny said.

"This doll is really sad," Lily said.

"I think the singing is helping," Aunt Sunny said.

Lily began to sing the song their mother sang to them when they couldn't get to sleep. "'Swing low, sweet chariot, coming for to carry me home,'" she sang.

"Um, is mustard yellow your favorite color?" Zinnie asked, holding up no fewer than six Dijon-colored scarves.

"Heavens, no, but it was all the rage in the seventies,"

Aunt Sunny said, removing a long blue skirt from a wardrobe and holding it up in front of her. "What about this for Forget-Me-Not? It's simple and plain and certainly blue."

"No!" Marigold said. "I mean, I think we should go for something more modern."

"We'd better keep looking," Zinnie said, not wanting to upset her star. "But Marigold, I warned you it has to be plain. That's what's in character for Forget-Me-Not!"

Marigold started to protest, but the conversation stopped when they heard Lily softly crying.

"Lily, what's wrong?" Zinnie asked, turning around.

"I want to go home," Lily said. "I miss Mom and Dad! I miss Berta!"

"Oh, Lily," Aunt Sunny said, closing the chest she had been searching through and rushing over to Lily, "you will see them soon, I promise."

"It's not the doll who's sad, is it?" Marigold asked.

"It's me, too!" Lily said, clutching the doll. "It's both of us!"

"We'll be home in a just a little more than week," Zinnie said.

"Is there anything that might make you feel better, dear?" Aunt Sunny asked.

"Maybe some champurrado," Lily said, wiping away a tear.

"The Mexican hot chocolate," Zinnie said to Aunt Sunny.

"Isn't it . . . a bit warm for that?" Sunny asked, dabbing her brow with a hankie. "It's eighty-five degrees out. Perhaps ninety up here."

"It's more of a Christmastime drink," Marigold said. "Berta made it special for us before we left because she knew we were going away for so long."

"I could make fresh-squeezed lemonade," Aunt Sunny offered.

"It's the only thing that might make me feel better," Lily said, wiping her tears. "The only thing in the world!"

"Then champurrado it is," Aunt Sunny said.

# 43 · Champurrado and Shooting Stars

They brought the doll downstairs so she wouldn't be lonely anymore, opened all the doors and windows, turned the fans up to high, and went to work. Though it took the sisters almost ten minutes on Aunt Sunny's old computer, they found a recipe for champurrado on the internet. Marigold tried to reach Mom and Dad in hopes that they could reassure Lily, but Mom's phone went to voice mail immediately, and the person who answered the emergency landline in Big Sur said that Dad was up in the tree.

"Stir over low heat for twenty minutes," Aunt Sunny said as she stood in front of the fan, reading the directions aloud. "You'd better pour us some ice water, Zinnia. We're going to have to stay hydrated."

As Zinnie filled tumblers with ice, Marigold peered over Aunt Sunny's shoulder to read the recipe.

"Uh-oh. Do you have *masa harina*? *Piloncillo*? Or a tablet of Mexican chocolate?" Marigold asked. "Do they even sell that stuff here? I think you can only get it at the Mexican markets."

"You don't have the right stuff?" Lily asked. Her lower lip was trembling. Marigold regretted opening her mouth, because she could feel her sister approaching the edge of a meltdown. "I wish Berta were here. She always has the ingredients for everything."

"Now, now. You never know what I have," Aunt Sunny said, disappearing into the pantry. "A little of this, yes, this will do. . . . We don't have that, but maybe I can use some of this . . . ," she said to herself. Then Aunt Sunny emerged with her arms full. She set a sack of corn flour, a package of chocolate, a bag of brown sugar, and a few cinnamon sticks on the counter.

"We can do it," Aunt Sunny said. "But I'm going to need your help, Lily. You're the expert here." Lily nodded.

First they simmered the milk with the cinnamon, sugar, and chocolate. Lily stood on a stool and stirred the mixture over the stove. Now that she was focused on an activity, her homesickness appeared to be fading. "It's kind of hot in here," Lily said, as if noticing the heat wave for the first time. Then she stripped down to her undies right there in the kitchen. "Much better." Zinnie mixed the corn flour with water, then added it to the pot on the stove. Lily kept stirring for another ten minutes until it was ready.

"Not sweet enough," Lily declared upon tasting the final product. Aunt Sunny added some maple syrup, which Berta never would have done, and when Lily took another sip, she grinned and declared it *"¡Delicioso!"*

For Lily's sake, they each took a mug of the thick, warm champurrado. It smelled good, but it was just about the last thing Marigold wanted to drink on a hot summer night. Even with the fans on and tumblers full of ice water, she could feel beads of sweat on her upper lip.

"Let's go outside," Zinnie said.

"Great idea," Sunny said. "Looks like we finally have a breeze."

They walked barefoot into the pear orchard, and all but Lily abandoned their mugs of champurrado on the little wooden bench by the back door. The temperature had dropped a few degrees, or maybe it only seemed cooler because they were coming from the warm kitchen. But as Marigold's feet sank into the cool grass, the crickets sang a green and summery song, and a gentle breeze lifted her ponytail, the night felt like the perfect temperature.

Aunt Sunny spread a thin cotton blanket on the ground, and they all sat down. Aunt Sunny began to tell them about what exactly caused a heat wave, but Marigold tuned out. She lay on her back and gazed up at the stars. She nearly lost her breath as her eyes traveled across the sky. She had never seen so many stars in all her life. They were faded and swirled together in some places and were shining bright and solitary in others. A plane pulsed toward the crescent moon. A purple-gray cloud sailed through the scene like a faraway ship. A shooting star dashed across the sky, quick as a blink.

Another breeze swept over her, and Marigold's eyelids grew heavy. Maybe it was all the time she spent in the salt water, or all the exercise she got walking back and forth from town all day, or the way Zinnie made her run around in rehearsals. Or maybe it was something in Aunt Sunny's food. But here in Pruet, Marigold had discovered a new kind of tired. At night her limbs were loose and happy, tingling with a memory of sun. And when her head hit the pillow on her boat bed, sleep became as sweet and irresistible as a bowl of peppermint stick ice cream.

She was drifting off now when Lily shook her back to consciousness. "Wake up, Marigold! Mommy is on the phone. She got our message, and she called us back!" Lily's hot little hands were gripping Marigold's shoulders. But it was too late. Even though Marigold wanted to tell Mom more about her plans and how it finally felt like destiny was on her side, she had already tasted a delicious spoonful of sleep, and all she wanted was another.

# 44 · The Search for Gus

The next day Zinnie decided that she couldn't put off finding Gus any longer. It was getting clearer with each rehearsal in the dance studio how much she needed him. After breakfast she asked Marigold, who they'd practically had to carry to bed last night after she'd fallen asleep in the pear orchard, if she would ask Peter to be Gus. If she'd convinced him to do the talent show by sailing a boat, maybe she could sail a bigger boat to get him to play Gus. But Marigold said "no way." Not only had she barely survived the first bet, she said, but she had lines to memorize. Zinnie was on her own for this one.

As Zinnie headed to the yacht club, she reminded herself that at least she wasn't going to have to give up her life's savings anymore. Last night, on the phone, Mom had said that she had talked about it with Dad, and they didn't think it was right that Zinnie should have to give up her entire envelope of cash for a talent show prize. They'd decided they would make a hundred-dollar donation to cover the cost of the prize. After all, Zinnie had shown great initiative and imagination in getting this talent show off the ground. She certainly didn't deserve to be punished for it.

Zinnie found Peter in the yacht club dining room, folding napkins for the lunch crowd. Zinnie begged him to play Gus, even offering to take over his napkin-folding duties until she left for California, but he said he was already going to embarrass himself enough by singing "Rocky Raccoon" in front of the whole town. The last thing he needed was to humiliate himself completely by portraying a chicken. "Some of us actually go to school here," he said.

"Do you know anyone who would do it?" Zinnie asked.

"Hey, Victor," Peter called to a teenager setting the tables. Then he leaned closer to Zinnie and whispered, "Victor's kind of crazy."

"Yeah?" Victor asked, looking up. "What's up?"

"My friend here wants to know if you'd dance around in a chicken suit in front of the whole town at the casino," Peter said.

"Is this a bet?" Victor asked, his eyes lighting up. "How much are you going to pay me if I do it?"

"It's for that talent show," Peter said.

"There's no payment," Zinnie said. "But if our play wins first place, there's a hundred-dollar prize. Only thing is that you'd have to split it with my sisters and Miss Melody's modern dance class."

"That's a lot of splitting," Victor said.

"You could have my share, too," Zinnie said.

Victor considered this. "I'll do it for five hundred," he said. "No, make it a thousand."

"I can't pay a thousand dollars!" Zinnie said.

"If you want me to dance in front of the town in a chicken suit, that's what it's going to cost you," Victor said.

Zinnie slumped in her chair and rubbed her eyes as Victor went back to his table-setting duties.

"You're not crying, are you?" Peter asked.

"No," Zinnie said. "I'm just frustrated."

"Hold on," Peter said. He went into the kitchen to get her a ginger ale, uncapped the small bottle, and placed it in front of her. He continued folding his napkins and asked her a lot of questions about Marigold, like if she ever read comic books and whether or not she liked the Beatles.

That afternoon, after another Gus-less rehearsal, Zinnie and Marigold went to the town beach. It was more crowded than usual. The heat wave hadn't broken yet, so they made a beeline for the water, where they stayed for most of the afternoon, playing Marco Polo with Kara and Tara. Zinnie asked the twins if either one of them would play Gus, but no luck. Then she stopped by the snack bar to ask Ashley if she would consider the role. "You want me to play a dancing chicken?" Ashley asked, nearly choking on her Hot 'n' Zesty Cheez Chips.

Zinnie nodded. "No one believes me, but it's the best role in the play. Trust me, you're going to get a lot of laughs."

"Do I have a sign across my head that says 'raving lunatic'?" Ashley asked, pointing to her forehead with a finger that was orange with artificial cheese dust.

"Uh . . . no," Zinnie said.

"Hello, that's your answer," Ashley said in a way that left no room for argument. "Didn't I tell you on like the first day I met you that I was looking for a boyfriend?"

As she bought an ice pop and walked back to her towel, Zinnie began to wonder: Should she make Gus not a chicken? Should she make him a brave lion instead? A surfer dude? A handsome prince? Should she cross out the lines about hip-hop and belly dancing so no one had to embarrass themselves? But no, she thought. She didn't want to do that. Gus was a chicken and he loved to dance and that was that!

That evening she decided to ask the tree. In fact, she decided to ask all the trees around Aunt Sunny's. She started with the big beech tree, moved on to the pear orchard, and finished with the maple at the end of the driveway, but not one of them had an answer.

# 45 · Guess Who's Gus

It wasn't until three days before the show, on the afternoon that the heat wave broke in a downpour, that it was finally decided who would play Gus. Zinnie, Marigold, Lily, and Aunt Sunny were at the church thrift store, searching for costumes. Aunt Sunny's attic hadn't turned up anything in the way of costumes except for the scarves.

The clothes section at the church thrift store was arranged by color. Zinnie was looking in the black section, where she'd found a pair of pants and a T-shirt that would work for her costume as the narrator. Zinnie had discovered in rehearsals at Miss Melody's studio that she was a good narrator because she was a natural at what Mr. Herrera called reading with expression. And her all-black narrator costume was the easiest one to find. It had taken her a total of five minutes to locate her wardrobe.

Her sisters' costumes would be more challenging. Right now Lily was wearing a pink-sequined tutu she'd found, which was two sizes too big. Marigold had just plucked a dress from a crowded clothes rack. It was light blue with a knee-length skirt made from layers of soft fabric.

"This should be my costume," Marigold said, holding it up against her body and staring at herself in the full-length mirror. "It's blue, and it looks like a fairy dress."

"It is elegant," Aunt Sunny said, examining the cornflower confection. "It must be from the nineteen fifties. And it's handmade, too. Someone put a lot of work into this little number." She ran her hands along the sides. "Such craftsmanship on this bodice. And this chiffon is just lovely for twirling."

Marigold twirled and gasped at how perfectly the dress floated around her. "Zinnie, it's perfect. It's like something a movie star would wear on Oscar night if she wanted to go retro! I mean, if she had the right jewelry. It's missing a certain bling."

"We can fix that," Aunt Sunny said, and checked the price. "And it's only ten bucks." Aunt Sunny pinched the waist of the dress. "I can take it in a bit here. Maybe lift up the straps. Oh, it will be charming!"

"You look like a princess!" Lily said, and clapped her hands. Lily had unearthed a bright yellow sweater that had shoulder pads and was covered with sequins and feathers. It was truly the ugliest thing that Zinnie had ever seen.

"But that's the problem," Zinnie said, feeling very plain with her black pants. "No one will believe that Forget-Me-Not is forgettable if you're clearly the most beautiful flower onstage. The whole point is that she's ordinary!"

"Well, that sucks," Marigold said, taking another long look in the mirror.

"Don't say 'sucks,'" Aunt Sunny said. "It's unbecoming."

"Hey, how about this?" Zinnie said, pulling out a denim blue dress that looked about Marigold's size.

"Ugh. That's nasty," Marigold said, and curled her lip in disgust.

"Come on, Marigold. Try it on," Zinnie said.

Marigold reluctantly handed the vintage fairy dress to Aunt Sunny and slipped behind the old shower curtain that hid the thrift store's dressing room.

A minute later she stepped out, looking pale and grumpy, not even having bothered to zip up the side.

"I like the other one better," Lily said. "It was much prettier."

"It's perfect," Zinnie said. "You look like Forget-Me-Not."

"I look ugly," Marigold said.

Zinnie rolled her eyes. She hated when her sister said things like this. The words were a fork in her average-looking heart. "Marigold, it's impossible for you to look ugly, and you know it."

"I'm afraid your sister is right," Aunt Sunny said.

"You could wear a potato sack and still be the queen of the castle, the belle of the ball, the darling of the dance."

"Hey!" Marigold said, the color returning to her cheeks. "Maybe I could wear the other dress to the dance!"

"Wonderful idea," Aunt Sunny said. "I'll get out my sewing machine tonight."

"Can I wear this tutu in the play," Lily asked, "if Aunt Sunny makes it smaller?"

"Sure," Zinnie said. "But you need to lose the yellow sweater."

"Okay," Lily said. "You wear it instead." She tossed the sweater to Zinnie, who sneezed from its big, dusty feathers. "Now you're Gus."

"Hey, she's right," Marigold said, laughing. "It's perfect for Gus! You can just take a break from being the narrator, throw on the sweater, and be the chicken. Besides, you've played animals before. Remember when you were Wilbur in *Charlotte's Web*?"

"Or the Frog in *The Frog Prince*?" Lily added.

They were right. Zinnie had played her share of animals, both at Miss Hadley's and at the Ronald P. Harp studio.

"You do keep saying it's the funniest part," Aunt Sunny said, "and you have a terrific sense of humor."

Zinnie looked at herself in the mirror. She had to admit that the sweater was very chickenish and that with only a few days left before the play, she had no other option.

# 46 · Making Waves

On the afternoon of the dance, after a morning of rehearsal and a lunch of tuna sandwiches (which Lily loved because Aunt Sunny didn't use too much mustard or too much mayonnaise), Aunt Sunny was about to send the girls to the general store. She was making her famous brownies for the dance that night, and she was out of a few essential ingredients. She was just jotting down a list of items for them to pick up when Tony appeared in the doorway, with a nervous smile on his face and a *National Geographic* magazine curled in his hands.

"Well, if it isn't the four prettiest girls in Pruet," he said. Aunt Sunny looked up from her list and smiled. Zinnie looked around. It took her a minute to figure out that he was counting Aunt Sunny as a girl, even though she was sixty years old.

"Hello, Tony," Aunt Sunny said. "What a nice surprise."

"I just stopped by to return this article you loaned me about tsunamis," he said, and placed the *National Geographic* on the little table in the entryway.

"What's a tsunami?" Lily asked.

"It's a really big—" Zinnie began, but Marigold slammed a hand over her mouth.

"It's a kind of dance," Marigold answered. Zinnie nodded, realizing that the last thing a little girl who was scared of the ocean needed to know about was enormous, deadly waves.

"My goodness, I'd forgotten all about this," Aunt Sunny said. "Thank you."

"Well, I was in the neighborhood, so I figured . . ." Tony paused for a moment. He shifted his feet. "Are you coming to the dance this year, Sunny?"

"I have to," she said. "I have three young ladies to chaperone."

Tony smiled. "Well, that's mighty good to hear. My band is playing, so let me know if you have any special requests. See you later!" Then he hopped in his truck and drove away.

Aunt Sunny studied the magazine. "He borrowed this a year ago," she said to herself. "Whatever made him return it today?"

"Duh," Marigold said. "He wanted to make sure that you were coming to the dance tonight."

Aunt Sunny's face turned pink.

"He likes you," Zinnie said, and when Aunt Sunny's expression didn't change, she added, "He thinks you're a hot tamale."

"He does?" Aunt Sunny asked.

"It's so obvious," Marigold said. "He wants to date you."

"And kiss you," Lily added. "And hug you, too!"

"Oh, well, I don't know about that," Aunt Sunny said, and waved them away. All three of them giggled. She handed them her list and some money. "Go on now, you're driving me batty."

"Is a tsunami really a dance?" Lily asked as they headed up the driveway.

"Yes," Marigold and Zinnie said at the same time.

"What's it look like?" Lily asked.

"Like this," Zinnie said, and shook her behind and waved her arms as Lily and Marigold laughed and laughed.

## 47 · The Hat Poem

Zinnie was out of breath and sweaty by the time she reached the end of the long driveway (the tsunami dance was quite a workout). That was when she saw the faded, grimy Red Sox hat perched on the mailbox with a note stuck through the hole in the back. She snatched it before her sisters could and pulled out the scrolled-up note that was tucked inside. Scrawled in boy's handwriting across the top were the words "To Marigold from Peter."

"*Ooh-la-la,*" Zinnie said. "A love letter . . . from Peter's hat. Love is in the air!"

"Hey," Marigold said, grabbing the note from Zinnie's hand.

"Hats can't write letters," Lily said.

Marigold unfurled the note. Zinnie peered over her shoulder and saw the note was actually a poem.

"But they can write poems," Zinnie said.

"Hats can't write poems either," Lily said. "Right, Zinnie?"

"Read it," Zinnie said, ignoring Lily. "Read us your love poem. From your boyfriend."

"He's not her boyfriend," Lily said.

"That's right, Lily. He's not my boyfriend, and it's not a love poem." Marigold sighed. "It says:

*Marigold, don't think that I'd forget*
*that you lost our little bet*
*you needed my help in the Cape Cod cat*
*so I'll see you tonight wearing this hat*
                                    *Peter*
*PS it's never been washed!!! Ha-ha-ha!"*

Marigold gave Zinnie an I-told-you-so look. "There, you happy?"

"I need to know exactly how this hat thing happened," Zinnie said as they turned the corner onto Harbor Road.

"Well, remember that day we went sailing?" Marigold asked. She recounted the day in extraordinary detail. For a girl who didn't like a boy, she sure did remember just about everything he'd said and done. By the time Marigold finished, they'd reached the general store. "See?" Marigold said. "It was just a bet; it had nothing to do with boyfriends and girlfriends."

"I love Peter," Lily said as they opened the screen door and the little bell chimed, "And I'm going to marry him and do the tsunami!" Lily danced into the store. Zinnie and Marigold looked at each other and tried not to laugh.

# 48 · Out-of-Town Heels

It wasn't like the Silver sisters knew everyone in Pruet. They hadn't even been here three weeks. But Marigold, Zinnie, and Lily were able to spot a stranger in town as quickly as anyone else, if not a little quicker, because they'd been strangers here themselves not so long ago. They were going about their usual business in the general store: Zinnie was gathering the items on Aunt Sunny's list in a basket, Lily was pondering the penny candy, debating if she should get Swedish fish or gummy worms, and Marigold was searching the magazine rack when a woman walked in on heels so thin and high and pointy, they could've been used to spear the little fish that swam in the estuary.

"Prada," Marigold whispered to herself.

"Excuse me, do you know where Charlotte Point is?" the high-heeled woman asked the teenager who worked at the counter. She was wearing red lipstick. "It's not coming up on my GPS, and I've been driving around for almost thirty minutes looking for it."

Marigold looked at Zinnie. Everyone knew that Charlotte Point was where Philip Rathbone's house was.

"I know where it is," Marigold said. "It's at the end of this road."

"Are you here to see Mr. Rathbone?" Zinnie asked.

"Yes," the mysterious woman said. She lifted her sunglasses. She had long eyelashes. "I'm one of his producers."

"Cool. We're from Los Angeles," Zinnie said, and cleared her throat. "And you can see Mr. Rathbone tomorrow night at the casino, where we're putting on a talent show. Mr. Rathbone is our judge. My play is called *How Forget-Me-Not Remembered*, and it's starring my beautiful sister, Marigold Silver." Zinnie pointed to Marigold.

"Uh, hi," Marigold said. Zinnie got a sinking feeling that she'd just embarrassed her.

"I know you," the producer lady said, aiming her sunglasses at Marigold. She tilted her head and narrowed her eyes. "What were you in?"

"*Seasons,*" Marigold said. "I was in three episodes."

"Oh, yeah," the producer lady said, and wagged a long, purple nail at her. "You were good."

"Thanks," Marigold said, her cheeks coloring.

"You really should come to the talent show," Zinnie said. "It's going to be great. Marigold is really good in it. Like, as good as she was in *Seasons*. Like, if you like *Seasons*, you'll love this play."

"I'm in the play, too!" Lily said. "I wear a pink tutu, and I go like this." Lily performed her two lines and finished with a twirl near the postcard rack.

"Maybe I'll come," the producer lady said. "What else is there to do out here in the sticks, right?"

"Right," Zinnie said, but something about the way the producer lady's lip curled when she said "the sticks" made Zinnie flinch.

"So Charlotte Point is at the end of this road?" the producer lady asked.

"Yes," Marigold said. "But there's no sign or anything. After the old schoolhouse turn left."

"Thanks. Ciao," she said, and click-clacked out of the general store.

# 49 · Transformations

"Twirl," Lily said, and clapped her hands as Marigold spun around in her vintage dress. The chiffon skirt floated around her like gauzy petals. "Faster! Faster!" Lily said.

"I can't," Marigold said, slowing down. "I'm getting dizzy." Lily laughed as Marigold staggered to the bed. But she might as well have been dizzy from happiness. She loved this cornflower-blue dress, even if it was a little plain. Aunt Sunny had taken in the sides, shortened the straps, and removed the one little stain on the sash. She couldn't see if it fitted because Aunt Sunny didn't have a full-length mirror, but she could feel it wrapping around her waist just right and then swishing out in silky lightness. Marigold stood up, regaining her balance. She was too excited for the dance, her first dance, to sit down.

"You look like a princess," Lily said, gazing at her older sister with her hands clasped in front of her chest.

"I feel like I need . . . something extra," Marigold said.

"You should fluff out all your hair and put flowers in it," Lily suggested.

"Hmm." Marigold crossed her arms and scrunched her lips to one side of her mouth.

"What's wrong?" Lily asked Zinnie as she walked into the room. "Are you sick?"

Zinnie stood in the doorway wearing the tie-dyed dress that had been Marigold's favorite less than a month ago. It was the one she had worn to her audition for the agent. After Zinnie had begged and pleaded, Marigold had let her borrow it. But it just didn't look right on Zinnie. It was too tight in some places and too loose in others and way too long.

"I look terrible," Zinnie said, flopped on her bed, and curled into a ball. "I'm fat and I'm short and I'm a frizz ball."

"No, you're not!" Marigold said. "You look . . . cute."

"Just tell me the truth," Zinnie said, her lip trembling. "I'm not stupid." She burst into tears.

"Don't cry," Lily said. Her own lips were trembling. When her older sisters cried, she did, too. Marigold pulled Lily onto her lap.

"You're pretty," Marigold said, and handed each of

her crying sisters a tissue. She put a hand on Zinnie's back. "You have the best eyes of anyone." Zinnie blew her nose. Loudly. Lily copied her and rested her wet face on Marigold's arm.

"This used to be your dress, and you looked like a mermaid or something," Zinnie said. "I look . . . like a blowfish." Marigold and Lily both laughed at this, but Zinnie didn't.

"What's a blowfish?" Lily asked, giggling through her tears.

Marigold sighed. "Do you even like wearing dresses, Zin?" Zinnie shook her head. Marigold looked just like Mom as she said, "If you could wear anything right now, would you pick jeans or a dress?"

"Jeans, obviously," Zinnie said.

"Well, maybe that's your style," Marigold said.

"My style is T-shirts with animals on them," Lily said, and dried her eyes.

"Go pick out your favorite T-shirt," Marigold whispered to Lily. Then Marigold pulled out her *Young & Lovely* magazines, which were stacked neatly by her bed with Post-its marking her favorite looks. As Lily debated between a zebra shirt and a frog shirt, Marigold flipped through the pages for inspiration. "I have an idea," Marigold said. "Take off the dress and put on your jeans. I'll be right back."

Zinnie shimmied out of the dress and put on her jeans and an undershirt. "Ah, so much better," she said, relaxing on the bed. Marigold returned with Aunt Sunny's sewing scissors.

"The zebra shirt is the best one," Lily said, putting it on.

Marigold held the dress up, considering it.

"Do you think Aunt Sunny and Tony will fall in love tonight?" Zinnie asked.

"I hope so," Marigold said, laying the dress on the floor. "He totally likes her."

"Aunt Sunny and Tony are going to fall in love?" Lily asked. "And get married?"

"Shh," Zinnie said, and whispered, "We're hoping they do, but we don't want to act too silly about it or Aunt Sunny will get shy."

"Oh," Lily whispered. "Is it a secret?"

"Kind of," Zinnie said; then she gasped. There was a terrible ripping noise. Marigold was using Aunt Sunny's sewing scissors to cut the bottom half of the silk dress. "Jeez, what are you doing, Marigold?"

"Oh, my goodness!" Lily said. "You ripped that dress. You ripped it in half!"

"Here," Marigold said, handing the mutilated dress to Zinnie. "Put it on."

Zinnie sighed and pulled it over her head again. Without the bottom the dress seemed to fit.

"Tuck it in," Marigold said, circling Zinnie.

Zinnie tucked it in.

"Not too much," Marigold said, and fluffed it out so

that it was a little bit baggy.

"You made that dress a shirt!" Lily exclaimed.

"Yes, I did," Marigold said.

"It feels like it fits," Zinnie said. "How does it look?"

"Much better," Lily said.

"Awesome," Marigold said. "Now for your hair. Be right back."

"Is she going to cut your hair, too?" Lily asked. Zinnie gripped her hair in fear.

Marigold returned with Zinnie's hair goop in her hand.

"That stuff doesn't work," Zinnie said.

"How are you using it?" Marigold asked as she read the directions on the back.

"I wash my hair; then I brush in the goop; then I blow-dry it," Zinnie said.

"You're blow-drying?"

"It says, 'Style as usual,'" Zinnie said.

"First of all, with this kind of product, you need to use your fingers to work it through your hair," Marigold said. "And the hair dryer is not your friend, okay?"

"But you blow-dry your hair all the time," Zinnie said.

"But I have straight hair," Marigold said, "and you're a curly girl." She told Zinnie to dunk her head in the sink and towel-dry her hair. Lily watched as Zinnie followed Marigold's directions. When Marigold felt Zinnie's hair had made the important leap from wet to damp, she smothered her hands in goop and twisted her fingers through Zinnie's curls until they looked like the cord on Aunt Sunny's old-fashioned phone.

"See," Marigold said, showing Zinnie her reflection in the little mirror above the sink. "You look great. And if we let it dry just like this, no frizz."

"Wow!" Lily said. She was sitting on the toilet lid, watching this makeover unfold as though it were the greatest story ever told.

"Cool!" Zinnie said as she looked in the mirror. "I'm always going to wear my hair like this." She turned her head from side to side, smiling the whole time.

Aunt Sunny appeared in the doorway in her usual khaki shorts, white T-shirt, and a navy blue sweater. "Why, Zinnia, you look so jazzy. Your hair is just a work of art!"

"Thanks," Zinnie said. "Marigold did it."

"And that blouse is just dazzling," Aunt Sunny said. "You all look great. So let's hop to it and get to the dance."

"But you're not dressed up," Lily said.

"The dance is for you, not for me," Sunny said.

"But you have to look beautiful so Tony will fall in love with you!" Lily blurted. Marigold and Zinnie shot her a silencing look. "Oops," Lily said.

Aunt Sunny laughed. "Is that so?"

"No, no," Zinnie said. "It's just that it's a special night. Don't you want to look special, too?"

"Can we just see what else you have?" Marigold said.

"I don't see why I need—" Aunt Sunny said.

"Please?" Marigold said.

"Pretty please?" Zinnie added.

"Pretty please with sugar on top and . . . a clam?" Lily added. "Because you like clams so much?"

"Gross," Marigold and Zinnie said at the same time.

"I can't say no to a clam," Aunt Sunny said. "Though it does sound positively disgusting."

Fifteen minutes later Aunt Sunny was wearing a long flowery skirt that Marigold said was so retro it was cool. Marigold paired it with a plain white blouse and a pair of silvery slippers that, like the skirt, dated back to the 1970s. Marigold wanted her to wear high heels, but Aunt Sunny just laughed. She had never, ever liked heels. But she had clearly liked nice clothes.

"Why were we looking in the attic for clothes for the play?" Marigold asked. "The good stuff is here in your bedroom."

"It didn't occur to me that you'd be so interested," Aunt Sunny said.

But Marigold was interested. Aunt Sunny's bedroom closet was brimming with stuff that Marigold said was "hip" and "chic" and "totally classic."

"You need some bling," Marigold said. Aunt Sunny, resigned to her niece's vision, showed Marigold her jewelry box.

"It's mostly junk," she said, but the girls thought it

was loaded with treasures. They kept pawing through it, even after they'd found a funky necklace for Aunt Sunny to wear. "A statement necklace" Marigold had called it.

"You may each pick one thing to keep," Aunt Sunny said, delighted that her nieces thought her collection was cool. Lily found a small hair comb made from tiny shells. Marigold placed it in her curls. Zinnie found a blue bracelet that Aunt Sunny said was "very art deco." Zinnie thought that it complemented her new top by bringing out the dashes of blue that were somewhat hidden in the pattern. Aunt Sunny agreed.

Just as Zinnie was slipping it on her arm, she spotted the true prize, a gold necklace with a sea horse charm. Zinnie gasped. "Look at that," she said, picking it up and admiring the sea horse's emerald eye. Marigold promptly plucked the necklace from Zinnie's palm and cooed with admiration.

"This is exactly what my dress needs," Marigold said, hanging it around her neck and affixing the clasp. The sea horse aligned perfectly with the sweetheart neckline of the dress. As Marigold did a quick and graceful turn, the emerald caught the light and shone, and the layers of the skirt twirled around her like a soft summer breeze. Zinnie was about to protest that she had seen it first, but by then it was too late; Marigold wanted it. And so it was hers.

"Look what I found," Lily said, lifting a piece of red

sea glass from a hidden drawer of the jewelry box. "Just what Peter wanted for his collection."

"Oh, yeah," Marigold said, and then explained to Sunny and Zinnie how Peter collected sea glass and had always wanted a red piece, the rarest color, but had never been able to find one.

"Let's give it to him," Lily said. "Please, Aunt Sunny?"

"I'm afraid that's the one thing in the box that I can't let go of," Aunt Sunny said.

"Why not?" Lily asked.

"Because it reminds me of Ham," Aunt Sunny said. "He found it and gave it to me when we were courting, and I felt like he'd given me a piece of his heart."

"But Aunt Sunny," Zinnie said softly, "doesn't everything in this house remind you of Ham? The pictures, the walls, the chairs, the beds . . . everything?"

"I suppose so," Aunt Sunny said, and then stood up and glanced at her watch. "Look at the time. We really need to get going. Oh, and let's not forget the brownies."

"We won't," Zinnie said, and added with an impish grin, "And Marigold, don't you forget your baseball hat!"

## 50 · An Invisible String of Hearts

They could hear the music from a block away. It was a Beach Boys song, the one about its being nice to be older. Their dad loved the Beach Boys. So did Zinnie. As they walked across the lawn, past the hydrangea bushes and the climbing roses, Zinnie broke into a skip. Aunt Sunny sang along to music, *"Do do do do dee da."* The casino was twinkling in the dusk. Fairy lights decorated the porch, and when they walked inside, paper lanterns hung from the rafters like brightly colored moons.

Tony spotted them from the stage, smiled, and leaned into his microphone as he sang the familiar lyrics. He and his band were wearing matching T-shirts that said TONY & THE CONTRACTORS. Kids were dancing in a circle in the middle of the floor. Adults chatted around the edges of the room, drifting in and out from the big porch with plastic cups and easy smiles. Little kids zoomed across the dance floor barefoot. Lily took off her shoes and joined them. Aunt Sunny placed her brownies with the other snacks on the snack table, and Jean clapped at the sight of her all dressed up. "You look gorgeous!" she exclaimed, and hugged Aunt Sunny.

"Hey, Marigold, I like your outfit," Peter said when he saw them. He was wearing a tie, and it looked like he had goop in his hair, too. "The hat's the best part."

"Thanks," Marigold said. "I kinda like it now. I might just keep it."

"No way," Peter said. "That hat is the most valuable thing I own."

"He's not kidding," Jean said. "I'm not allowed to touch it. Once he left it at my sister's house in Maine, and there were actual tears."

"Mom!" Peter said, turning bright red. "Stop!"

"Sorry," Jean said, and covered her mouth.

"Maybe you should give it back," Zinnie said to Marigold.

"No," Peter said. "She has to wear it to the end of the dance."

"Fine with me," Marigold said. "How was the sailing race?"

"I came in first place," Peter said with a grin. Jean pulled him in for a hug, but Peter resisted her.

"Sorry," Jean said. "It's just that I'm so proud. Peter is a fantastic sailor."

Zinnie then spotted Ashley and Kara and Tara, who were in a big group, taking turns dancing in the middle. She ran over to say hi.

Tony & the Contractors were good, playing songs both the kids and grown-ups liked. Ashley air-guitared to "Hound Dog," and Zinnie pretended to drive a car and honk the horn to "Drive My Car." She was glad she was wearing her favorite jeans, because she could do some of her break dancing moves, like the worm, and not worry about anyone's seeing her underwear. Lily did the tsunami in her tutu. Peter gave Lily a piggyback for almost three songs in a row. Even Marigold was getting into it, twirling in her pretty dress and leaping across the room. When Tony played "California Girls," Marigold, Zinnie, and Lily danced in the center for the whole song.

Then Tony tapped the microphone. "This one is for a very special lady," he said. "One of the finest women I've ever known. And she looks so darn pretty tonight, I can hardly believe my eyes. Here goes." Tony began playing the guitar very softly.

Zinnie guessed he was talking about Aunt Sunny, but she was totally sure of it when she realized he was playing "Here Comes the Sun" by the Beatles. She looked for Aunt Sunny, who was where she'd been most of the night, standing by the snack table, talking to Jean. Only now she was swaying to the song with a shy smile on her face. Tony was gazing at her, and she was gazing back. Zinnie could practically see a string of hearts between them. Their makeover had been a true success! Zinnie looked around for Marigold.

"Dance with me!" Lily said, and put her arms around Zinnie's waist.

"We need to find Marigold and tell her that our plan worked," Zinnie said, taking Lily's hand and weaving through the crowd. Everyone was dancing to this song, even the grown-ups.

"What plan?" Lily asked.

"You know," Zinnie said, leading Lily toward the porch. Maybe Marigold had stepped outside for some fresh air? It was kind of crowded in here. "The one where we get Aunt Sunny to—" She stopped in her tracks. There was Marigold. Sitting on the steps with Peter. He was leaning in close. And then he was kissing her. On the lips.

"Where we get Aunt Sunny to do what?" Lily asked.

"Never mind. Come on," Zinnie said, yanking Lily back inside. She did not want to ruin another kiss for Marigold.

# 51 · Marigold, Full of Stars

After the dance a group of kids was going to Edith's for ice cream. Marigold and Peter walked at the back of the group, smiling at each other every few steps but not speaking very much. This was okay with Marigold. She was busy reviewing the kiss in her mind so that she wouldn't forget it.

It had happened like this: She was taking a punch break after dancing in the circle with her sisters to "California Girls." Lily and she had tangoed, with Lily wanting to be dipped every other step, and then she had tried to follow Zinnie's break dance moves, which were kind of crazy. She was so thirsty! She had just finished her third cup of punch when Peter tapped her on the shoulder.

"Want to see the Big Dippah, Marigold?" he asked.

"What's a dippah?" she asked, smiling. She liked

the way he said her name now, no doubt about it.

"You know, the stahs?" he said.

"Oh," Marigold said, "the Big Dipper!"

"You want to see it or what?" he asked.

"Sure," she said, and followed him out to the lawn.

As they looked up into the night sky, he showed her not only the Big Dipper but also the Little Dipper and Orion's belt and another constellation called Cassiopeia, which was shaped like a W.

"Cassiopeia was a queen who thought she was better than everyone else," he said as he took a seat on the steps of the big porch. "You know, I used to think you were stuck up."

"You did?" Marigold asked, though really this didn't surprise her. She plopped down onto the step next to him, her dress spreading out around her.

"I thought that you thought you were too good for Pruet," he said. "I thought you hated it here."

"I didn't like it at first," she admitted, "but I like it now." As she leaned back on the porch steps, she realized that she really did like Pruet. She liked how quickly she fell asleep in her boat bed after swimming at the beach and playing tag in the pear orchard with her sisters. She liked that she could actually see the stars here. And sailing. She had loved the wind on her face and how far the boat tipped without turning over. And she liked Peter. She liked that he was so nice to Lily. She liked that he knew so much about sailing and baseball and nothing about skateboarding or surfing. She even liked his stupid hat. She was filled with so much like for Peter that she punched him lightly in the arm. And that's when he leaned over and kissed her. She lost her breath and felt herself blush. It was soft and short and real. There were no cameras, no director, no set. There was just a boy in a tie, a girl in a hat, and a skyful of stars.

## 52 · Amanda Arrives

Peter took Marigold's hand as they walked to Edith's Ice Cream Shop. It was a little awkward because Peter kept jumping up to grab branches, accidentally yanking Marigold along with him.

The line at Edith's was long, and Peter offered to stand in line and get the ice cream (rocky road for him, peppermint stick for her) while Marigold waited for him on the little bench outside. She had just sat down when a big black SUV with tinted windows pulled up in front of the store. The window rolled down halfway.

"Marigold?" a girl's voice said from inside the SUV. As the window went down, Marigold saw that the girl inside was Amanda Mills, the pop singer who was going to star in *Night Sprites*. Marigold felt a little buzz that not only had Amanda remembered her name but she had actually asked whoever was driving the car to stop so that she could talk to her. Though it made sense that Amanda was here because of the movie, she was so out of context that for a moment Marigold felt like she was dreaming.

"Hi," Marigold said, standing up from the bench and walking over to the SUV.

"You're in this, too!" Amanda said. "That's so cool. Now I have a friend on set!"

*I'm your friend?* Marigold thought, and tried not to look as thrilled as she felt for fear it would seem uncool. "Well," Marigold said, "I'm not exactly in it. Yet."

"Then what are you doing here?" Amanda asked.

"Oh, um, I'm staying with my aunt," Marigold said.

"You must be dying!" Amanda said. "There isn't a Sephora for seventy-five miles. I just looked it up on my phone. Luckily, *Young & Lovely* sent me a whole bunch of sample stuff. I'm going to be on the October cover."

"Wow," Marigold said, in total awe. She peered into the SUV. There was a driver up front and a woman snoring in the back.

"That's my mom," Amanda said.

"Oh," Marigold said. Marigold looked at the woman sprawled in the backseat in her hot-pink tracksuit, a tiny string of drool hanging from her mouth and her bare feet curled up. She didn't look like a mom, and that's when Marigold remembered the stories she had heard about Amanda's mother: that she had been to jail for something; that she had abandoned Amanda when she was little but come back for her once she'd been discovered on *America Sings*.

"You're not going to believe this," Amanda said, "but some lady asked Phil to judge a talent show that the locals are doing." Marigold gulped. She felt sick. "I guess the winner gets to have a walk-on role in the movie or something. Anyway, I'm totally going, too, because it's going to be hilarious. I'm going to help him judge."

"You are?" Marigold asked.

"Well, not officially, but I bet he'll ask my advice since I won *America Sings*, the biggest talent show in the world."

"Maybe some of them are talented," Marigold said. "You never know, right?"

"Wait, are you *in* it?" Amanda asked.

"No," Marigold said, without even thinking. "No way."

"For a minute I was like . . ." Amanda made a face. "Because I'm totally going to tweet about it. Maybe I'll even post the worst ones on YouTube. We have to sit next to each other!"

"I don't think they allow cameras," Marigold said.

"Who cares? Hey, after the talent show tomorrow there's going to be a barbecue at Phil's place. You can come with me if you want."

"Really?" Marigold asked. "That would be great." This was exactly what Marigold needed: a real introduction to Philip Rathbone. She was suddenly realizing that if she wanted to be in this movie, she shouldn't be in a silly, unprofessional talent show. That was probably the last thing she should do. Instead, she needed someone important, like Amanda, to make the connection for her. Then he would take her seriously.

"Maybe there's still a part for you," Amanda said.

"Do you think? That would be awesome," Marigold said.

"You never know, but it's worth a shot, right?" she asked with her trademark wink.

"Yes," Marigold said with a distracted smile, because although she was thrilled at this unexpected gift of glimmering opportunity, she was already anxious about telling Zinnie that she could no longer be in the play.

"God, the people around here are such hicks," Amanda said. "I just saw a grown man in overalls. And look at that loser and a half," she said, pointing toward Edith's Ice Cream Shop. Marigold turned to see Peter coming out of Edith's with two large ice cream cones, both of which looked like they were about to tumble over. He was staring at them, as if this would help him not to drop them, when he tripped over a step.

As Marigold watched him regain his balance,

managing to lose only one scoop off the left cone, she saw Peter through Amanda's eyes. His jacket was a little too big for him, and his pants were a little too short. His ears were sticking out from under his baseball cap. She couldn't believe that less than an hour ago she had kissed him. Marigold felt so confused. Her mouth went dry. Her ears started to hum. She wanted to disappear.

"Hey, um, do you think you could give me a ride?" Marigold asked. "I need to get back to my aunt's."

"Sure thing," Amanda said. "I can show you my latest video on the way."

Marigold ran to the other side of the SUV and climbed inside.

## 53 · Temporary Blindness

The next day, the day of the talent show, it was so windy that they didn't even bother carrying the beach umbrella out of the car. "If we open it up and hold on, the wind will swoop us away over the sea," Aunt Sunny said.

"Maybe it would drop us on a forgotten island," Lily said.

"Let's go there in our imaginations instead," Aunt Sunny said, and she and the girls took the wood-planked path to the estuary side of the beach. A strong breeze blew, filling Zinnie's ears with swirling air and billowing out her T-shirt. It was odd to go to the beach on such a blustery day, but earlier that morning Aunt Sunny had insisted there was nothing to soothe a nervous soul like the fresh ocean air. They would have to get to the casino a few hours early to help Jean set up, but Aunt Sunny assured them that there was plenty of time for an early lunch and even a quick dip.

"You're nervous, aren't you?" Aunt Sunny asked when Zinnie had barely touched her pancakes, her favorite breakfast. Aunt Sunny was right. Zinnie was too nervous to eat. It wasn't just that the whole talent show had been her idea and she desperately wanted it to go well, or that Philip Rathbone himself was going to be judging the contest and would determine on the basis of her play whether or not Marigold got to be in *Night Sprites*, or even that she was going to be playing Gus, the chicken, in front of so many people. It was also that Marigold had been acting really weird all morning. She was speaking in a more high-pitched voice, she wasn't making eye contact, and she was chewing her nails, a habit she'd quit in fifth grade.

Zinnie wondered if it was the kiss that had turned Marigold into such a weirdo. Isn't that what all the songs about kissing and falling in love said? That it made you crazy? Now that she thought of it, the latest single by Amanda Mills was called "Kiss Me to Crazytown." Had Marigold, in fact, been kissed all the way to Crazytown?

When they reached the estuary, there was a wooden sign that read FAST CURRENT, SWIM AT YOUR OWN RISK. NO LIFEGUARDS. Zinnie had never noticed it before. As the breeze lifted her curls into the wind, she wondered if that sign was always there or if today was particularly dangerous.

"That's the spot," Aunt Sunny said, and pointed to a sandy little nook up the beach that was sheltered by two big dunes. They made their way there and set up camp. Zinnie tried to spread out her towel while standing up, but it was too windy. It kept fluttering over her head. She had to hunker down and secure it with rocks. Marigold simply sat on her folded towel and gazed out at the estuary.

"I have quite a surprise for you girls tonight," Aunt Sunny said, with one hand holding the hat on her head as she unfolded her beach chair and planted it in the sand. The chair part was so saggy that it touched the sand when she sat on it.

"What is it?" Lily asked, plopping down next to Aunt Sunny without even bothering to sit on a towel. She was holding the rock that Peter had given her.

"It wouldn't be a surprise if I told you, now would it?" Aunt Sunny said, rustling Lily's hair.

"What if we guess it?" Lily asked.

"I'll never let on," Aunt Sunny said. "I'm like a Swiss vault."

"What do you think it is, Marigold?" Zinnie asked, noticing that once they were sitting down, there was hardly any wind in their little corner of the beach. It was toasty warm.

"Dunno," Marigold said, picking up a fistful of sand. She stared at it as she let it slip between her fingers.

"I'm hungry," Lily said, and fluttered her lips.

"Me, too," Aunt Sunny said, and sat up, looking around her. She sighed and tapped her head. "See, I'm so excited about the surprise that I've gone and left the sandwiches in the car. Never mind. I'll go get them. You girls stay here. Don't anyone go in the water until I'm back. Marigold is in charge."

"Okay," Lily said. She was now burying her legs in the sand, covering everything except Peter's rock, which was balanced on her right kneecap.

Once Aunt Sunny had disappeared completely down the path, Marigold turned to Zinnie and took a deep breath. "I need to talk to you," she said.

"Is it about the K-I-S-S?" Zinnie said, squinting in the sun.

"No." Marigold sighed. "Wait, how did you know about that?"

"I kinda saw it," Zinnie said, and bit her lip.

"That's weird," Marigold said. Zinnie felt a sting of humiliation; it wasn't like she'd meant to see it. "But no," Marigold continued, "it's not about that. Actually, I have to tell you that I can't be in the play."

"Ha-ha. Not funny," Zinnie said.

"I'm not joking," Marigold said.

"What?" Zinnie studied her sister, not under-standing. It was like Marigold had spoken to her in

Kawooluh, the ancient Night Sprite language.

"I'm serious," Marigold said. "I'm sorry."

"It's in four hours, Marigold," Zinnie said. "You have to do it."

"Yeah," Lily said. "You have to. You're the star."

"I can't," Marigold said.

"Why not?" Zinnie asked. Her lower lip started to tremble.

"I'm a professional actor, and it got out to the actors' union that I was doing this. And they won't let me."

"That's a lie!" Zinnie said. "You're lying! Tell me the truth."

"Stop yelling," Lily said, putting her hands over her ears.

"I just can't," Marigold said. "Okay. I can't!"

"But you're going to ruin everything!" Zinnie said.

"Stop it," Lily said, jamming her feet in the sand.

Zinnie stood up. She should have known this was going to happen. Yesterday, before the dance, when Marigold gave her a makeover, had just been a freak accident. This whole summer had been a fluke. Here was the Marigold she knew, who took what she wanted and didn't care about anyone else, who changed the radio station every time Zinnie started to sing along, and who didn't allow her to sit with her and her friends in the school cafeteria.

Zinnie paced, the anger building inside her with every footprint in the sand. Each memory of Marigold's dismissing and belittling her was like another stick thrown on Zinnie's fire. She turned to Marigold, who was pouting as if Zinnie were the one who was acting like a brat. What had she expected? That she could just ruin her play and Zinnie would accept it?

"How did you get so mean?" Zinnie asked her. "Mom's not mean. Dad's not mean. I'm not mean. Lily's not mean. So why are you?"

Marigold threw off her sunglasses and sprang to her feet. "Because you copy everything I do, and I hate it. I hate it so much. You copy what I say, you copy what I do, you copy what I wear, and you even copy how I walk. You tried to be an actress because I'm an actress. You figure out what my favorite song is, and then you make it yours. You even try to make my friends your friends. I just want some space to be my own person without you following me everywhere and breathing down my neck. I just want my own life!"

"Fine," Zinnie shouted, her hair flying in her face. She looked Marigold right in the eye. She pointed at her with a shaky finger. "I'll stop copying you. I used to look up to you, but I don't anymore. You're a bad sister." Zinnie watched, not breathing, as Marigold's face paled, then reddened as if she'd been slapped, but she wasn't finished. "You're too scared to tell me the real reason why you're quitting. I always thought that you were brave and smart and perfect, my strong older sister. But you're not. You're just a chicken."

Marigold's eyes filled. She sucked in air and turned around. Then she screamed. Not a scream of anger but a scream of fear. "Oh, my God," Marigold shrieked. "Oh, my God, where's Lily?"

## 54 · The Kind of Scared That Makes You Faster

They spotted Lily in her red bathing suit, being carried by the current to the roaring mouth of the ocean. The girls sprinted up the beach, trying to stay with her. Fueled by fear, Marigold and Zinnie ran faster than they ever had. But still they couldn't seem to catch up. It was difficult to run on the sand, and the wind knocked them about, pushing them sideways, slowing them down. They shouted Lily's name in wild, panicked voices that scraped their throats, but Lily did not wave or call back. Could she hear them? Was her head above water? Was she facing up or down? It was hard to tell. The estuary was choppy and rapid.

Then it felt like Aunt Sunny appeared from out of nowhere. She was swimming on a diagonal across the estuary in fast, clean strokes. It was as though she had swan dived from atop the dune, though that would have been impossible. Marigold and Zinnie clung to each other and watched as the gap between Aunt Sunny and Lily grew smaller and smaller and at last, at last, was closed. They held each other even tighter as Aunt Sunny pulled Lily, again on a diagonal, back to the shore in slow, even strokes. As they got closer, Marigold and Zinnie could see Lily's little feet kicking, but they didn't let go of each other until they heard her little voice exclaim, "Again!"

## 55 · Today of All Days

"Lily," Marigold said, rushing to embrace her littlest sister and wrap her in a towel. Zinnie hugged her from the other side.

"I did it," Lily said as Marigold dried her off and Zinnie kissed her wet head. Lily was so thrilled that she didn't even realize that her teeth were chattering. "I swam all by myself. I was so b-b-b-brave!"

"Yes, indeed," Aunt Sunny said, who stood breathless and dripping next to her. "But do you remember when we talked about how important it is to have an adult with you when you go swimming?" Lily nodded reluctantly. "And do you remember how before I left to get the sandwiches, I told you girls that no one was to go in the water?"

Again, Lily nodded, looking at the sand. "Am I in deep trouble?"

"No," Aunt Sunny said. "You are not. But you must promise me that you will never go in the ocean without a grown-up." Lily nodded. "Promise?"

"Promise," Lily said.

"And you must always do as I say," Aunt Sunny added. "Is that understood?"

"Yes," Lily said.

"Now tell us," Aunt Sunny said, "why did you go in today? Why today of all days?"

"Marigold and Zinnie were fighting," Lily said. Marigold and Zinnie exchanged a quick and heated glance, from which Marigold turned away first. All three sisters were quiet and still, their faces as serious as that old-fashioned doll's they'd found in the attic.

"I see," Aunt Sunny said, and flashed Marigold and Zinnie a look that chilled their very bones. "And why did that make you want to go swimming?"

"I thought they'd be so surprised that they'd stop. And it worked," Lily said.

"It certainly did," Aunt Sunny said.

Instead of leaving right away, Aunt Sunny insisted that they stay for a bit. They ate a civilized lunch and upon Lily's request had a tea party with the lemonade. Then Zinnie and Marigold played with Lily. They buried her in the sand. They chased her through the dunes. They built a castle for her rock. They did all this and more with Aunt Sunny close behind, keeping a hawk's eye on them. And though they spoke to

Lily, laughed with her, and played whatever part she wanted them to in her imaginary games, they didn't say a word to each other.

"It's time to go now," Aunt Sunny said when a third game of jewelry store came to an end. She told Marigold and Zinnie to gather and carry all their belongings as she walked Lily to the station wagon and belted her in. Then she took the two older girls aside.

"I'm very disappointed in you two," she said. "How could you have let this happen?"

"She told me she wasn't going to be in my play anymore," Zinnie said, pointing to Marigold. "And we got in a big fight."

"I have a right to change my mind," Marigold said. "She called me names. She said I was a liar."

"You are!" Zinnie said.

"What has gotten into you?" Aunt Sunny said. Her voice was low and calm, but without its usual warmth. "Nothing is more important than looking out for one another. Nothing is more important than your sisters. Do you know what could've happened today?"

Marigold nodded and bit her lip, staring at her feet. Tears dripped down Zinnie's chin.

"I didn't scold you earlier," Aunt Sunny continued, "because I don't want Lily to have any more traumatic memories of the ocean, but make no mistake about it, she could've been lost forever."

# 56 · What Now?

After they returned from the beach, Marigold took Lily upstairs to change out of her bathing suit and Zinnie tried to call Mom and Dad. Aunt Sunny had confirmed that this qualified as an emergency, and she was allowed to make a long-distance call. However, Mom's phone was breaking up so much that they couldn't carry on a conversation beyond clarifying that none of the sisters was in any danger. They couldn't reach Dad either. No one was answering the landline number, and his cell phone went right to voice mail. Aunt Sunny suggested they have a powwow in the kitchen. She cut two pieces of blueberry pie, poured two iced teas, and asked Zinnie what she planned to do about her situation.

"I guess I'm not going to do my play," Zinnie said as the ice crackled in the glass. "I guess the whole thing's off."

"What?" Aunt Sunny asked. "After all your hard work? Surely there's a solution." She turned her wrist to look at her watch. "You still have a few hours."

"I've lost my star actress," Zinnie reminded her. "How can I have a play without a star?"

"Why don't you play that part?" Aunt Sunny asked. "Forget-Me-Not was a part you were born to play. She's wise and funny just like you. And after all of your rehearsals, you must know the lines."

"But I'm not a good actress," Zinnie said, taking a bite of pie. "Ronald P. Harp told me."

"Who on earth is Ronald P. Harp?" Aunt Sunny asked, spearing a forkful of blueberries. "And why are you listening to him?"

"He's an acting teacher," Zinnie said. "He told me I wasn't good enough to be in his acting class."

"Well," Aunt Sunny said, dabbing the corners of her mouth with great dignity "this isn't his acting class, is it? This is the Pruet Talent Show, and around here we do it for fun, not profit. *Hmph*."

"But what if people think I stink compared with Marigold?" Zinnie asked.

"There won't be any comparisons," Aunt Sunny said, "because she's not in the play anymore. She's not even in the talent show."

Zinnie thought Aunt Sunny made a good point. Ronald P. Harp was very far away. And so was Los Angeles. Most people would never have seen Marigold act before. (Even though *Seasons* was an award-winning show, it was on a small cable network.) She'd started this play to promote Marigold's dream, but in the course of it, she'd discovered her own, which was to be a writer.

"And what about Lily and Miss Melody's modern dance class? Do you want to let them down?" Aunt Sunny asked.

"I guess I could be Forget-Me-Not," Zinnie said. "I mean, I did write it. And whoever played the narrator could just read the script. Narrators do that all the time."

"Exactly. Why, I don't think I've ever seen a narrator not read from a script," Aunt Sunny said. "You've lost your first mate, but you're the captain of this ship. Haul up the mainsail and set for the seas." Zinnie smiled in spite of herself. Aunt Sunny could make anything seem like an adventure, but she still wasn't sure. "If you had been able to reach your parents, what do you think they would tell you?"

"That's easy," Zinnie said. "Dad would say 'the show must go on.'"

"Why is that?" Aunt Sunny asked.

"This kind of stuff happens in movies all the time," Zinnie said. "Sometimes Dad needs to be on the set to write new scenes while they're shooting the movie because an actor leaves or a producer changes his mind about something."

"I see," Aunt Sunny said.

"But Dad will do anything for a movie, anything. He'll even go for a few days without sleeping. And if anyone loves to sleep, it's Dad," Zinnie said.

Aunt Sunny smiled, stirring an extra spoonful of sugar into her iced tea with her special extra-long iced tea spoons. "And what about Mom? What would she say?"

Zinnie took another bite of pie and pictured Mom giving her advice. "She'd look at me like this," Zinnie said, tilting her head the way her mother did when she was listening. "She'd probably ask me, 'What's the worst thing that can happen?'" Aunt Sunny laughed. Zinnie knew it was because she'd perfectly imitated Mom's voice. "And I'd tell her, 'Well, I could mess up my lines or Marigold could laugh at me, or no one could like my play.' And then she'd probably say, 'Would that be the end of the world?'"

"Would it?" Aunt Sunny asked.

"It wouldn't be great," Zinnie said.

"But what if everyone loved it?" Aunt Sunny asked. "What if you and Lily and Miss Melody's class have the time of your lives? What if Marigold is impressed by your talent and courage? What if you discover that you *are* a good actress? What if—oh, I can just picture it—you get a standing ovation?"

"That would be awesome," Zinnie said.

"Isn't worth the risk?" Aunt Sunny asked.

Aunt Sunny didn't have to wait for an answer. Zinnie gave her a smile that said it all. Zinnie finished her pie, downed her iced tea, and went to find Ashley. Sure enough, Ashley was at the casino, warming up her vocal cords. Ashley readily admitted that she was loud and funny, which were great qualities for a narrator, and she agreed to play the part without hesitation. The only thing she wouldn't do was be Gus, the chicken. "I won't go *bock bock bock* in public. Especially not in some nasty sweatah!" *Sweatah.* While it had taken Zinnie a while to get used to the Massachusetts accent, she now couldn't imagine Ashley without it.

"But I can't be both Forget-Me-Not and Gus, because they're in a scene together. If we win second place, I'll give you the whole hundred bucks," Zinnie said.

"I'll be the narrator. and that's all. Take it or leave it."

"I'll take it," Zinnie said. The audience would just have to suspend their disbelief as Zinnie went back and forth between Forget-Me-Not and Gus. *This is for fun, not profit,* she reminded herself.

# 57 · The Story of
# Stanley Toots I, II, and III

Marigold sat on Lily's boat bed as her littlest sister slept next to her, curled in a square of sunlight. Neither one of them had moved from her position since they'd returned from the beach over an hour ago and changed out of their bathing suits. Marigold did not want to let Lily out of her sight ever again.

She wished she had never come to this place, she thought as she hugged her pillow. Their lives in California were as separate as their bedrooms. Marigold had auditions, Zinnie had all her school activities and clubs, and Lily had Berta. In L.A., Zinnie didn't need her to be in a play, and Lily didn't need her protection. And it was better that way, she thought as a lump gathered in her throat, because she was a terrible sister. Zinnie was right.

There was a knock at the door.

"Marigold?" Aunt Sunny said from behind the closed door. "May I come in?"

"Sure," Marigold said, taking a deep breath and wiping her eyes.

"Well, it's not the warmest invitation I've ever received, but I'll take it," Aunt Sunny said, stepping into the room and closing the door behind her. She nodded in Lily's direction. "Still out like a light?"

Marigold nodded and then burst into tears. "I'm sorry," she said. She tried to rein it in, but she couldn't. Once the tears began to fall, it was a downpour.

"I know you are," Aunt Sunny said. She sat across from Marigold on Zinnie's bed and took her hand. "I know." As Marigold wiped her eyes and the tears slowed to a trickle, Aunt Sunny lay back on Zinnie's bed. "I'd forgotten how comfortable these beds are." She sighed and stared at the ceiling. "You know, I once lost sight of a child at the beach."

"You did?" Marigold asked, now hiccuping. "When?"

"I was thirteen, maybe fourteen."

"I'm twelve," Marigold said.

"I know," Aunt Sunny said. "So I was about your age, and it was the first day of my first job, a babysitting job. Oh, I can see the little boy now. His name was Stanley Toots the Third, and he had a face only a mother could love, with a curl right in the middle of his forehead. Like the poem."

"Stanley Toots the Third?" Marigold laughed.

"I know it's a funny name. But the Tootses were quite a prestigious family around these parts, and I was considered lucky to get the job."

"Really?" Marigold asked. It was hard to imagine someone being lucky to get a babysitting job. Maybe it was because she had two little sisters, but babysitting had never appealed to her.

"Oh, yes," Aunt Sunny said. "Stanley Toots the Second owned great swaths of waterfront real estate from here to Falmouth. And Stanley Toots the First was a captain of industry. Anyway, Stanley Toots the Third was my responsibility that day. He was next to me one moment; then I stopped to chat with Beau Williams, a very handsome lifeguard, and when I turned back, Stanley the Third was gone without so much as footprint in the sand by which to track him."

"That guy wasn't a very good lifeguard," Marigold said.

"Good point," Aunt Sunny said, laughing. "I never thought of that. Anyway, that was my last babysitting job until . . . gosh, until this summer."

"What happened to Stanley?" Marigold asked.

"Why, he'd decided that he didn't like me and that he would walk back home. The whole hour I'd been searching the beach in a state of total panic, he'd been sitting on his own kitchen counter with his hand in the cookie jar. And Mrs. Toots did not spare me. She let me sweat it out and look for him, even though she knew he was perfectly safe. Oh, was she ever furious with me. Not that I can blame her. She had every right to be."

"What did she do when you showed up at their house?" Marigold asked.

"She read me the riot act and fired me on the double," Aunt Sunny said. Marigold laughed. Aunt Sunny did, too. "I laugh now, but really, I felt just awful."

"But I'm Lily's sister, not her babysitter," Marigold said. "And she wasn't at home eating cookies. She was in the water. She could've drowned."

"But she didn't," Aunt Sunny said. "And everyone makes mistakes, Marigold."

"And Zinnie hates me too," Marigold said.

"She doesn't hate you. But you must admit, you've put her in a pickle," Aunt Sunny leaned on her elbow. "Why did you drop out?"

Marigold was too exhausted to tell any sort of lie. "I saw Amanda Mills last night. We're friends from L.A. Kind of."

"Who's she?" Aunt Sunny asked.

"She's a huge star. She's has her own TV show and everything."

"Never heard of her," Aunt Sunny said.

"She sings that song 'Kiss Me to Crazytown,'" Marigold said. Aunt Sunny looked at her blankly. Marigold hummed the chorus, but because she was tone deaf, this didn't help. Aunt Sunny shook her head. She probably wouldn't have recognized it anyway. "Well, Amanda is the star of *Night Sprites*," Marigold said. "And she invited me to this supercool party at Phil's house tomorrow. . . ."

"Now he's Phil, huh?"

"And I realized that if the star of the movie introduced me, I might have a fighting chance to actually be in it. I also realized that Zinnie's play isn't very . . . professional."

"It's her first play," Aunt Sunny said. "No one is born a professional."

"Well," Marigold said, "Amanda basically said that she thought it was stupid. If I'm in it, it's like I'm admitting that I'm not good enough to be in the movie." Aunt Sunny narrowed her eyes with skepticism. "Aunt Sunny, I need her to introduce me to Phil Rathbone, and she's going to the talent show to make fun of it." It felt good to get the whole thing off her chest and out in the open.

"That's lousy," Aunt Sunny said. "I don't like this Amanda. She can go eat her socks!"

"I know it sounds bad, but I really want to be in this movie." Marigold started to tear up. "It's my dream. Should I really give that up? I wasn't trying to be mean to Zinnie, I swear."

"And what do you think?" Aunt Sunny said, plucking a tissue from a box and handing it to Marigold.

"Do you think Zinnie's play is stupid?"

"No," Marigold said. She blew her nose and thought. "At least I didn't until I talked to Amanda."

"Why should her opinion matter more than yours?" Aunt Sunny asked.

"It just does." Marigold sighed. She didn't know how to explain all of Hollywood to Aunt Sunny.

"I bet Amanda would like to have a sister like Zinnia," Aunt Sunny said. "Or a friend like Peter."

"Oh, God," Marigold said, remembering the third person she had betrayed in the last twenty-four hours. "Peter."

"He called here, looking for you," Aunt Sunny said. "He thought you'd been kidnapped. When I told him you were safe and sound in your bed, he hung up. This has to do with that Amanda character too, doesn't it?"

"Yes," Marigold said, wiping her eyes. "And I feel bad. I feel bad about everything. I feel bad about Lily. I feel bad about Peter. I feel bad about ruining Zinnie's play."

"I don't think you have ruined her play," Aunt Sunny said.

"Really? What's she going to do?" Marigold asked.

"She's down at the casino right now, figuring it out," Aunt Sunny said. "You know Zinnia. She's like a Cheerio. Hard to sink." The grandfather clock chimed six o'clock. "Oh, goodness, we need to get to the casino ourselves. Show starts in half an hour. Wake up your sister and get her dressed in her costume, won't you? Your surprise is arriving any minute, and I need to get downstairs." Aunt Sunny sat up. "Up she goes," she said as she stood up and headed toward the door. She stopped just short of the door and turned back. "Marigold," she said, "don't waste too much time feeling bad. Remember, it's never too late to do the right thing. I've forgotten who said that, but it was somebody very prominent."

"Was it Stanley Toots the First?" Marigold asked.

"No, I don't believe it was." Aunt Sunny laughed and smiled at Marigold in a way that made her feel that despite all her betrayals, she was, deep down, still a good girl. It was a great relief.

"Aunt Sunny, you would've been a really good mom," Marigold said.

Aunt Sunny took a deep breath, put a hand on her heart, and tapped it twice. "Ah, me," she said. "Ah, me."

# 58 · Backstage at the Casino

Zinnie peered out from behind the simple curtain that Jean and her husband, Mack, had rigged up. The casino was packed. Jean and Mack were greeting people as they entered, searching for any empty seats, and helping others find a place to stand. Little kids were sitting on the floor to make room for the adults. Aunt Sunny and Tony were sitting together in the front row, though Tony would have to come backstage any minute. He was in charge of all the music. The producer lady was there, too. She was wearing those same crazy heels and texting furiously.

The judges' table was front and center. There were three seats for three judges. Ashley's dad, who owned the car dealership on Route 6, was one of them. Jean thought he'd make a good talent judge because he'd been in so many commercials. Some people thought this gave Ashley an unfair advantage, but he promised to be objective. Right now he was talking to Kara and Tara's parents. Zinnie could hear him advertising his terrific bargains on preowned vehicles even over the noise of the casino. Clearly, Ashley had inherited her loud voice from him.

Edith was the second judge. She was wearing a flowery dress and reviewing the list of participants. Zinnie had never seen her without her apron on. Mocha Chip was curled up at her feet as usual.

A hush fell over the casino as Philip Rathbone, with his signature messy hair and round sunglasses, walked in and took the third seat at the judges' table. He was followed by Amanda Mills, who traipsed through the crowd, glowing like the movie star she was. Behind her was Marigold, biting her nails. It looked to Zinnie like Marigold was trying to say something to Amanda, but Amanda was ignoring her. As Zinnie watched them take their seats, she realized that this was the real reason Marigold had dropped out of the play: she didn't want to embarrass herself in front of Amanda. Zinnie felt she'd been punched in the gut, and then the hurt started to climb up her throat, but before the tears came, Zinnie took a deep breath and slammed the curtain closed. *Marigold deserves to be ignored,* Zinnie thought, *and I won't let her ruin my play.*

Lily twirled toward her. "Why isn't Marigold in the play anymore?"

"She just doesn't want to be," Zinnie said.

"She needs to lose the attitude?" Lily asked.

"Something like that," Zinnie said, and laughed. "Lily, you're so . . ."

"I know, I know," Lily said. "'I'm so smart.'"

Zinnie watched as midtwirl, Lily's eyes grew wide and a huge smile spread across her face. Zinnie felt a big, warm hand on her shoulder. She turned around. Her father! He was looking a little . . . well, like he'd been living in trees for the past month. His beard had grown out, and he had a serious tan. But his eyes were the same, big and soft and brown and full of love. He knelt down and opened his arms.

"Daddy!" Zinnie said, and jumped right into a hug.

"Daddy," Lily echoed, and flung herself on the pile. "Are you the surprise that Aunt Sunny was talking about?"

"Yep," Dad said, and squeezed them tighter. "You didn't think I was going to miss Zinnie's first play, did you? Or Lily's acting debut?" Zinnie kissed his scratchy cheek. She wasn't nervous anymore. She was just excited. "Mom's here too," Dad said. Mom crept up behind them and kissed them all over their faces.

"Hello, my loves!" she said. "Oh, how I've missed you."

"How was Canada?" Zinnie asked.

"It was a lot of work," Mom said. "I'm glad I did it, but I'm also glad it's over. And I am so happy to see you! Where's Marigold?"

"She's not in the play anymore," Zinnie said with a huff.

"Why not?" Dad asked.

"Too cool for school," Lily said, and they all laughed, wondering where she'd picked that one up.

"Uh-oh," Mom said.

"Uh-oh is right! I'm going to have to do a costume change onstage tonight. Meanwhile, she's sitting out there, hanging with her movie star friend," Zinnie said.

Jean's voice came over the microphone: "Hey, everybody! We're running a little late, so if you could take your seats immediately, we'd appreciate it!"

"We'd better go," Dad said, kissing his two youngest daughters on their heads. "We'll surprise Marigold after the show. And Zinnie, remember, in show business, things change at the last minute all the time. Go with the flow, okay?"

"Okay," Zinnie said, taking a deep breath for courage.

"Break a leg!" Mom said, giving them one last squeeze, and then they quietly made their way to the back of the auditorium.

Zinnie took Lily's hand in hers as Jean continued: "It's time for the twenty-first Annual Pruet Talent Show, the first in many years. Most of you know me, but for those who don't, I'm Jean, and I'll be your MC for the evening." Everyone clapped. "I can't tell you how happy I am to see all of you, supporting the young talent of our coastal town. I want to start off by saying that we wouldn't be here tonight if it weren't for the hard work and inspiration of some very special girls from California. Silver girls, where are you?"

"That's us," Zinnie whispered to Lily, and together they walked out onstage. Zinnie waved, and Lily hid behind her.

"There's one more," Jean said, looking around. Zinnie looked at Marigold, but Marigold just stared at the floor, her pale cheeks burning red. Lucky for her, Jean didn't spot her. "Well, that's most of them anyway. Put your hands together for the Silver sisters."

Zinnie watched as Amanda leaned in and whispered something to Marigold, and Marigold shook her head in response.

"*Woo-hoo!*" Mom called from the audience. Dad did his two-handed taxicab whistle.

"Okay, let's get this party started. The judges will be awarding first, second, and third place. First-place prize is a walk-on role for Mr. Rathbone's film *Night Sprites*!" The audience roared. "The second-place prize is one hundred dollars cash." The audience roared again. "I know. Not bad, right? It kind of makes me want to participate too. And the third-place prize is a gift certificate for four ice cream cones at Edith's Ice Cream Shop." Jean looked over at Edith, who took a little bow to another round of applause. Mocha Chip wagged his tail and gave a little howl.

"So, everybody, please turn off your cell phones and welcome our first performers, Kara and Tara Malloy, who are doing a gymnastics routine."

Zinnie helped Lily find a seat on the floor and then slipped backstage, since she was in charge of making sure kids were ready when their names were called. She listened as people cheered for Kara and Tara. Tony cued the music, and the show began.

# 59 · Lobster Boy

"You can probably see their panty lines from, like, outer space," Amanda said as Kara and Tara took their places onstage.

"Totally," Marigold said, and giggled, but she withered a bit inside as she said it. It was true that Kara and Tara's routine was far from professional; they weren't at all synchronized, and Tara couldn't get all the way to the ground in her split. It was also true that you could see their bunched-up underpants under their leotards, but not every girl had her own personal dance instructor and stylist.

"I've got to tweet about this," Amanda said, poking at her phone. "Darn. I can't get any service in here."

"Too bad," Marigold said, but felt relieved.

As the show continued, Amanda didn't have anything nice to say about anyone. Even Grace, who just played the recorder. "That girl needs a hairbrush!" Amanda said, and gripped Marigold's hand.

"I know," Marigold said, but she could see Grace's fingers trembling as they covered the holes on her recorder and instantly felt bad. On the one hand, Marigold would never have believed that the pop star Amanda Mills would be holding her hand, whispering to her like a friend. On the other hand, she wanted to tell her to be quiet and just let Grace finish her piece.

But if she thought that the incident with Grace made her uncomfortable, it was nothing compared with when Peter stepped onstage with his guitar. His face was bright red, and Marigold could tell how much he hated being up there. "I don't like getting up in front of people," he'd told her that day they went sailing. And as she watched him now, it was clear he'd really meant it. He looked miserable.

"He looks like a lobster," Amanda said. Peter's face was all flushed and perspiring. Even his neck was blushing, which only seemed to make his hair look redder. And it didn't help that he was wearing a red T-shirt. There were dark spots under the arms where he had sweated right through it.

"A sweaty lobster," Amanda said. "With big ears." Marigold managed to get out a chuckle from between her clenched jaws. Maybe Peter wasn't the cutest guy in the world, but Amanda had no right to say these things. She didn't know him. She hadn't seen him when he was sailing and knew exactly when to pull the halyards and let the boom fly. She hadn't watched him find a perfectly smooth rock for a small, scared Lily. She hadn't kissed him.

Peter adjusted the microphone, and it made a horrible high-pitched, squeaking noise. Amanda covered her ears. Phil Rathbone flinched. Marigold wanted to evaporate.

"Sorry," Peter said, his voice cracking. He dropped his guitar pick, and his hand shook so much that he had a hard time picking it up. Marigold's stomach was starting to hurt.

"Superfreaky lobster boy," Amanda whispered to Marigold, and giggled.

Marigold didn't take her eyes off Peter, who was taking a breath, trying to compose himself. Unfortunately, he was breathing right into the microphone but didn't seem to realize it. Marigold looked at her own hand now and noticed that she was also shaking. Was it out of sympathy for Peter? Or was it because Amanda was making her so angry by giggling uncontrollably?

*I'm sorry,* Marigold tried to tell Peter telepathically. *You don't have to do this.*

But Peter didn't seem to get her message. Instead, he started to sing his song, "Rocky Raccoon," by the Beatles. He was a little shaky at first, speaking rather than singing, but then he relaxed. He never fully broke into song. It was kind of like he was telling a story while playing the guitar. But he was good at it. Phil Rathbone was smiling and nodding as Peter played. This shut up Amanda, who wouldn't dare dislike something that Phil Rathbone approved of.

When he finished his song, Marigold caught his eye and flashed him a huge smile. He didn't smile back.

# 60 · Two Marigolds

As the show continued, Marigold couldn't focus. She couldn't concentrate on the animal impressions, the dance numbers, or the song from *The Little Mermaid*. Her stomach ached. It was as if two versions of herself were wrestling in her gut. First, there was L.A. Marigold. L.A. Marigold was confident and powerful. She loved sitting next to Amanda, who smelled like apple shampoo and whose skin sparkled. When Amanda giggled with her or nudged her with her golden arms, Marigold felt looped into her circle of brightness. For just a second, when the L.A.-girl version of herself was winning the wrestling match, Marigold felt she belonged right there next to Amanda. She felt like someone ought to snap a picture of them and put it in the pages of *Young & Lovely*, because that's what they were.

But there was also Pruet Marigold. Pruet Marigold was confident, but not in a movie star way. Instead, she was confident in a way that let her sail a boat almost by herself and allowed her know exactly the outfit that would make Aunt Sunny find love. And Pruet Marigold hated that Amanda had laughed at Peter when his voice squeaked. It made Pruet Marigold sick to think about the look he had given her. It was a look that said, "You suck." It was the opposite of how he had looked at her before they'd kissed. Pruet Marigold didn't belong whispering with Amanda, but not because she wasn't famous enough. Pruet Marigold didn't belong next to her because she didn't like her.

Then Zinnie's friend Ashley stepped onstage, looking like someone in a painting with her dark hair pulled up in a bun.

"The last thing that one needs is to win a gift certificate for ice cream," Amanda said, not even bothering to whisper. Marigold shrank in her seat. She could tell that not only had people around them heard her, but so had Ashley. She was staring right at them with her hand on her hip and her mouth bunched up on one side.

"What is she doing?" Amanda asked.

"I'm waiting for you to shut your trap so I can sing my song," Ashley said. The audience snickered. Somebody even whooped. Marigold watched with fascination as Amanda blushed and bored holes in the floor with her eyes. Ashley, the snack bar girl, had intimidated Amanda, the international pop star, into silence!

"Thank you," Ashley said. "Now I will sing Schubert's 'Ave Maria.'" She nodded at Tony, and he began playing the piano. What happened next was nothing less than magic. Ashley's voice was as bright as a July noon; it was as clear as a Los Angeles sky swept clean by a week of rain; it was as warm as the column of sun that streamed into Aunt Sunny's kitchen in the morning. It was pure talent.

The wrestling match in Marigold's gut stopped. Both sides of her paused, sat up, and listened. She didn't understand the words. She couldn't even say what language they were in. She knew that the song seemed to fill up the small, dark room inside her where she felt she had been hiding since yesterday, when she had run away from Peter, told Zinnie off, and lost sight of Lily. She couldn't be sure if was the L.A. or the Pruet side of herself that first reached out to the other, only that by the end of the song, there was just one Marigold.

Ashley, looking as surprised by the miracle of her voice as anyone, beamed at the audience. Flushed and a little shaky, she took a bow.

"Go, Ashley!" Marigold heard Zinnie call from the wings. "Go, Ashley!"

# 61 · Forget-Me-Not

Because Zinnie had backstage duties, she and Jean had decided it would be best if her play were the last act in the talent show. It started off great. As the chorus of wildflowers Miss Melody's modern dance class was step ball changing and back brushing in perfect time to the jaunty ditty Tony had composed for the show. Their fluttering hands were delicate petals in a believable summer breeze. Ashley was a bold narrator with her accent and hand gestures. She definitely had what Ronald P. Harp would call presence.

Zinnie was funny as Forget-Me-Not. Marigold thought that Ronald P. Harp wouldn't approve of her over-the-top facial expressions and hand gestures, but they worked just fine here at the casino. People laughed at the spots where they were supposed to laugh, like when Forget-Me-Not tried to join the Goatsbeards' party and didn't know the secret handshake, or when she tried to attend a Ladies' Tresses' dance circle but was too clumsy.

"Oh, my God, the short one with the black hair is mouthing everyone else's lines," Amanda said, elbowing Marigold. "Watch." Marigold hadn't noticed until Amanda pointed it out, but she was right. Zinnie was mouthing everyone's words! Her lips were moving right along with Ashley's! The only time she stopped was when she was speaking.

"I have to put this on YouTube," Amanda said. "It's too hilarious."

"Don't," Marigold said, grabbing Amanda's hand as she reached for her camera phone.

"What? Why?" Amanda freed her hand from Marigold's grip. "It's going to be so funny. I'll tweet it, and I bet it will get like a million hits."

"No," Marigold said, picturing people laughing at Zinnie from behind the safety of their computers. "I'm serious. It's not nice."

"She'll never even know," Amanda said. "Oh, my God, look at that yellow sweater. This is too funny."

Marigold turned to see half of Zinnie's body stuck inside that disgusting yellow feather sweater. Even though it was the narrator's job to play Gus, the chicken, Zinnie was doing it! She was going to play both roles! That is, if she could ever get the sweater on.

"Uh, one second," Zinnie said to the audience. Her

voice was muffled through the polyester, and Marigold could see she was starting to panic. She was trying to stick her head through one of the sleeves, and it looked like she was stuck.

"This is amazing," Amanda said, laughing and aiming her camera phone at the stage.

"Shut up," Marigold said, "and put your camera away."

"Why are you being such a freak?" Amanda asked.

"Because that's my sister," Marigold said, "and no one is allowed to make fun of her except me!"

Then she stood up, kicked off her wedges, and marched onstage, deciding that the only way to not be a chicken was to be a chicken.

# 62 · The Chicken Dance

When the tacky yellow sweater was finally off her head, Zinnie couldn't believe her eyes. Marigold had helped her. And what's more, she was now throwing the sweater over her own head. Zinnie's jaw hung open as Marigold fluffed up the feathers on the shoulders, tucked her thumbs under her armpits, turned to the audience, and said: "*Bock-bock-bock*, what's a flower fairy like you doing on a lonesome road like this?"

"Uh . . . ," Zinnie said, unable to hide her amazement, "I'm looking for the people who are going to pave over my flower field to make a supermarket. I must stop them before it's too late."

"Well, you've found the right chicken," Marigold said, and added a few more *bock-bock-bock*s. Then Marigold did some short, quick head movements that made her look like a real chicken. *She is such a good actress,* Zinnie thought. "That's where I'm headed," Marigold said. "See, they're going to have a big poultry section in that supermarket, but I'm hoping once they meet me and see what a talented dancer I am, they'll realize that chickens deserve to live and decide to go vegan." The audience laughed. "I can take you to their home—it's right down the road—but the only problem is I'm not sure which style of dance will impress them the most. Can you help me decide?"

"Okay," Zinnie said. "Let's see your ballet moves!"

"Here goes," Marigold said, and she did some pirouettes, but in a very chicken-like way. *"Whoa, whoa!"* she said, landing the last pirouette on her butt. The whole audience laughed. Zinnie couldn't help it. She laughed, too. She'd had no idea that Marigold could dance like that.

"Hmm. I don't know if ballet is your best bet. Let's see some Latin moves," Zinnie said. "Try a salsa or a tango!" Zinnie heard her dad's distinctive laugh.

"Cha-cha-cha!" Marigold said, grabbed Zinnie, and tangoed the full length of the stage, to the delight of the audience.

Ashley cleared her throat. "So . . . um, the chicken continued to try many styles of dance, including hip-hop, belly dancing, and even Bollywood."

To Zinnie's surprise, Marigold was really getting into it. With every new style of dance that Ashley listed, Marigold became more ridiculous and silly.

People were laughing so hard that Zinnie broke down and started laughing, too. Trying not to laugh only made her laugh more. But Marigold stayed in character. She kept a serious look of surprise on her face as she hopped wildly around the stage.

"Then they—" Ashley started, but she had to stop and wait for the audience to quiet down. "Then they met a little girl named Hope. She was practicing her own ballerina moves." Out twirled Lily. She must have been very excited by all the laughing and clapping, because she completely forgot her lines and twirled until she was so dizzy that she almost fell on her face. But she didn't, because just as she was about to tumble over, Marigold stepped up and caught her.

There was an awkward moment of silence until Marigold whispered something into Lily's ear. Lily regained her balance, sprang to her feet, and said, "Hi there!" The play continued, with Tony improvising on the piano as Marigold, Zinnie, and Lily, as Gus, Forget-Me-Not, and Hope, skipped across the stage to the field of flowers. Miss Melody's class showed their technique and training as they waved their scarves with grace and expression.

Lily even got her line right as she called out, "Mama and Papa, you must not build that supermarket or the enchanting flowers will die!" She was supposed to say the lines into the cell phone prop that

Zinnie had carefully tucked into the tutu before the show, but Lily addressed her own mom and dad in the audience instead. And when it was time for Zinnie's closing monologue, Marigold took Lily by the hand and stepped quietly to the side, so that Zinnie could have the spotlight all to herself.

# 63 · Forgiveness

After the performance Marigold felt like a Fourth of July sparkler. All her acting experience had been in her acting class and on the set of *Seasons*. She had never acted in front of a crowd before, and she had found it thrilling to look out and see so many people watching her with great big smiles on their faces. Marigold had glowed as if the audience's laughter were a great beam of energy shining directly on her. And when she took her bow with the rest of the cast, she was filled with so much lightness, she couldn't be quite sure that she was touching the ground.

As she scanned the audience, her heart nearly popped with surprise and happiness when she saw her parents cheering. Mom and Dad were standing up, clapping wildly. Then Aunt Sunny, who was sitting nearby, stood up and clapped. Soon the whole audience was on its feet. Marigold waved to her parents, though she wasn't sure they could still see her through the standing ovation. After she took her final bow, she ran off the stage, up the center aisle, and right into their arms, not caring if Amanda saw.

"You're here!" Marigold said.

"You were fantastic," Dad said.

"You're such a wonderful actress," Mom said.

Her sisters weren't far behind her. Mom picked up Lily and pulled Zinnie in for a hug. As Jean made some announcements about the judges' tallying the scores, Dad leaned over to Marigold and whispered, "I was so glad to see you up there. There was a rumor that you weren't going to be in the play."

"Was it in the *Hollywood Reporter*?" Marigold asked. "I thought you knew better than to believe show biz rumors!" Though she was joking around with Dad, she knew that she had something important to do, and she didn't want to wait another minute. She leaned over to Zinnie and whispered, "I'm sorry."

"It's okay," Zinnie said, and though Marigold searched Zinnie's face for hurt and anger, there was none. Her sister's eyes were shining, and her cheeks were rosy and round with happiness. It could have been because Zinnie's play had been such a success that now Marigold's bad behavior didn't seem like such a big deal. But when Zinnie went one step further and embraced Marigold in a bear hug, Marigold knew that she had been totally forgiven.

Marigold was suddenly aware of a big difference between Zinnie and her. Marigold could hold a grudge for days or longer, even after several apologies. She collected her hurts the way Peter collected his sea glass. Zinnie, on the other hand, was quick to forgive. All Marigold had to do was say sorry, and *poof!* The fight was all over, and Zinnie had her arms around her. This was part of what made Zinnie so, well, so Zinnie. Tony played a few lively chords to get the audience's attention, and Jean hushed the crowd. And for a split second, as Marigold hugged Zinnie back, their long-standing roles reversed: it was Marigold who wanted to be more like her sister, instead of the other way around.

# 64 · The Piping Plover Society

After the prizes had been handed out and the crowd had thinned a bit, Marigold was still riding high. In fact, Marigold didn't think she had ever felt more exhilarated, even though they had only won second place. Ashley won first place, and Joey and his animal impressions came in third.

Amanda was long gone. Maybe she was going to tweet about it, but Marigold hoped not. She didn't have time to look for her and ask, because people kept coming up to her and telling her how funny she was. Aunt Sunny gave her a huge hug and a big kiss on her cheek. "I'm so proud of you," she said. Marigold put her hand to her face and felt a lipstick mark. Aunt Sunny was wearing lipstick!

When she turned around to tell Zinnie, she found herself looking right at Phil Rathbone. It was the moment she'd been waiting for. And yet she couldn't find any words. She stared at him. She smiled weirdly. She wished she had thought to take off the feathery sweater.

"Uh . . . hi there," he said. "I'm Phil Rathbone."

"I know," she said. "I'm Marigold Silver."

"Nice to meet you," he said, and extended his hand. She remembered that a firm handshake was sign of confidence and shook his hand heartily. It may have been a little too hearty, because Phil Rathbone shook out his hand a little and said, "That's quite a handshake you've got."

"Thanks," Marigold said. "I'm an actress, you know."

"I can see that," he said, and smiled. "You were very funny. You make an excellent chicken."

"Thanks, but um . . . in L.A. I mean," Marigold said, "I was on *Seasons*."

"Oh," he said, his eyes twinkling with recognition, "so you were. You do drama and comedy. Very impressive."

"Yes," Marigold said, standing straight and tall. "And I really want to be in *Night Sprites*." She could see Aunt Sunny out of the corner of her eye, lingering by the punch table, within definite earshot of Marigold and Phil Rathbone.

"I'm afraid it's totally cast," he said, and Marigold's heart dropped an inch. "I suppose I could always use another extra. You don't want to be an extra, do you?"

Marigold thought about it. She really didn't. She was a real actress, and she wanted a real part.

Phil Rathbone must have gathered this from her expression. "That's what I thought," he said. "But tell you what, I'll keep my eye out for you. Now, if you'll excuse me, I need to mingle. I built a house here last year, and the locals seem to really dislike me. I wish I knew why."

He was about to walk away when Marigold placed a hand on his arm. "It's because of the piping plovers," she said.

"What do you mean?" he asked. "What are piping plovers?"

"The little shorebirds. When you built your house, you destroyed their nests."

"I did? Oh, no. My lawyers didn't tell me that. They just said there was a problem and they would make it go away. Then I came here and found myself very unpopular."

"But . . . how did you not know?" Marigold asked.

"I have six houses," Phil Rathbone confessed. "And each house has its own staff. I don't always know the details. If I did, I wouldn't have time to make movies."

"Well," Marigold said, "if I were you, I'd think about making a donation to the Piping Plover Society. A big one."

"That's a great idea. I didn't even know there was a society. Who do I talk to about that?" he asked.

"That lady right there," Marigold said, and pointed to Aunt Sunny, who was chatting with Dad. Aunt Sunny smiled and looked away, as though she hadn't been listening to the whole conversation. "Her name is Sunny."

"The truth is, I'm a big environmentalist," Mr. Rathbone said. "I've even hired a producer to help me find an environment-related documentary to produce." He nodded in the direction of the high-heeled woman they had met in the general store.

"You see that man Sunny's talking to?" Marigold asked, pointing to her dad. "He's just finished a documentary about the tallest redwood."

"Really? Hey, thanks for the tip," he said. "And have your agent send me your stuff."

"Okay," Marigold said. "I will."

As they shook hands again (this time Marigold was more gentle), Peter walked right past them. He didn't even look at her. After Marigold and Mr. Rathbone said one last good-bye, she turned quickly to follow Peter.

"Peter," she called over everyone's heads. "Peter, wait." He turned around at the sound of his name, but when he saw that it was Marigold, he shook his head and kept walking.

"I don't think he wants to talk to you right now, honey," Jean said matter-of-factly. She put a hand on Marigold's shoulder. "He's more sensitive then he looks, and he was pretty bummed out after the dance."

"I know," Marigold said. "I want to say I'm sorry."

"I don't know if he's ready," Jean said, giving Marigold a little squeeze. "He'll come around. Give him some time."

*But we're leaving the day after tomorrow,* Marigold thought. *I don't have time.*

# 65 · A Piece of Her Heart

After a dinner of grilled hamburgers and a game of flashlight tag in the pear orchard, Mom and Dad tucked the girls in.

"I can't believe you survived sharing a room with these two for three whole weeks," Dad said as he kissed Marigold good night. Mom was sitting on Lily's boat bed, brushing her hair.

"Ugh, me either," Marigold said.

"Hey!" Lily and Zinnie said at the same time.

"Just kidding," Marigold said. "They weren't so bad. Except Zinnie never puts her clothes away, and she stays up late reading with her flashlight, and Lily wakes us all up before sunrise."

"We weren't so bad?" Zinnie said. "Please. You're the one who snores."

"No, I don't!" Marigold said.

"Sometimes," Zinnie said. "It sounds sort of like a whistle. Like this." Zinnie did one of her perfect imitations. Mom laughed, but Marigold did not find it funny.

"I do not snore," Marigold said.

"Okay, girls," Mom said. "You'll be back to your own rooms in just a few days. So try to enjoy this togetherness while it lasts. Unless of course you'd all like to move into one room back in L.A. Marigold's room is the biggest, so . . ."

"No!" Marigold said.

"We could turn Zinnie's room into a gym." Dad said.

"No way!" Zinnie said.

"And Lily's room into my office," Mom said.

"No way, José!" Lily said. They all laughed.

Marigold was looking forward to being back in her own room with its lavender walls, fluffy pillows, and iPod docking station next to her canopy bed. She needed her privacy. After all, she was starting seventh grade in a month. The thought of it shot a dart of worry into her heart. But then she heard Mom singing Lily the song about the chariots swinging low. As she pulled the sheet up to her chin, she had to admit that there was something about sleeping in the same room as her sisters that made her feel extra safe and cozy inside. *Maybe I could share a room with them.* Marigold wondered about it as her mom sang. Visions of Zinnie's clothes cluttering her closet and Lily's toys on her floor quickly entered her mind. *Nah,* Marigold said to herself, and curled up on her side, amazed that she'd even had the thought.

Mom and Dad gave them each one last kiss and went to settle in on an air mattress downstairs. The house quieted down, and the moon cast a pale glow on the bedroom. Usually Marigold fell asleep right away, but not tonight. After several minutes of tossing and turning, she sat up in her boat bed.

"What's up?" Zinnie asked Marigold.

"Can't sleep," Marigold said.

"What are you thinking about?" Zinnie asked.

"I don't know what will make Peter forgive me," Marigold said.

"What did you do to Peter?" Lily interrupted.

"You're still awake, too?" Zinnie asked.

"Would I be talking if I was asleep?" Lily said.

"Good point," Zinnie said.

"I hurt his feelings," Marigold said.

"Say you're sorry," Lily said, and sat up.

"He's not ready to hear it," Marigold said. "Jean said so."

"Maybe that's it," Zinnie said. "He doesn't want to hear it. You need to think of a way of saying sorry without actually saying it."

"What do you mean?" Marigold asked.

"Like when he gave you the hat, he was saying that

he liked you without actually saying that he liked you, right?" Zinnie asked.

"And when he gave me the rock," Lily said, "he was saying that he loved me."

"Like 'actions speak louder than words' kinda thing?" Marigold asked, twirling her hair around her finger.

"Exactly!" Zinnie said.

"But what could I give him?" Marigold asked. "He likes baseball. He likes stars and constellations."

"Maybe you could get him, like, those sticky stars to put on his ceiling," Zinnie suggested. "Or a book about constellations."

"He likes sea glass," Lily said.

"Oh, yeah," Marigold said. "He does." She thought about his collection and how he wanted a red piece.

"Aunt Sunny has a red piece in her jewelry box," Lily said.

"I remember," Zinnie said. "But Ham gave it to her. It was the one thing that we couldn't pick out."

"But maybe if I traded back my sea horse necklace, she would consider it," Marigold said. "And she was wearing lipstick tonight." Not only had she been wearing makeup, but Aunt Sunny had had a new look about her lately, something rosy and light about her face. Marigold had the feeling she knew what it was. She had felt like that once, too, right after Peter had kissed her.

"So?" Lily asked. "What's lipstick got to do with it?"

"A lot," Marigold said, and stood up. "I need to go ask Aunt Sunny."

"Now?" Lily asked. "In the middle of the night?"

"Yes," Marigold said. "It's important."

"I'm coming, too!" Lily said.

"This is so romantic," Zinnie said, clapping her hands, and hopped out of bed.

# 66 · The Flower Brigade

The girls tiptoed past their sleeping parents on the air mattress to Aunt Sunny's bedroom. She was sitting on her bed in her bathrobe and slippers, reading the latest *National Geographic* with her glasses perched on the end of her nose. There was a giant red frog on the cover.

"Knock, knock," Marigold said.

"My goodness, what is this, the flower brigade?" Aunt Sunny asked.

"I have something to ask you," Marigold said.

"We all do," Zinnie said.

"Even Benny," Lily said, and held up her bunny. "It's for Peter. Beautiful Peter."

"Beautiful Peter?" Aunt Sunny asked. "I'm intrigued."

Marigold held out the sea horse necklace. "I was

wondering if I could trade this for something else from your jewelry box."

"But you love that necklace," Aunt Sunny said. "It looks just darling on you. What would you trade it for?"

"The red sea glass," Marigold said. "You see, Peter has a collection, and he's been looking for a red piece his whole life. And I just know that it would mean a lot to him." Aunt Sunny put her glasses on her head and bit her lip. "I know Ham gave it to you, and it felt like he was giving you a piece of his heart, but . . ." Marigold couldn't find the right words.

"We were thinking that maybe if you let it go," Zinnie said, finishing her sister's thought, "there would be a little more room in your heart for Tony."

Aunt Sunny regarded her nieces thoughtfully. There seemed to be many things crossing her mind at once. Then she sighed. "It's funny," she said, "how I didn't see it until now."

"See what?" Marigold asked.

"How tightly I've been holding on to him." Then she stood up and opened the jewelry box. She handed Marigold the red sea glass, kissing her hand as she passed it along. As Marigold put back the sea horse necklace, Aunt Sunny remarked what a lovely birthday present it would make for a teenager. Perhaps someone's thirteenth birthday.

Marigold wrapped the sea glass in tissue paper and attached a little poem, which she had written in private:

*Here's a piece of sea glass that is red*
*in hopes you'll forgive me for being a butthead*
*good-bye is something I must say*
*before I go back to L.A.*

*Marigold*

Now she just needed to make sure she was able to give it to him in person before she left.

# 67 · The Lucky One

"Boy, your girls had me laughing last night," Edith said as she handed Mom and Dad sugar cones of her signature flavor, the very one for which she'd named her beloved dog, Mocha Chip. Marigold, Zinnie, and Lily already had servings of their favorite flavors: lime sherbet for Marigold, double chocolate for Zinnie, and strawberry for Lily. They were seated at the best table, the one next to the jukebox. Marigold made sure to sit on the side that faced the big window in case she happened to see Peter walking by. The red sea glass and the poem were in her shorts pocket, and she was determined to give them to him today, no matter what.

Even though their parents had both been to Pruet before, the girls wanted to show them all the places they had come to love in the past three weeks. They'd already been to the general store, where they bought a few postcards to hang on the fridge back home, and to the library, where Zinnie returned the book about putting on a play, and to the town beach, where Ashley was enjoying her status as the new town celebrity. In between selling ice pops and candy bars, she was signing autographs. Last on the list was Edith's ice cream. This afternoon Aunt Sunny was taking a nap, the first one in three weeks, but had instructed them to please bring her back a pint of mocha chip.

"These girls are made for the stage," Edith said.

"They were great, weren't they?" Mom said as she paid for the ice cream and stuffed the change in the tip jar.

"Now, I knew Zinnie was a cutup from the minute she walked through my door," Edith said, "but Marigold is a riot, too. And the little one! Oh, how she lights up a room with those cheeks! All three of them are stars. We're going to miss them around here."

"Thanks," Dad said. "That's really nice to hear. And this is the best ice cream I've ever tasted, by the way."

"I aim to please. Let me give you an extra scoop on the house," Edith said, gesturing for Dad to give her his cone.

"Excuse me if I don't refuse," Dad said, handing Edith his cone.

Mom sat next to Marigold and put an arm around her. Marigold rested her head on her shoulder and felt her whole body relax.

Dad flipped through the music selections at the jukebox. "Oh, this is a good one," he said. He pressed a few buttons and put in a quarter. "My Girl" piped through the speakers. "Come on, Gwen, won't you dance with me?"

"I'd love to," Mom said.

"You're supposed to eat sitting down," Lily said. "That's what they say at school. Bottoms on the chairs!"

"I think we can get away with it this one time," Mom said, standing up and taking Dad's hand with the hand that wasn't holding the cone. "After all, it's summer." Lily grinned and joined in. Zinnie did too. Edith turned up the volume so that the song filled the shop. Dancing with an ice cream cone was a little messy, especially for Lily, but nobody seemed to mind.

"Come on over, Marigold," Dad called. "You're my girl, too!"

Marigold was about to give in and join them, even if she was wearing her linen pintuck top in the perfect shade of pink that would most definitely be ruined by a drop of lime sherbet. She stood up but paused when she noticed the black SUV with the tinted windows heading toward the bridge. She knew that it was Amanda, heading out of town. Marigold was surprised to find that she felt sorry for the movie star. Amanda may have had all the things that Marigold longed for— an acting career, the most incredible wardrobe, and even her picture on the cover of *Young & Lovely*—but when Marigold saw her parents and sisters dancing and singing with wobbly ice cream cones in their hands, she knew that she was the lucky one.

"I need to make one more stop," Marigold said as the Silver family walked by the Pruet Yacht Club. It was four o'clock, and Marigold knew that that was when sailing practice was finished. Marigold's hands started to sweat, even though she had been charged with carrying Aunt Sunny's pint of mocha chip.

"At the yacht club?" Mom said.

"I just need to drop something off for someone," Marigold said, handing Aunt Sunny's ice cream to Mom.

"Peter," Zinnie and Lily said at the same time.

"Let's go find him," Lily said, but Zinnie held her back. "Zinnie, let go. He's my boyfriend."

"I think Marigold might want to do this alone," Zinnie said. Lily began to protest, but Zinnie cut her off. "Besides, we don't want Aunt Sunny's ice cream to melt. Come on, race you to the end of Harbor Road!"

As Zinnie and Lily sped away, Mom took Dad's hand, turned to Marigold, and said, "See you back at the house."

Marigold took a deep breath, waved at the clipboard guy, and headed toward the docks.

Peter had just finished tying a dinghy to the dock and was walking in Marigold's direction. Marigold felt her tummy flutter when she saw his red hair and baseball cap. She couldn't help smiling. But when he saw her, he looked away.

"Peter," Marigold said, and she stood in his way to try to stop him from passing her.

"I'm not talking to you," Peter said, shaking his head.

"Wait," Marigold called. To her surprise, he actually turned around. She held up the envelope and said, "This is for you."

"I don't want it," Peter said.

"Please," Marigold said, holding it in her outstretched arm. "I'm really sorry. I was a jerk. And I can explain, sort of. But I think this might say it better than words."

"If I take that envelope, it doesn't mean I like you," he said.

"Okay," she said. "We're having a picnic on the beach tonight. Your mom and dad are coming. I hope you will, too." She handed him the envelope, which was crumpled from spending the day in her pocket. He held it in his hand, noticing its weird shape. Marigold smiled because she knew there was no way he could guess what was inside and she could tell he was curious. Then, feeling that she had said what she'd come to say and done what she'd come to do, she turned around, walked down to the dock, and went back toward Aunt Sunny's, where her family would be waiting for her.

## 68 · Sisters

That evening, Marigold, Zinnie, Lily, their parents, Aunt Sunny, Tony, Jean, and Mack had a great big picnic on the estuary side of the beach. The sky paled as the sun dipped behind the dunes, but the air stayed warm. The sand was cool beneath their feet as they kicked off their sneakers and flip-flops and searched for a good spot. They wanted to find the best place to enjoy their last night. As they spread their picnic blanket and unpacked the food from the coolers, a few piping plovers raced near the shore.

Aunt Sunny had invited Peter, but to everyone's disappointment, he'd said he had to go to a very important sailing team meeting. As the captain, he'd said, he really had to be there. Zinnie knew Peter was mad at Marigold, but still, she couldn't imagine anyone missing this feast. They ate lobster rolls, drenched with drawn butter, that Dad had picked up from the fish market and tomatoes from Tony's garden. Jean brought potato salad and summer squash, and Mom couldn't resist buying a blueberry pie from the farm stand. And of course Aunt Sunny made her surprise brownies. Zinnie thought it had been a summer full of so many surprises that she wasn't sure another one was possible.

But just then she saw Peter walking toward them. Zinnie watched as Marigold's face lit up, her eyes round with anticipation. When Jean asked him about the sailing team meeting, Peter said that he was on his way, but he wanted to stop by here first. Then Peter nodded at Marigold, and the two of them walked to the water's edge to talk away from everyone else. Zinnie couldn't be sure what happened, but when they came back to join the group, Marigold had a secret smile on her face and she was wearing his old, stinky Red Sox hat.

Lily asked if it was finally time for her to show Dad and Mom that she wasn't afraid of swimming anymore. It had been a full half hour since she'd eaten, and she couldn't wait a minute longer. "Mommy, will you come with me?" she asked. "Aunt Sunny said I can't go in by myself."

"I'd love to," Mom said. The two of them stripped down to their bathing suits and raced to the water. Mom held out her hands to carry Lily in, but Lily jumped in all by herself. Dad watched in amazement.

"How did you do it, Sunny?" he asked.

"It was a group effort. Your daughters make a good team," she said, resting her head on Tony's shoulder as he played a quiet song on the guitar.

"Did I tell you girls about the fairy rings?" Dad asked Zinnie and a very distracted Marigold.

"No. What are fairy rings?" Zinnie asked.

Dad explained that they were perfect circles of redwood trees, created by one mother tree that had died and sent her seeds out around her. He showed them a picture on his phone of him standing in one. The trees surrounded him like great columns. Dad zoomed in on the image. "They share a giant interconnected root system underground, and this helps keep them resilient," he said. "It reminds me of you girls and how you'll always have one another to keep you strong." Zinnie thought it was a magical image.

Marigold was not as fascinated. "That's cool, but I'm going to go look for sea glass," she said. Then she headed toward the ocean side of the beach.

Zinnie stood up, about to follow her, but something made her stop. She realized that Marigold probably just wanted to think about Peter. As she watched her sister walk away, she thought of the hollyhocks Aunt Sunny had planted and how she had said that they needed space between them or they wouldn't reach their full height or bloom brightly. Her dad was right about sisters being like a circle of redwoods; their roots were intertwined. But Zinnie thought that sisters were also like those hollyhocks: They needed their own patches of dirt and bits of sunshine in order to grow. Besides, she wanted to know more about fairy circles.

So Zinnie sat back down and took Dad's hand. She buried her toes in the warm sand, and he described what it had been like to sit in the arms of the tallest living thing, a tree that may have been a thousand years old; how he'd smelled the fog, tasted a huckleberry, heard a salamander slither across a leaf, and seen what felt like the whole wide world from its branches. As Zinnie leaned against his shoulder and listened, her imagination sparked and crackled. Her dad's stories seemed to stir up her own. She had the feeling that the idea for a new play was forming, maybe something about fairy circles. She wasn't sure. It wasn't a thought she could grab onto or describe just yet. But she could sense it in the air around her, in the late-summer breeze tousling her curls, like a secret whispered by the sea.

# AUNT SUNNY'S SURPRISE (PEPPERMINT) BROWNIES

## INGREDIENTS

BROWNIES:

- 1 stick butter
- 1 cup sugar
- 4 eggs
- 1-pound can liquid chocolate syrup
- 1 cup flour
- ½ cup chopped walnuts (optional)

FROSTING:

- 3 cups powdered or confectioner's sugar
- 4 tablespoons butter
- 3–4 tablespoons milk
- ½ teaspoon peppermint extract (add more to taste)
- a few drops green food coloring

## CHOCOLATE TOPPING:

   3 tablespoons butter
   3 squares bittersweet chocolate

# DIRECTIONS

### BROWNIES:

Preheat oven to 350°. In a large mixing bowl, cream the butter with the sugar. Add the eggs, mixing well. Then add the remaining brownie ingredients and mix together. Bake in a lightly greased 10" x 15" jelly roll pan for 30 minutes. Let cool.

### FROSTING:

Sift the powdered sugar into a large bowl. Next, cream the butter and sugar together. The consistency of the frosting should be creamy; add milk, up to 4 tablespoons. Mix in the remaining frosting ingredients and spread evenly over the cooled brownies while they're still in the pan. Let set for 20–30 minutes.

### TOPPING

Melt the butter and chocolate squares in a saucepan over low heat until thick, stirring frequently so the mixture doesn't get burned. Pour the topping over the brownies still in the pan. Tilt the pan so the topping coats the brownies evenly. Once the topping has set, the brownies are ready to cut and enjoy!

# Acknowledgments

Thanks to my beloved agent, Sara Crowe, for her unwavering belief in me. Great heaps of gratitude to my brilliant editor, Alexandra Cooper, for her vision and wisdom and for loving these girls as much as I do. Thank you to the whole team at HarperCollins, especially Alyssa Miele. I am indebted to Kayla Cagan and Vanessa Cross Napolitano for their encouragement, thoughtful feedback, and friendship. Thank you to my whole family, especially my mom and dad. Thanks also to the late Dorothy W. Gifford, also known as Aunt Dot the Great, teacher, sage, and fairy godmother. Giff, you've been my best friend from the get-go. And Maryhope, every day I count my lucky stars that you are my sister. As always, love and thanks to JLD, my sweetheart and secret weapon. And to HHD, who inspires and delights me beyond compare, thank you for opening my heart wider than I thought possible.

For more fun and sun with the Silver sisters,
turn the page and catch a glimpse of
their next summer vacation in

# the Brightest Stars of Summer

# 1 · A Young Star

It was guaranteed to be one of the highlights of the summer, maybe even of the year, maybe even of their lives, and Zinnie didn't want to miss a single moment. She plucked her mininotebook out of her back pocket, uncapped her favorite purple pen, and took a good look around.

She was at a special early showing for the cast and crew of the movie *Night Sprites* because her very own and soon-to-be-famous older sister, Marigold, had a part in it. Marigold played a small role, but she had got to say two whole sentences on camera, and it was a pretty big deal.

Being in a movie was Marigold's dream come true, and it only took one glance at her enormous smile, made extra shimmery today by the lip gloss their mother had allowed her to wear for this special occasion, for Zinnie to be certain that her sister was truly a star.

Zinnie couldn't help but feel that she'd had a big hand in making it happen. After all, it had been her idea to have a talent show last summer in the town of Pruet, Massachusetts, where the director, Philip Rathbone, had a vacation home, and where the three Silver sisters had spent a few fun-filled weeks at their aunt Sunny's cottage. And it was Zinnie who'd written the play in which Marigold had performed so outstandingly that Mr. Rathbone had noticed her. And it was Zinnie again who encouraged Marigold to send Mr. Rathbone her headshot a few weeks later, along with a letter telling him how nice it had been to meet him.

Zinnie had even helped Marigold write the letter, making sure it had both personality and good grammar. Zinnie was pretty certain that it had been that letter that had sealed the deal and made Mr. Rathbone think of Marigold when, after the rest of the movie had been filmed, he'd decided that the story needed an opening scene that wasn't even in the book: a scene where a normal, human girl was sitting by a tree reading, not knowing that she was falling into a dream woven by the Night Sprites.

Zinnie imagined Marigold's letter and headshot landing in Mr. Rathbone's mailbox on the very day he had the idea. She could just picture him sitting at a big desk, puzzling over which young actress would play this small but crucial role. Then his eyes growing wide with delight as he opened the envelope containing Marigold's headshot and realized he'd actually met the perfect girl that summer. "Mildred, get this girl in here for an audition right away!" Zinnie imagined him saying to an assistant, just like the old movies she and her dad saw at the cinema that showed classics every Tuesday night.

Regardless of how it had happened, Marigold had gotten the part on the spot. And now, a few months later, here the Silver family was, making their way down the aisle of the movie theater to see Marigold on the big screen in what was sure to be the biggest hit of the summer.

This wasn't any old Cineplex at the mall; it was a fully restored historical movie theater from the 1940s in downtown Los Angeles, grand and ornate. Zinnie thought it was perfect for the exclusive advance screening of a major Hollywood movie. She paused in the aisle before following her dad down the row to their seats. She narrowed her eyes, hoping to land on the perfect details to capture this epic moment. Mrs. Lee, her sixth-grade English teacher, always said that when it comes to writing, "It's all about the details."

*Red curtains hang gloriously in front of the screen,* Zinnie wrote in the dim light. *Velvet seats snap open like hungry mouths.* She read her work over and imagined Mrs. Lee smiling out of the corner of her mouth and tapping her pencil to her lips the way she did when she thought something was really good.

Mrs. Lee was a real author. She'd had an actual book published. Zinnie had seen it at the library and at the bookstore. It had even won an award and had one of those shiny gold stickers on it. Zinnie wasn't sure if she wanted to write books or plays or—like her father—movies, but she knew that she wanted to be a writer and that getting into Mrs. Lee's Writers' Workshop in the fall was a top priority. Mrs. Lee selected ten students from the seventh and eighth grades, and those students spent the afternoons attending plays and films and going to museums in Los Angeles, visiting bookstores and libraries, and, of course, writing. They even took a group field trip to England over spring vacation, and Zinnie was dying to go on it. One of the best parts was that the members of the Writers' Workshop were excused from mandatory afterschool sports.

This was an even bigger deal to Zinnie than the trip to England. She'd endured soccer last fall, and that had been almost as bad as basketball in the winter, though not as terrible as track in the spring. Track was lonely and boring, and it didn't help that she was always in the very back, "bringing up the rear," as Miss Kimberly said when Zinnie finished far behind everyone else. Zinnie had come to truly hate that expression.

Getting into the Writers' Workshop was not going to be easy. Students could submit a poem, a play, a story, an essay, or even a graphic novel. The work was supposed to be submitted by the end of the school year, but Mrs. Lee said that she understood how sometimes the summer could offer a new perspective, so she'd read applications through July tenth, at which point she was going on her annual summer retreat to Laguna Beach, where she planned to finish writing her latest novel. During the final school assembly, Mrs. Lee said that the only rules were that the writing had to feel true and original. "And it really needs to be the very best example of your work," she'd added, standing at the podium in one of her signature colorful scarves.

Zinnie wasn't going to need the extra time. She'd turned in a story on the last day of school. It was about a band of young warriors from a forgotten land, seeking to overthrow a demon king by unlocking spells that had been dormant for centuries. Zinnie felt good about it: it had action, plot, and, she thought, good use of setting, something they had focused on in English class this year. Mrs. Lee said that a writer is, in a way, always writing, and that little notes she'd taken over the years had sometimes been exactly the inspiration she'd been looking for later.

"Let's sit down," Marigold said. "It's going to start any minute!"

"Okay," Zinnie said, and scooted down the row, taking a seat next to their dad. Marigold, their mom, and finally the youngest sister, Lily, who was decked out in a fairy costume, followed her down the row.

Since Mrs. Lee always said that three was the magic number, Zinnie wanted to capture one last detail before the movie started. She looked around the theater. There were crystal chandeliers, golden balconies, and a ceiling with angels painted on it. Even with the splendor around her, Zinnie turned to Marigold for the final detail for her notebook. With her beauty and confidence and unpredictable moods, Marigold was an endlessly fascinating subject, especially today.

Marigold tossed her long, shiny hair and snapped a selfie with her phone. She leaned toward Zinnie, and before Zinnie even had a chance to pose, she took a picture of the two of them, giving Zinnie a little rush. There was almost nothing that Zinnie liked better than to be included in her sister's glamorous world, and Marigold had been in the best mood all day.

She'd even offered to let Zinnie borrow anything she wanted from her closet. *Anything.* This was unheard of. Zinnie had been bold enough to ask to borrow the jean jacket, the one that had become Marigold's unofficial weekend uniform. Perfectly shrunken and faded, it was her trademark piece. Zinnie had been expecting rejection, but Marigold said, "Sure," and handed it to Zinnie as if she had a million of them. For a second

Zinnie wondered if she hadn't aimed high enough. Was there something else she could have asked for?

The theater lights dimmed. Marigold beamed as she stared up at the screen. *Future star shines bright in the darkness,* Zinnie scribbled in her notebook, even though she could no longer see the paper.

## 2 · A Bad Feeling

The movie had only been playing for a minute or two when Marigold started to get a bad feeling. She couldn't explain it, but as the music swelled and she watched the scenery unfurl on the giant screen— the turquoise sea, the rocky beach, the steep cliffs—she became a little queasy.

She had asked her mother once why sometimes she knew which way something was going to go, good or bad, right before it happened. Like the time she'd known that she was going to get that part on the TV show *Seasons* before she'd even stepped into the room to audition. Or when she'd felt in the pit of her stomach that seventh grade was going to be a really tough year even before the first bell rang. "That's your intuition," Mom had said. "Your gut instinct. And you should always listen to it."

Right now, her gut instinct was telling her that something was wrong. The first scene was supposed to take place at the edge of the forest, where a girl was sitting under a tree, reading a book. A girl played by Marigold. But the landscape in those fast and sweeping panoramic views suggested that the girl was being skipped over and the audience was being taken directly to the lagoon where the queen of the Night Sprites lived. The bad feeling landed in her belly like a penny at the bottom of a fountain.

Marigold had an important line in this movie. It was the first in the film: "Where does the magic of a summer evening come from? It's hidden deep in the twilight, though perhaps is closer than you ever imagined." She had practiced it until it was like a favorite song playing on a loop as she walked to school or drifted off while doing homework.

Now, a few months after shooting her scenes, she was more than ready to hear that line outside her head. She was expecting it to fill the theater, just as she had envisioned so many times. But instead of her voice opening the movie, Xiomara's song flowed from the speakers.

Marigold's scene had been cut.

*Wait. What?*

This couldn't be happening to her! Or could it? Everyone said that bad things happened in threes. She didn't believe it, but here it was: the third bad thing.

The TV show Marigold had been on for six whole episodes had been canceled this fall. Then two weeks ago her agent, Jill, had announced that she was quitting the business and moving to Costa Rica to discover the meaning of life. Jill had assured her that a part in the summer's hottest blockbuster would mean that she'd be able to find another agent in no time, and Marigold had believed her. But now she wasn't even in the movie!

Marigold wanted to reach up, rewind the action, and zoom in on the tree under which she was meant to be sitting. But of course she couldn't. All she could do was grip her velvet armrests and try not to cry.

Marigold could still see that tree where they had filmed just two and half months earlier in Griffith Park, the huge park in the middle of Los Angeles. The tree had tangled, knotty roots that rose above the ground to create a shady, comfortable reading nook for a girl her size. On that perfect day in April, as one of Mr. Rathbone's assistants adjusted Marigold's costume, Marigold had wondered how many trees they'd looked at before they found this one. *It's the best tree,* she thought as she relaxed against the cool bark, *for the best day.*

She'd arrived early on the set. A guy with crazy pants had done her hair and a lady with light and careful fingertips had applied her makeup. Marigold was more nervous than she'd thought she would be.

Her mouth was dry and her hands were clammy, but she wasn't so nervous that she forgot her lines. And when Mr. Rathbone called "Action!" Marigold was such a natural that she'd done the scene in just one take.

Marigold had returned from spring break ready to tell everyone about her big day. For weeks it was all she could talk about. It wasn't just because she wanted to relive her dream on a daily basis—it was also because she thought it would give her that something extra she needed to be accepted by the girls in her class.

Her intuition had been right about seventh grade. It was different from sixth in a way that was hard to put her finger on. It wasn't just because they were actually allowed to choose some of their classes (French or Spanish? pottery or dance?), or even that they were allowed to use their phones during the school day. It was something much bigger and more difficult to name.

In sixth grade, all thirty-five girls in her class at Miss Hadley's School had pretty much been friends. Some girls were closer than others, like Marigold and her best friend Pilar, but overall there weren't any groups. She didn't think twice about where she sat at lunch or who she walked to gym class with. And the birthday party rules from elementary school were still in place: girls invited either the whole class or just one or two close friends.

In seventh grade things changed.

The year had started off okay, but as the fall crept toward winter, cliques started to form. There was one group calling themselves "the Cuties" who were all on the swim team and who'd gone on a ski trip together over winter vacation.

In the week they'd spent at Mammoth Mountain, they seemed to have shared a lifetime's worth of secrets and what they called "location jokes." Marigold learned these were jokes she'd only understand if she'd been at the *location* where the joke happened, and they'd all happened during the ski trip. By the time spring vacation rolled around, the Cuties were wearing their hair the same way, sitting together at the smaller lunch table (the one with only enough room for eight people) closest to the windows, and constantly saying the word "amazing."

Marigold, who'd always been confident, was suddenly timid about speaking up in front of the Cuties—and she'd gone to kindergarten with most of them. She was also weirdly shy about using the word "amazing." It was like those girls owned the word, which didn't make any sense. How could anyone own a word?

She thought there was no better way to get her classmates' approval than to make sure that they knew she was going to be in the *Night Sprites* movie. Her entire class had read the books, and it seemed like the whole world was waiting for the film, which would be released on July first—the day her life would change forever.

Marigold started talking about being in the movie every chance she could get: in homeroom, in the locker room, walking to class. "I just can't wait until July first!" she'd said more than once. This did get everyone's attention, but only for a few days. After listening to several stories about "the shoot," the Cuties lost interest, and they still didn't invite her to sit at their table.

It wasn't until Pilar talked to her in the lunch line that Marigold finally started to understand.

"People think you're bragging," Pilar said as she grabbed a yogurt and put it on her tray.

"Do *you* think I'm bragging?" Marigold asked. Pilar bit her lip as she selected a turkey sandwich. "Pilar?"

"Maybe?" Pilar said, looking up at Marigold from under her long, dark eyelashes.

"I think everyone is jealous," Marigold said, picking out a ham and cheese on whole wheat. Pilar froze, her brow pinched. "I mean, not you, but everyone else. The Cuties for sure. They're such jerks."

"They aren't so bad," Pilar said, and then she checked to see if anyone had overheard. Marigold felt her throat constrict. Was Pilar becoming one of them?

It was true that Marigold had been spending less time with Pilar since she'd been cast in *Night Sprites*. She'd had a bunch of auditions that she'd missed school for, and she was now taking an improv class and a voice-over class in addition to her acting class. It was also true that Pilar had asked her to hang out a lot and she'd almost always had to say no. Had Marigold been a bad friend without realizing it? Didn't Pilar understand how important acting was to her?

The truth, Marigold knew, was that she hadn't signed up for all the extra classes just because acting was her passion. It also gave her an excuse not to fit in.

"I'm so busy this weekend because I have auditions," she'd said once when she wasn't invited to a birthday party. (Pilar had been invited to that one.) Another time she'd said, "I have to go to acting class after school today," when she knew a bunch of girls from her class went to the new frozen yogurt place that let you sample every flavor, but didn't ask her to come along.

Marigold realized that even if Pilar did get more invitations, she probably still really missed having her best friend around. Marigold had an idea.

"Hey, do you want to try the Cupcake Café this weekend? We can do a taste test and see if the cupcakes there are as good as the ones at the Farmers Market."

"I went last weekend," Pilar said.

"Without me?" Marigold asked.

"It's been open for a whole month, Marigold."

"But we were going to go together, remember?"

"I already asked you to go twice and you said you were busy."

"I was," Marigold said, her voice high and pleading.

"You're always busy," Pilar said as she grabbed an orange juice and headed toward the seventh-grade tables.

"But I really was," Marigold said, following her friend.

Pilar said "Hi" to the Cuties as she passed their table and they said "Hi" back, but to Marigold's relief, Pilar didn't sit with them. Instead the two of them sat at their regular table with the usual girls. But for that whole lunch period, Marigold felt like Pilar wanted to be somewhere else.

Now Marigold was the one who wanted to be somewhere else. Anywhere but here in this fancy, old-fashioned movie theater, watching her dream go down the drain. She grabbed her mom's hand.

"They skipped it," she whispered.

"Maybe they moved it," Mom said. A tear rolled down Marigold's cheek. "Do you want to leave, honey?"

"No! We need to stay in case it's in there somewhere," Marigold said.

"We'll stay," Mom said, and wrapped an arm around her daughter.

The rest of the movie was torture. Marigold couldn't enjoy a single scene. Zinnie, on the other hand, loved it. She was laughing like crazy when Xiomara entertained the ravens and crying when it appeared that all hope was lost. Marigold kept shooting her dirty looks, but they were wasted—Zinnie didn't even notice. Not until the very end, when she turned to Marigold and, as if it was just dawning on her that something was amiss, said, "Hey, wait a second. Where was your scene? Did I miss it?" And Marigold had to cover her face with both hands to keep from screaming.

"Do you want to stick around and talk to anyone?" Mom asked, stroking Marigold's hair.

"I just want to go home," Marigold said, still hiding her tear-stained face. "I want to call Pilar." How could her dream be taken from her like this? How was she ever going to face her classmates? Now no one would know about her most perfect moment on earth, sitting under that tree, saying her lines like a real movie actress. Now the only people who would ever know that she was in the best, most successful movie of the year were the handful who had been there on that April day. It was, she thought, the cruelest location joke of all.

# EXPLORE THE SUMMER MAGIC OF CAPE COD WITH THE SILVER SISTERS!